"Because *Midnight Black: The Purge* by R.J. Eastwood is a political thriller set in the future (not my first choice in fiction, I almost passed on selecting this superb book to read and review. How glad I am that I didn't. Eastwood's impressive bio on Amazon, plus the fact that his first novel has so many positive reviews made me curious. That curiosity was amply satisfied. I absolutely loved the concept behind the fascinating plot of *Midnight Black*. It's both unique and frightening in its implications. And then there's the author's considerable skill as a writer: Eastwood's experience as a producer and director of feature films and documentaries shows throughout the story. The plot moves swiftly and Eastwood makes it so easy for readers to visualize the settings which change like scenes in a movie. This movie-like presentation is most appealing as the author engages all our senses and draws us into the plot and reveals his characters. When *Midnight Black* finally draws to a close, readers feel as if they have truly lived in this future world, but hope they never will. Curious? You should be. This is powerful writing and well worth your time. Don't be surprised if you read it in one sitting. I did!"
Reviewed By Viga Boland for Readers' Favorite

• • • •

"Eastwood has panache in his style of writing reminiscent of Michael Crichton: crisp prose, intelligently humorous dialogue, and structure that provides just enough momentum for his writing to feel dangerously comfortable."

• • • •

"Eastwood's prose is crisp and his settings breathtaking. His short chapters and constant shifts in story line create powerful suspense."

• • • •

"R. J. Eastwood's writing is never predictable,

There is always a surprise at every turn."

• • • •

*"Eastwood's use of imagery is always real
and effective, and the dialogue is crisp and believable."*

• • • •

*"I certainly hope there are many more stories to come
From the fertile and creative mind of Mr. Eastwood."*

• • • •

*Mr. Eastwood's work has been awarded the
2018 Readers' Favorite Award for Fiction -
The 2018 Award for Book of the Year from
Book Talk Radio & The 2017
Author's Circle Award for Fiction*

Midnight Black
The Purge

. . . .

A Novel By
R. J. Eastwood

Join the author online at his Author's homepage.

www.robertjemeryauthor.com[1]

Contact the author at:

Media8@verizon.net

Consider writing a review.

To Angie and Al who gave me life, to my children who joined me for the journey, and to my wife Susanne who threatened me if I asked her to read one more revision. Thanks to my patient editor Jennie Rosenblum, and Bonnie Mutchler for the great cover design.

MIDNIGHT BLACK

The Purge

Chapter 1

The Execution

I *kick in the front door and call his bastard name... like the coward he is, he scurries on his hands and knees like a rodent into an oversized closet, cowering behind boxes and hanging clothes, his legs bent to his chest, his arms wrapped around his knees, his fingers intertwined so tight they're turning white... his head is bent forward, eyes shut, like if he doesn't look at me, I'm not there and I won't do what I came to do. I'm yelling at him to open his eyes, to look into mine, but he won't, and he doesn't. My hand is tightly wrapped around the handle of the Glock. The little slug's head comes up, his eyes go first to the gun, then up to me... he's gonna' plead for his life, but I'm not offering options here, forget it, they'll be no negotiations. Before he breathes a word, I squeeze the trigger... damn, it sounds like a cannon blast in this closet... the bullet rips away his right kneecap... he howls, his leg jerks and flops like a pig being slaughtered, its jugular vein sliced through. My second shot explodes his left kneecap, scattering flesh and bone, his body's oscillating like an electric toothbrush, his mouth opens wide... all that comes out is a chilling scream. Go ahead, you pussy, make all the noise you want, nobody's coming to help. Look at me, asshole, look at me before your lights go out, before you meet your maker, whoever the hell that is... Satan maybe. I make sure he knows in whose holy name I commit him to hell.*

"Diedre... her name was Diedre."

I squeeze the trigger... the bullet races down the barrel at twenty-five-hundred feet per second, seventeen-hundred miles per hour, striking his forehead just above and between his eyes, leaving not a neat hole, but tearing off the top of his skull, splattering flesh, bone, blood, and brains over boxes, clothes and walls... Lucifer's bastard son is dead... score one for Lady Justice...... I should post his bloodied carcass on the Internet and let the world see what I did, what I had to do in Diedre's name. Hell, they post everything else on the damn web...... An earsplitting siren breaks the silence, I flinch and step back and spin around... it sounds like it came from inside this closet......whoa, there it is again, it's loud... make it stop! Now I feel a sharp stab to the middle of my back, then zap, zap, an electrical charge is stinging me. For God's sake, stop it! ... My eyes are closed, but damn it, they can't be, I'm right here in this closet, I can see jerk-off lying dead up against the wall. My eyelids begin to flutter like a butterfly before popping open and I focus... damn it, damn it, someone's in my face and the fool's yelling.

"Get up, get your lazy ass up!"

Jesus, it's Quasi! What the hell is he doing here?

Chapter 2
This Place Sucks

My name is **William Evan 'Billy' Russell,** the only child of Amelia and Alistair Russell from Orban, Argyll, Scotland. Seeking greater opportunities, mom and dad immigrated to Providence, Rhode Island, USA. Dad had lined up an engineering job there, I was born there. From my earliest childhood, no one called me "William', just Billy, and that was fine with me. 'William' always sounded so damn formal. How is little 'W-i-l-l-i-a-m', people would say… it reaches my ears like fingernails on a blackboard…… Why can't I recall my parents' faces now? My mind blanks each time I try. Being in total isolation for the past fifteen-years has wiped my memory clean… this stinking hole in the ground will do that. On the day we arrived, they made it crystal clear who was in charge by stripping us naked and marching us past a line of leering, catcalling inmates… message received, sir, you humiliated us, you're in charge, sir. They issued us identification number's—mine is 11349556. I would be known only as 556… it's stitched on the back of the only two shirts I was issued… I guess they knew I was coming. After a few weeks, I wished someone, anyone, would call me by my name… even William would do… but no one does… I am 556 for the duration, so get used to it. I was twenty-six years old when I arrived, six-feet tall, weighed in at two-hundred and ten pounds. I'm still six-feet, but now I'm one-hundred and ninety pounds of muscle thanks to six days a week hard labor. My hair remains dark brown except for strands of white that have invaded my temples. There are dark circles under my light brown eyes and my face has forgotten how to smile…… Where do I begin to describe fifteen years living underground like a sewer rat, never seeing the surface, the sky, or whatever the hell else might be out there in no man's land? One day runs into the next without reference to anything but the semi-dark, dusty mine shafts, the incessant noise of heavy equipment, the Neanderthal guards, and the windowless steel boxes we eat, sleep and live in. Each minute, each hour, each day plays out without place, time, meaning or documentation. When melancholy sets in, as it often does, I remind myself this is not my permanent reality, if I survive my life will resume where it left off, albeit scarred physically and mentally. That's what has kept me going, that's what has kept me sane...... We live in four sleeping bays, cold, dark, gray steel boxes housing fifty men per bay. I'm in Bay 3-East. There are two rows of twenty-five cots, two-feet apart in earshot of every snort, belch, cough, sneeze, grunt, and fart. A lot of the crap you hear these men mumbling in their sleep is enough to induce your own nightmares. The nights are long, sleep is dicey at best knowing at daybreak we'll be jolted awake by a screaming siren blast that scrapes deep in your bones. Most mornings my face and torso are covered in sweat, the two-week-old sheet beneath me damp. My muscles ache, they always do first thing. When that blast goes off, we have ten seconds to get our asses up or one of the trained gorillas will zap you with an instrument resembling a cattle prod. When an inmate fails to get up, it's a sure sign they experienced permanent cessation of their vital functions during the night. If anyone has an emotional breakdown, suicide is looked upon as an act of self-kindness... we've had our share of those. Friendships, fraternization, physical or otherwise, are strictly verboten. Good luck with that. There're dangerous dudes here. You learn quickly who to avoid if you know what's good for you... don't want to become some big guy's homeboy. Problem is, when you stack men like cordwood, treat them like shit, elevated testosterone levels will lead to an occasional Battle Royal. When the lid blows, the instigators are quickly identified and dragged off by goon's expert in inflicting grievous bodily harm. We have no contact with the outside world... nothing, nada, zip. A family member could die back home and you'd never know it... there's no existence beyond the one we inhabit. If you get sick, forget about it. I've watched men succumb to painful, ugly deaths with zero medical attention. We're all expendable here, replacements are on the way. Oh yeah, cigarettes are free and everyone smokes, including me. There's a constant white haze in the air 24/7. As for food, trust me, it ain't gourmet. Breakfast is a *bowl of oatmeal, a slice of brown bread, and black coffee... I've come to hate oatmeal. Lunch is a sandwich of mystery meat on brown bread, dried fruit to keep scurvy away, and all the water you want. Dinner is hot soup made of mystery meat and vegetables... heavy on the veggies... a slice of brown bread and all the water you want...... The one shining haven in our bleak existence is the library... it's housed in yet another cold, gray steel box. Two months after arriving, I was allowed one-hour in there on a Sunday, our only day off. There are no physical books, we read on computers. Via a special portal to Amazon ©, we have access to books, magazines, and articles, but zero access to current information about what might be happening back home. Bummer. We know nothing of this place other than its name, so I rolled the dice, typed the name in the search box, and low and behold, up it came. Turns out Planet Europa... yes, we're on Europa, the armpit planet of the universe... is the smallest of the four Galilean moons orbiting Jupiter and the sixth-largest moon[1] in the Solar System[2]. Its surface is frozen, 160 degrees Celsius, with a tenuous atmosphere of oxygen[3]... tenuous because it's not enough to keep us alive. Heat and oxygen are pumped into every nook and cranny where we live and work. There's plenty of water in natural underground reservoirs treated first to remove traces of iron-nickel alloy and foreign bacteria before we use it. If the life support systems fail and the backup generators fail, we all die... so far, so good......The entire operation is a major technological accomplishment on an unforgiving planet. Elevators take us deep into dark, dusty mines where we harvest a nonmetallic ore called Phostoirore. It's French, pronounced Phos-twa-ore. It smells like rotting chicken parts... an odor that will forever be embedded in my sinuses. The single structure on Europa's frozen surface is a giant landing-launch facility for Europa-1, 2, and 3, the ships that rotate hauling Phostoirore back to Earth. Once liquified, Phostoirore becomes a super-efficient, super clean energy source that's replaced all other fuel sources*

---

1. https://en.wikipedia.org/wiki/List_of_natural_satellites

2. https://en.wikipedia.org/wiki/Solar_System

3. https://en.wikipedia.org/wiki/Oxygen

on Earth. The French mining conglomerate, MAXMinerai, runs the operation... never heard of them before arriving here. But, here's the kicker... we inmates provide cheap labor and MAXMinerai profits high. Ten to one more than a few politicians back home pocketed enough cash to get this place designated as an official penal colony. The one good thing is that engines powered by Phostoirore have made it possible to travel the three-hundred and ninety-million miles between Earth and Europa in one year, one week, and a day...... Now, much to my dismay, here comes nature's mistake, an oaf of a man we call Quasimodo because his shoulders hunch forward like his head is too heavy for his corpulent body. His first name is Vladimir... don't know his last. He speaks with a heavy European accent, I have yet to determine what country he's from. Between his accent and his fractured English, it's often difficult to tell what the hell he's saying. We nicknamed him is Quasi for short, but never to his face... not if you hope to keep breathing. The mere sight of him sticks in my throat like the smell of the ore. Within a few days of my arrival, I pegged this asshole the one human being to be avoided whenever possible. He's ill-tempered and quick to find an excuse to abuse inmates. I learned the hard way my dry wit would not serve me well here. One day, I suggested to a few fellow inmates Quasi was abandoned at birth and raised by feral cats. I was zapped in the back with one of those damn cattle prods... Quasi was standing behind me, he had heard every dumb word that came out of my smart-ass mouth. So, this morning, Quasi comes stomping in with his usual pissed-off look he thinks intimidates us... it doesn't, but who's gonna" tell him. His voice is deeper and more threatening than usual, a sure sign he had a bad night.

"Grover, Henley, Russell stood by beds."

The word is 'stand', asshole. We must be in serious trouble, that's the first time anyone has called us by our names since we arrived in this stink hole.

"The rest of you, you know drill. Move it."

In unison, everyone answers in a chorus of disinterested voices.

"Yes, sir!"

Quasi follows them to the door until they've all filed out for the morning latrine break, then on to the mess hall for the morning bowl of yummy oatmeal and black coffee. Henley leans close and whispers.

"What in the hell have we done now?"

Grover cranes his head and looks down the aisle to Quasi.

"God only knows."

There are three unwritten rules we adhere to religiously... avoid making friends because they'll turn on you to save their own asses... never ask an inmate what crime they committed that got them sent here... and never ask a guard a question unless you ask for permission. I know nothing about Grover or Henley other than we've shared quarters and toil together in the mines. Chris Henley showed up about five years ago, Grover two years before that. Henley, who's about my age, is a smallish, wiry white guy with a wisecracking mouth only a mother could tolerate... it's caused him to incur Quasi's wrath on a few occasions. Leon Grover is black, tall with broad shoulders, he pretty much keeps to himself. Leon's pushing sixty and has a bad cough. With a smug look, Quasi comes strolling back.

"You three have appointment with Commandant. Get dressed."

Oh crap, the Commandant, that spells trouble big time. As usual Henley can't keep his mouth shut.

"What's the Commandant want with us?"

Quasi scowls, gets in Henley's face.

"Where written you ask question?"

Henley opens his mouth again, Quasi places his prod within an inch of his nose.

"Keep mouth shut. Get dressed."

Chapter 3
Get Out of Jail Card

*A**ll inmate sleeping bays,** showers, latrines, mess hall, staff quarters and support facilities are on the same level some forty-five feet below the surface and eighty-five-feet above where the mine shafts begin. Since the Commandant's office is at the far end, we trek for almost ten minutes through a maze of dark, narrow passageways and a series of airlocks that seal off sections in case of an emergency. The Commandant's name is an Oleg Maksymchak, a former colonel in the Ukrainian army. Colonel Maks, as we call him, encourages the guards to employ harsh measures for the slightest infractions... trust me, the last thing these sadistic bastards need is encouragement. Maks is a short man... five-seven if he's lucky. I've only seen him a couple of times during his inspections of the mines marching around quick step with a couple of his aids like he was Napoleon Bonaparte reincarnated. All short men have Napoleonic complex's... at least that's been my experience. When we enter his office, 'Napoleon' is sitting behind his desk with an austere expression that would melt ice. I notice right off his chair has been jacked up high to make him appear taller. Quasi clicks his heels and salutes. Overview*

"Commandant... inmates Grover, Russell, Henley."

Little Napoleon takes his time sizing up each of us. He picks up a sheet of paper, holds it above his head, and shakes it.

"This communiqué arrived last night. It authorizes me to send you home on Europa-2 when it departs later today. It's quite unusual that I should receive such short notice."

The three of us exchange nervous glances.

"It appears whoever pulled your ticket feels you would be of more use back there. Lucky you."

My brain is slow in processing the words. We're leaving this shit hole and returning to Earth... is that what he said? Surely, I misunderstood. Henley opens his mouth to speak, the Commander gives him a sharp look.

"Which one are you?"

"478."

"Not your number, your name."

"Christopher Henley."

"Well, Henley, do not speak until I say you may. You do, however, get to listen. Do I make myself clear?"

Like a good inmate, Henley nods.

"You will receive further instructions when you arrive back on Earth. Officer Sokolov will see that you are properly prepared for departure."

Sokolov, so that's Quasi's last name, sounds Russian. Commandant Oleg's words are finally beginning to sink in... for reasons unknown, we're being sent home and someone, it seems, is in a rush to get us back there. Why?

"Now, you may ask questions. Russell, you go first."

"Although this news pleases me, Commandant, may I ask why?"

"I'm not privy to why. Grover, you look unwell?"

"A bug, I think, sir. It's getting better."

"Do you have a question?"

"I have none, sir."

"Henley?"

"No, sir."

"Very well, you are dismissed."

Oh hell, Henley's raising his hand. Let it go, Chris, let's just get out of here.

"I do have a question."

"No more questions, you're dismissed. Enjoy the journey home."

And that, hopefully, is the last we'll ever see of Colonel Maks... soon we'll bid adios to Quasi and the rest of the goons.

• • • •

AS WE MAKE OUR WAY back, there's a new spring in my step along with a wave of apprehension, not only for what I will or won't find back home, but what the future holds for me in a world I barely remember. So, for reasons unknown I bid you goodbye, Europa, may your permafrost one-day melt and knock you off your axis into oblivion.

"This doesn't pass the smell test."

Grover shoots me a stern look.

"Never mind what it smells like, we're going home, that's all that counts."

Henley is smiling from ear-to-ear and whispers the same line he uses at the end of every mine shift.

"What did the shepherd say when he saw the storm coming?"

Grover is trying to stifle a laugh.

"Let's get the flock out of here."

"Leon, you remembered."

"How can I ever forget, Chris?"

Today, this glorious day, I take my final shower on Europa washing off the stink and grime of this garbage pit of a planet for the last time. I stand in the shower allowing the hot water to cascade over me, its thera-peutic powers magically restoring life to my aching muscles. Then we're off for our last bowl of oatmeal. For as long as I live, I will never again eat oatmeal, nor will I trust anyone who does. We're issued clean clothes… or-ange jumpsuits, white socks, new brown shoes, and a small zippered pouch containing a toothbrush, toothpaste, shaving cream, razor, a bar of soap, a comb, a laminated credit-sized card bearing our photo and ID number, and a green badge with only a black barcode along the bottom edge, which we're instructed to pin to our chest. That's it, that's all I have to show for the past fifteen-years. Not much of a resumé, but it is what it is. So now Quasi's growling like the angry animal he is.

"ID card is only proof you exist. Lose it, you become non-entity."

Thanks, you jelly-faced prick, livestock is treated with more dignity... I'll miss you like the loss of a limb. One of Colonel Maks aides shows up and has us sign release papers, which I don't bother to read and scribble my name on just to be done with the isolation, the mines, the bad food, the living conditions, the inmates, the cruel guards... done with it all.

Chapter 4
The Long Trip Home

*E**uropa-2 is a newer, bigger version** of the ship that brought me here fifteen years earlier. It's the length of one and a half football fields and half-again wide... one massive cargo-hold for Phostoirore, plus a latrine, a shower, and a mess hall we share with four guards and a flight crew of nine. Twenty of us from the four Bays are stacked on double bunks in a small, foul-smelling gray steel box. Grover's in the bunk above me, Henley's to my right. Why some men are wearing green badges and others red hasn't been explained...... The first twenty days out prove uneventful and boring as hell with nothing to do but eat and sleep. In the mess hall, there's an eight-foot wide, three-foot high glass portal providing a magnificent vista of space. When I looked out the first time, it blew my mind as I stared in amazement at the wonders of the vast Universe. The sights are spectacular, beyond belief, beyond anything I could have ever imagined. How fortunate I am to experience this... how very small and insignificant it makes me feel. Henley, Grover and I discuss at length how these sights have affected us, how they've given us a profound and spiritual appreciation for our short existence. If every living soul on Earth could spend a few minutes gazing out that portal, see what we've seen, experience the deep emotions we have, perhaps then all of mankind would come to appreciate how unique our lives are, how small we and our planet is to all that's out here.*

• • • •

ON THE THIRTY-THIRD day, *things take an unexpected turn. Leon is constantly coughing and having trouble breathing. He was always hacking back on Europa, but never this bad. Truth is, over the past fifteen-years we've seen this all too often... excessive mine dust and cigarettes resulting in deadly pulmonary infections. I have no idea how I've avoided it... maybe my good Scottish genes. Each day Leon's getting worse... he's spitting up* *flecks of blood and yellow-green stuff and gulping for air. Chris reports it to one of the guards, but the goon just smirks and waves him off... they'll be no medical assistance provided, end of discussion. We do our best to comfort Leon, get him to drink lots of water, but beyond that, there's little else to be done. On the morning of the twenty-fifth day, we awake to find him dead, his shirt soaked in his blood. As if Leon Grover was nothing more than a dead animal carcass, two guards hauled him off... to where we never knew.*

• • • •

THE LONG TRIP BECOMES increasingly boring *as each day passes. We wile away the hours eating three meals a day, taking occasional showers, gazing out at space, and sleeping... mostly sleeping. I've never slept so much in my life. Even on the last day of the trip, when I was super excited to be returning to Earth, I slipped into a deep slumber. Suddenly, I'm shaken awake by loud strange sounds and vibration, and for a few frightening seconds I have no idea where I am. I bound to a sitting position.*

"What, what?"

Chris leans over from his bunk and whispers.

"It's engine trust, we've begun our descent to Planet Fucking Earth."

"Jesus, how long have I been sleeping?"

"Oh, I'd say just over a year now."

"Whew, that's what it feels like."

Rubbing the sleep from my eyes, my face stretches into a wide grin, and I blow a hard sigh of relief.

"I thought we'd never get here."

Chris laughs... it's more of a snicker.

"Ye of little faith."

"Is today, Sunday, January 27th?"

"Unless they changed the calendar while we were gone it is. Why?"

"Tomorrow's my birthday."

"Whoa, happy birthday, dude, perfect time to return home. How old?"

"Forty-three."

"I'll have the goons bring a cake. Blow out the candles and you get a wish. What might that be?"

"That Europa explodes into a million pieces."

"That's the best you can come up with? First thing I'm gonna" do is get laid."

"Good luck with that, Poncho. What's your second choice?"

"To get laid a second time."

"And a second good luck with that. Me, I want a nice hot bowl of oatmeal."

• • • •

*AS SOON AS THE SHIP **is securely docked,** an announcement comes over the loudspeaker.*

"Passengers and crew members will disembark before cargo offloading begins."

Two gorillas that could have been crowd favorites in the Roman Colosseum in a previous life enter swinging their ever-present cattle prods. In a raspy, nicotine-soaked voice, one of them bellows.

"Okay you ground-crawlers, listen up. We've arrived at Base-Arizona. When we disembark, follow me single file to the delousing room to ensure none of you vermin are carrying foreign matter back to our beloved planet. When we enter the processing area, those wearing green badges line up at the door with the first letter of your last name. Those with red will follow officer Higgins here."

Ground-crawlers, vermin? I should rip his rancid tongue out and stick it up his ass. Not today, Billy Boy, not today, play nice...... Once off the ship, we're stripped naked and led into a windowless cement-block room where a fine green mist that smells like mint is released from overhead nozzles, presumably sanitizing us vermin and lowly ground-crawlers. We're issued new clothes... briefs, socks, T-shirt, long-sleeve shirt, pants, and a hip-length wool-lined jacket, all in brown... we look like what I remember UPS delivery men looking like. To celebrate my return to a planet a hell-of-a-lot more inviting than frozen Europa, I've sworn off cigarettes... Grover's ugly, painful death was not wasted on me......Raspy Voice rounds us up, we're off to the processing area. I'm understandably apprehensive, no, terror-stricken, of what will greet us. When I left, technology had elevated the world to the next level, some of it good, some not so good, much of it is addictive to the point of distraction. I can only wonder what awaits us now. We march single-file down a long, dark hallway. I'm half-way back in the line, Chris is behind me whispering low.

"Jesus, what's in store for us? Maybe nothing good."

"I vote for good. Hey, if we get separated, it's been nice knowing you. Hope you get laid."

"Count on it, Billy, count on it. I wish the hell Leon was with us."

"Yeah, me too."

At the end of the hallway, Raspy unlocks and swings open a steel door... bright light spills in. When it's my turn to step through, I hesitate. But this is Mother Earth, this is home, what am I frightened of? Pony up, Big Boy, take those last few steps to your future, there's light at the end of the tunnel, go to it. Raspy pokes me in the middle of my back with his cattle prod.

"Move it before you get a taste of this."

I glance back and squint at Chris, he shakes his head and rolls his eyes. Drawing in a quick, deep breath, I take a hesitant last step through the doorway.

Chapter 5
Welcome to The New World Order

A *guard brandishing an automatic weapon greets me as I step into the processing area. His finger is on the trigger, ready to mow down anyone who gets out of line. Another guard is holding back a German Shepherd that's straining at its leash anxious to sink his teeth into those who would dare piss him off. The processing center is one big open area. By God, there's color, a relief from gray, steel walls. These are painted a pastel green, the floor off-white tile. There're thirty to forty other inmates from who knows where already milling about, some with green badges, others with red, all looking as confused as me. The guards quickly round up those wearing red badges and lead them from the area. Now, it's only the green badges awaiting instructions. At that moment, reality bites hard... I'm a stranger in a strange land without the slightest clue why I've been returned, where I might be going, or what's to become of me. A loud speaker blares.*

"Attention. Green badges, line up at the door with the first letter of your last name."

All the doors are painted black and stand out against the green walls like a bad omen. The doors begin to my left with the 'A's through 'C's. I walk down the line until I find the one with P, Q, R" sign over it and line up behind three guys ahead of me. I look around for Chris, he's in his line... he waves, I smile and wave back. Thirty-five nervous minutes later, I'm at the head of the line staring at the black door wondering what happens on the other side. I'm about to find out because the heavyset guy that was in front of me comes out wearing a grim expression... not a good sign. For a fleeting moment we make eye contact... I think he's going to say something, but he doesn't, he looks away, turns left, and wanders off like he's unsure of where he's supposed to go. The light over the door flashes green, I search for

Chris again, but don't see him. Take a deep breath, Billy, put one foot in front of the other and march with courage to your future.

Chapter 6
Light at The End of The Tunnel

The room is stark white, **the walls bare**, *the exposed overhead fluorescent lights far too bright. A single white chair is positioned in front of a white desk, its surface is clean except for a clipboard and a nameplate that reads, 'Donald P. Costigan'. Typing on a computer keyboard to his left is a waif of a man wearing a dark blue suit and open collar gray shirt... the only color in an otherwise disorienting white Cyclorama. Costigan is bald with a pale complexion and hollow cheekbones that gives him a pinched, pissed-off look. With his eyes glued to the monitor, his right hand shoots up, his index finger points to the white chair.*

"Sit."

Like the good prisoner I was trained to be, I do as he instructs without comment.

"Your identification card—give it to me."

Damn! I forgot about the card. While I'm fumbling around for it, his right hand shoots up again, and he snaps his fingers twice.

"I don't have a year and a day—your card!"

Hey, shit-face, don't snap your fingers at me. I find the card in my left pant pocket and hold it out to him.

"Here is it."

He snatches it from my hand and inserts it in a slotted instrument next to his computer.

"Let's see what your story is."

He studies the screen for several seconds before mumbling.

"William Evan Russell—11349556. Born, Providence, Rhode Island. Graduated the New England Institute of Technology with a Criminal Justice Associates Degree. Five years as an undercover agent with the DEA. Hmm, the old Drug Enforcement Administration. Stationed in Providence, Rhode Island. Confirm that information."

"Yes, that's correct."

"Providence seems an odd place for a DEA undercover agent."

"My assignment was all of New England."

He raises an eyebrow, turns to his computer screen and studies.

"Says here you were sentenced to twenty-years after committing a crime of passion. Why a crime of passion?"

He turns and stares at me and for a few uncomfortable seconds, we size each other up.

"The sentencing guidelines called for twenty to forty years. My wife was raped and brutally stabbed to death. I executed the human garbage who did it. The judge took pity on me and gave me twenty."

"Sorry, your wife must have—"

Her name must be right there on the monitor... it offends me that he doesn't use it.

"Her name was Diedre Elizabeth Russo, Russell."

"Russo, sounds Italian."

"Sicilian."

"Is there a difference?"

"She thought so."

"Northern Italians might take issue."

"That would be their problem."

Costigan raises an eyebrow like maybe he thinks I'm an arrogant asshole, taps a few computer keys, and leans close to the monitor. Whatever he sees causes him to groan.

"Whoa, you really did it up big—shot the guy in both kneecaps before blowing off the top of his skull. Hmm, pretty darn cruel. Why the kneecaps first?"

"A bullet to a kneecap is as painful as it gets. I wanted him to suffer."

"It appears you accomplished that alright."

Costigan shakes his head and blows a quick, hard breath like he finds the whole affair distasteful.

"No matter the circumstances, Mr. Russell, you are not judge and jury. You do not get to summarily execute someone."

Ever so slightly, the right corner of my mouth curls into a grin.

"In that circumstance, I was judge, jury, and executioner."

"A decision for which you paid an extremely high price. From what I hear, Europa is most inhospitable."

"It is that."

"Well, now, let's see what the world has in store for you now."

"I wasn't told anything other than I was being sent back."

"It's a bit more complicated than that. As of now you're on parole with a work assignment."

What? What parole, what work assignment? Costigan's eyes whip back to the monitor.

"Let us see who's come to your rescue. Whoa, you hit the jackpot—the World Military Drug Enforcement regional facility in Boston. Lucky you, you get to play police officer again."

"Military? Boston?"

"I did not stutter, Mr. Russell. Lucky you, you get to play police officer again."

"But I—"

His hand shoots up.

"Stop—just listen. You are scheduled to fly to Boston later today. There you'll check into your authorized quarters and report to your assignment by ten AM tomorrow."

My head is swimming, he tossing stuff out fast, none of which I understand.

"I have housing at the other end?"

"That *is* what I said. As for the details, that will be clarified when you arrive. Any deviation in this itinerary and you'll be marked AWOL, and they *will* come looking for you, so do show up."

"None of this was explained before I left."

"That's why you get to spend this precious time with me."

I don't appreciate the little twerp's condescending tone and Id' like to tell him so, but I won't, I'll keep cool just to get through this.

"My parents live in Providence and have no idea I'm back. Is it possible I can see them first?"

He taps a few keys and leans close to the screen.

"Hmm... according to these records, your parents are deceased."

My spine stiffens... his words hit me like a slap in the face.

"That must be a mistake."

"No, no, says here they died in an auto accident four years ago."

Jesus, what? If that information is correct, why would the scabs on Europa have kept it from me? No, it has to be a mistake... another William Russell maybe.

"Are you sure?"

"According to this, yes."

"I was never informed."

"Well, you know now, Mr. Russell."

What a brutally callous thing for you to say, you pinch-faced son-of-a-bitch.

"I want to see the accident report."

He turns to me, his eyelids compressed, his jaw tight.

"Would you care to rephrase that?"

Now you've pissed him off good, Billy Boy, soften your tone.

"I'd like to see the accident report to confirm it was actually my parents."

"As a former cop, surely you know how to obtain the report. Now then, if you can contain yourself long enough for me to finish."

I'm crestfallen at the thought I will never see my parents again and try to hold it together. The little man opens a drawer, withdraws a red covered paperback book, sets it in the middle of the desk, and places his right hand flat atop it.

"This is the Redbook. It is the bible by which the new world government runs our fragile planet."

Whoa, what's he talking about?

"A world government, when did that happen?"

"Following the Pakistan-India incident."

"The what incident?"

"Didn't they tell you anything up there?"

"Nothing."

"Well, they don't pay me to give history lessons, just sit and listen."

He's drumming his fingers on the Red Book's cover.

"This book will familiarize you with all you need to know to survive the new world order. It is not casual reading, it *is* mandatory. Are you with me so far, Mr. Russell?"

Don't say anything that will bring you trouble, just nod and get the hell out of here.

"Hand me your badge."

I remove the green badge and hand it to him. He withdraws my ID card from the slot and tosses both in the waste basket behind him.

"I dare say, Mr. Russell, you look a bit confused."

"You're moving fast."

"Then I suggest you pay closer attention."

Screw you and the horse you rode in on Donald P. Costigan. His right hand disappears under the desk... he's reaching for something, there's a buzzing sound, a door opens behind him. Another guy enters like his only job is to wait in the dark for Mr. Pinch Face to buzz him in. This one is tall and rangy with a hangdog expression that suggests he's in need a decent meal. In his right hand is an instrument resembling a small hair dryer.

"Harvey here is going to insert a GPS tracker in your left forearm. It is to remain there for the length of your parole at which time it will be removed."

"How long am I on parole?"

"One year beginning tomorrow... if you show up. If for any reason that tracker is removed during your parole period, they'll come get you."

"What if it stops working?"

"Never had one fail yet."

Harvey taps me on the shoulder.

"What?

"Expose your left arm."

As soon as I remove my jacket and roll up my shirt sleeve, he swipes an alcohol pad over my forearm, presses his hairdryer down, and pulls a trigger. I feel a slight sting. He slaps a band-aid over the spot.

"You'll experience minor swelling for a day or two, that's normal. Keep it clean."

Then, as if he had given me nothing more than a flu shot, Harvey leaves through door number two. Costigan picks up the clipboard and extends it to me.

"This form confirms you understand all that has taken place here. Sign it."

Without reading it, I scribble my signature and hand it back. My new best friend smiles when he sees my scrawled signature. From his middle drawer, he takes out a stack of oversized, tan envelopes and leaf's through them.

"Russell, Russell, Russell—here it is."

He dumps the contents on the desk.

"A travel voucher for the flight to Boston, one for a taxi to transport you to your new quarters, as well as the addresses for your assigned quarters and where you'll be working. Oh yes, and this identification-debit card. Because the operation on Europa was run by a private enterprise, you earned spendable work credits."

"Credits?"

"Six-hundred to be exact—wow, forty whole credits for each year you were there. Lucky you. That should carry you until your salary kicks in unless you go on a spending binge. Paper money is no longer in use, so use that debit card for all purchases."

He holds the debit card up and waves it around.

"This is the only one you'll receive... lose it and you no longer exist."

He slips everything back in the envelope, places it inside the Red Book, and puts everything in a large manila envelope and pushes it toward me.

"Your employer will be notified that you've arrived, processed, and are on your way. You'll be flying out of Flagstaff Pulliam International Airport. Pulliam is not affiliated with this facility other than we ship you guys out from there. I caution you to be on your best behavior while mingling with the general public. Have I made everything clear enough?"

"Yes."

"We're finished here, Mr. Russell, out the door, turn left, board the bus to the air terminal. And please, try not to kill anyone else unless it's in the line of duty."

To say I detest this son-of-a-bitch is an understatement. My instinct is to slug him hard enough to force his jaw to the back of his head... that would earn me a trip back to glorious underground Europa. But I'll be damned if I'm gonna" let him have the last word. Shooting to my feet, I plant both hands on the front of the desk.

"I suggest you work on improving your bedside manner, the next guy might not have my patience."

Costigan feigns a sigh.

"Allow me to give you some advice. What you left behind fifteen years ago bears little resemblance to what you'll find out there now. There is a new world order, one you will find unrecognizable, but will be required to conform to like everyone else. I suggest you get with the program quickly or you may find yourself in trouble yet again. Next time they'll throw away the key. Now then, out the door, turn left, follow the signs to the bus."

Swooping up the envelope, I back my way to the door never taking my eyes from him.

"I question the origins of your mother... bovine perhaps."

The apathetic jerk shrugs, goes back to pounding on the keyboard as if I was nothing more than an inconvenient interruption in his otherwise mundane existence.

I *purposely slam the door, hoping it pisses off Costigan and scan the lines of men standing silently in paralyzed despondency, all waiting to be humiliated by the Mr. Pinch Faces of the world. Chris is nowhere in sight, I assume he's still being processed. I hope whoever he's facing is a little more civil than Costigan. Making eye contact with the next guy in line, I offer a friendly warning.*

"Enter at your own risk."

He gives me the evil eye as he passes, disappearing through the black door to the inner sanctum of abuse.

"Okay fella, but don't say you weren't warned."

My mind shifts to thoughts of my parents... I can't believe they're gone, that I'll never again see them. The last time was the day of my sentencing. Either my memory has completely failed or it's playing dirty tricks on me... I can't conjure up their faces. Why? Diedre, sweet Diedre, my beautiful late wife... I see her hazel eyes, her light brown hair, but for the love of me, I can't assemble a complete image of her face either. Okay, move on, don't dwell on it or it'll drive you nuts. The bus, find the bus. There, to your left, an overhead sign pointing the way to the ground transportation to the airport. Two steps are as far I get when a loud commotion breaks out... it's coming from the opposite direction and someone's shouting.

"Stop! Stop or we'll shoot!

Now the PA system is blaring.

"Code red, all officers to the processing area. Code red, all officers to the processing area."

I spin around to see what all the commotion's about. There, I see it, back by the first black door, a young guy is running at breakneck speed past the front of lines of men waiting to be processed, and he's coming directly at me. Guards are hot on his heels, their weapons at the ready... one of them is trotting behind that angry looking German Shepard straining at its leash, teeth showing, drool dripping from its open mouth. The loudspeaker blares again.

"All returnees, stay in your line, stay in your line!"

The guy that's running doesn't look older than his late twenties. He's flying as fast as he can one leg stretching far in front of the other in a desperate sprint to outrun the guards. I see a red badge pinned to his shirt... I don't recognize him... he wasn't on the ship with us. Holy crap, now one of the guards is raising his automatic weapon... he looks like he's gonna" shoot and I'm in his direct line of fire. Get out of the way, Billy, get the hell out of the way! But for whatever dumb reason, I freeze. The kid's coming at me fast... either I move or he'll run me down, or worse, I'll catch a bullet. Now he's twenty-feet away, fifteen, ten, five. I've got to get the hell out of his way! Too late, there's a burst of gunfire—bang, bang, bang, bang, bang—the bullets rip into the guy's back, his head snaps back, his eyes bulge, his mouth flaps open, his arms fly up and out and his hands land squarely on my chest almost knocking me over. He's clawing at me, his bulging eyes locked onto mine as the last seconds of consciousness ebb away and he slides to the floor landing flat on his face at my feet. My God, his shirt's ripped away, his back's exposed, he's bleeding like a sieve... the middle of his spine has been blown open. The guard turns the German Shepard loose. Before I can react the damn thing leaps over the dead guy slamming into me with the full force of his body and knocking me to the floor. He's growling, teeth showing, saliva dripping... the beast is going for my leg just as the guard grabs his collar, pulls him back, and shouts at me.

"Roll over, on your belly, do it now!"

Shaking, I do as he tells me and roll over on my stomach.

"You know this man?"

"No, no, sir."

"Why was he running to you?"

"He wasn't, he wasn't, I was in his way."

Now guards are standing over me with automatic weapons pointed at my head.

"Don't lie to me."

"I'm not."

In the commotion, I hear a familiar voice.

"What's going on out here, I heard gunfire? Oh my, what happened to that man? Oh God, his back! Is he dead?"

"He's a red badge, Mr. Costigan. He was making a run for it."

"Jeez, there's blood everywhere!"

"We have this under control, sir."

"The hell you do, why is this other man lying on the floor?"

"We think he might have known the guy."

"Are you people totally incompetent? I just processed and released him. Get him up off the floor."

"Really, sir, we have this under control."

"Get him up, damn it, do it now."

"Yes, sir."

I look up, the guard frowns and nods to two other guards who help me to my feet... I'm visibly shaking.

"Russell, show him your ID."

"It's in the envelope."

"Are you dense? I didn't ask you where it was, show it to the man."

The guard snatches up the envelope from the floor and hands it to me. My trembling hand rifles through it, finds the card, and I hand it to him. He examines it, then holds it up to Costigan.

"Can you verify this, sir?"

"What did I say that you didn't understand, officer? I processed this man out just minutes ago. Give him his ID back and let him be on his way."

"Yes, sir."

The guard hands me the card, I stuff it back in the envelope.

"Officer, apologize to this man."

"We're just doing our job, Mr. Costigan."

"Badly, it seems. Do it, please."

The guard is glaring at me... he's pissed., he doesn't want to do it. He shoots a grim look to Costigan then to me.

"It was a misunderstanding."

That's as close to an apology as I'm getting. Costigan tugs at my sleeve, pulls me aside and pats me on the arm.

"For heaven's sake, Russell, be watchful, it's a perilous world you've returned to."

"Who was that poor guy?"

"Red badges are transferred to other correctional facilities."

I'm still shaking... Costigan pats my arm again.

"Sorry you had to see this. Go now, catch that bus."

Is this the same Donald P. Costigan who moments ago took perverse pleasure in treating me like dirt? Now he's concerned for my well-being? Okay, man up, say something nice.

"I thought I was in trouble for a minute there. Thank you."

Damn if he doesn't smile wide and pat me on the arm a third time.

"You're welcome. On your way now, and be careful."

He strolls back to his office, but when he reaches the door, he turns back and grins like he knows something I don't.

"Still think my mother was of bovine origin?"

"Ah, sorry, bad choice of words."

"Yes, it was. Have a good life, Mr. Russell."

With a wry, satisfied smile, passive-aggressive Donald P. Costigan enters his super-white office, hopefully to be gone from my life forever. The loudspeaker blares.

"Everyone stay in line until the prisoner is removed. Step out of line and you will be arrested."

Two guys in white uniforms arrive with a stretcher and lift the dead guy onto it face down leaving his mutilated spine exposed. I'm suddenly feeling sick and nauseated and need to make it to a restroom before I lose it right here. Turning to my left, I see a men's room sign and make a beeline for it. Inside, one of the guards, who only moments ago had his automatic weapon pointed at my head, is taking a wiz at a urinal... his rifle propped against the wall next to him. We make eye contact, he grins, but says nothing. Entering a stall, I lock the door, spin around and miss the commode by six-inches as a projectile of greenish liquid propels from my mouth to the floor. I cough, I gag. The guy at the urinal calls to me.

"You alright in there?"

"Yeah, yeah, I'm fine."

"Sure? I can call somebody."

"I'm okay, Officer, thanks."

"Okay, suit yourself. Close call back there."

"Yeah, close call."

Right, you prick, you were all set to blow my brains out a few minutes ago. When I'm certain he's gone, I make it to one of the sinks and douse cold water on my face and look in the mirror... I'm white as a ghost. Get it together, Billy Boy, what's past is prologue, as the saying goes, nothing matters now but your future, moment by moment, one step at a time. Go find the damn bus and get the hell away from this place. When I exit the men's room, the dead guy is gone... two men are mopping the blood from floor. Taking a deep breath, I follow the signs to bus transportation. When I reach the exit, there's a checkpoint... the guard stops me.

"Your ID."

"Yes."

I dig it out of the envelope and show it to him.

"Okay, through this door, board the bus."

"Which one?"

He gives me a strained look.

"There's only one, it's white and it's big, can't miss it."

Is everyone here a smart-ass? Outside, just like he said, there's a big white bus. As I board, a guard holding an automatic weapon is standing by the seated driver. I smile, they don't. A dozen men dressed exactly like me are already in their seats... I don't see Chris among them. There's an empty row all the way in the rear, I take the window seat. A guy comes down the aisle and slips into the seat next to me and nods.

"Hi."

"Hi."

"Did you see what happened back there?"

"I was the one the he ran into."

"Yeah, yeah, now I recognize you. God, they shred that guy's back to pieces."

"That they did."

"Sick, really sick."

He puts out his hand, I take it and we shake.

"Europa?"

"Yeah."

"Fred, 498."

"Billy, 556."

"Oh, yeah, I remember seeing you on the trip."

"I recognize you too."

"What bay were you in?"

"Three-East."

"I was in Two-West. Boy, we had some humdingers in there. You took your life in your hands if you looked any of them in the eye."

"Same in bay three, man."

"Funny we never crossed paths in the mines."

"We could have."

"Europa, one God-awful, dangerous place, alright. At least we both made it out."

"Yeah."

"Where are they sending you?"

"Boston."

"Never been there. I'm off to Colorado."

As bad as I want to converse with a real person, I have no interest in talking to a former fellow inmate about the good old days. I turn to the window hoping he gets the message... thankfully, he does. Minutes later, the bus is full and still there's no sign of Chris. Hopefully, he's on the next one. As the bus pulls away, I glance out the back window... there's Europa-2 perched on its launch pad. My God, that sucker is huge... may I never see that hunk of steel again...... Once we clear the base the desert takes over... I'm overwhelmed by the sights. There's a couple of inches of snow on the ground and there's cactus, succulent plants, and pine trees, magnificent mountains in the distance, blue sky, and the sun is out. After fifteen-years of isolation living underground, what more could an ex-prisoner from Europa hope for? I could disappear in the desert and live off the land... how difficult can that be after what I've endured? Dumb idea, they'd come looking for me and that would be the end of that or worse... they'd do to me what they did to that poor guy back in processing. You're a free man now, Billy Boy, time to live like one. Yeah, right, easier said than done... I'm on parole and attached to their GPS tracker. What I really want to know is who sprung me from hell five-years early and why?

• • • •

AN HOUR LATER WE ARRIVE *at the Flagstaff Pulliam Airport. The place is crowded with passengers coming and going. The very sight of real people and not inmates gives me a high. It takes me a few minutes to figure out where to go, but I follow the signs and find the check-in counter without having to ask for help... baby steps. The attractive older lady behind the counter informs me the flight to Boston is delayed.*

"A mechanical problem, shouldn't be more than an hour to an hour and a half."

I give her my voucher, she issues me a boarding pass.

"Been through here before?"

"No, first time."

The voucher and my standard issue brown outfit are glaring neon signs that telegraphs where I just came from, so what's with her insolent question? I'll bet she uses that line with every parolee she meets just to amuse herself. Not nice, lady, not nice. She smiles her practiced smile and hands me a small brochure.

"This is the terminal layout showing where you'll find available services."

"Food?"

"There's several fine restaurants on the second-floor concourse as well as a fast-food court. Be at gate 7A at least a half hour prior to departure."

"Thank you."

"I hope you come through and visit again sometime. Have a nice flight, sir."

Wow, she's milking this for all its worth... I'm tempted to tell her to screw off. Ignore her, Billy, move on. So now I have time on my hands, no guards to harass me, how to spend it? Hopefully, I'll run into Chris before my flight leaves. Topping my bucket list is female companionship, but that'll have to wait... not too long, I hope. Right now, I'll settle for real food, no oatmeal or brown bread... the food court is my destination. I see a sign pointing the way and head in that direction. I'm almost there... I just have to follow my nose now. Whoa, I'm there and overwhelmed... there's a smorgasbord of whatever one desires... pizza, Chinese, burgers, sandwiches... it's all there. I settle on the fast food burger joint and order a double patty, with cheese, fries, and a Coke and use my debit card for the first time. Will miracles never cease, I have real money to spend. The meal costs me seven credits. Finding a seat at the open table area, I dig into the burger. My tongue comes alive alerting whatever part of my brain dealing with pleasurable sensory sensations just how wonderful real food can be. And the fries, they're incredible. Savoring each bite as if it's pure ambrosia, I wolf down the burger and order another... there went another four and a half credits. I wolf down the second burger... my stomach sends a signal I shouldn't eat anymore. Finding a seat in a quiet corner, I watch in awe as the parade of humanity passes me by... white, brown, black, tall, short, fat, skinny, they're all there in different shapes, colors, and sizes, some with happy faces, some not. It's mankind's very own alien society. Reminds me of the Intergalactic Café scenes in those old 'Star Wars' films that I saw on YOUTUBE years after they were released. Shamelessly, I leer at every fetching woman that passes to the point of embarrassment. I haven't seen or touched the female species in fifteen years and dammit, I want one. I catch the eye of one lovely blond creature who looks my way, realizes I'm sizing her up, smiles knowingly, then fades into the crowd never to be seen again...... The announcement finally comes that my flight is ready for boarding, I make my way to the gate. My seat is halfway back on the right side... a window and an aisle... mine is the aisle. An announcement is made... the flight to Boston will take three and a half hours. The very idea that I'll be among humans who actually converse with one another gives me yet another high. Maybe I can engage at least one in real conversation that excludes any mention of ore mines, bad food, or cruel guards. A smiling, white-haired elderly lady... a grandmother for sure... stops at my aisle and places a small bag in the overhead rack.

"Hello, young man."

I toss her a wide, friendly smile.

"Hello."

"The window seat, it's mine."

"Oh, right, sorry."

Stepping into the aisle, she slides past me, sits herself down, buckles her seatbelt, and looks out the window with a sigh.

"They're forecasting snow for Boston."

"Really?"

"Not looking forward to that."

She folds her hands, places them in her lap, and promptly falls asleep dashing all hope of a conversation. Not even the noise of takeoff wakes her... she's one hell of a sound sleeper. All around me, I hear others chatting easi-

ly. It's exhilarating and I want desperately to join in. I settle for a brief encounter with the flight attendant who asks what I would like to drink and whether I prefer chips or pretzels. Later, when I visit the restroom the same attendant smiles her practiced smile and asks if I'm enjoying the flight... fine, I tell her. She turns away to attend to her duties dashing any hope we might exchange pleasantries if only for a brief few moments. When I return to my seat the old lady is still in a deep sleep. Each time she exhales she emits a soft wheezing sound. With nothing else to do, I take out the Red Book. First page lists 'The Peoples Cooperative Populist Party, One World in Unity—World Headquarters Marseilles, France.' Second page is a litany of the most serious threats to present day society... overcrowding, poverty, drug use, and rampant disease making governing 'difficult.' Difficult? Sounds like it's a bit more than difficult. The next three pages present a blueprint of the government's plan to deal with these issues. None of them strike me as workable concepts. Subsequent pages are a manifesto of rules, regulations, and laws by which the populace is to abide, stated in language that sends a clear warning to anyone foolish enough to challenge authority. I skip ahead, looking for an explanation of the Pakistan-India event that Costigan had referenced, but find none. Just what had caused every country on the planet to agree to a world government? What could be more drastic than that... headquartered in France yet? In my wildest imagination, I can't envision how a world government would even function. Okay, I've read enough of this dystopian tome... back in the envelope it goes...... I must have dozed off because I don't remember the rest of the flight until the announcement comes that we would be landing at Boston's Logan International Airport in twenty-minutes. The old lady opens her eyes and yawns.

"How was your flight, young man?"

"Fine. How was your nap?"

"I sleep well on planes."

"Yes, I see that."

"I'm visiting my daughter's family in Boston. I'm so grateful for my two lovely granddaughters. Do you have a family?"

"No, not married."

"Ever been?"

"Once, a long time ago, but she died."

"Oh, so sorry. Children?"

"No."

"What brings you to Boston?"

"A new job."

"What is it you do?"

"I'm a police officer."

Her brow furrows, she makes a smacking sound with her lips.

"My, my, in this frightening world, we need lots of you. I pray one day we go back to the way it was, before those madmen took over, back when we had our own Constitution, not theirs. But I can't imagine it will happen in my lifetime."

I want to ask her a million questions, but I dare not... I'd have to explain why I don't know the answers. The wheels touch down and in short order, we're at the terminal and off-loading.

"Well, the best of luck to you, young man. And for heaven's sake, help us stay safe from the madness."

"I promise. Enjoy your visit with your family."

Her brow stretches up and she chuckles softly.

"I will if my son-in-law holds his acid tongue. His mother must not have breastfed him."

She laughs, tosses me a friendly smile, and strolls off down the aisle. There goes my limited contact with a fellow human being... except to thank the flight attendant on my way out for the soft drink and pretzels.

Chapter 8
A Slow Ride to Hell

It's 10:32 PM. I'm moving freely through crowds of ordinary everyday citizens... it's intoxicating and intimidating, but I can't shake the feeling people are staring at me. The signs to ground transportation lead to the baggage area and the revolving doors to the outside. The cool night air smells sweet and pure, unlike the stink of human sweat and the putrid odor of Pistoriore. Damn, I want a cigarette. I notice there's no private vehicles coming or going, just a long line of identical red vehicles with the words 'Ministry Taxi's - Electric Powered' stenciled in white on the rear doors. Digging out the address to my destination and the travel voucher, I approach the first taxi parked at the head of the line. The dark-skinned driver looks young, maybe in his mid-twenties. He's leaning against the front passenger door and smiling as I approach. Everyone in a service job has a practiced smile.

"Halooo, you need ride?"

"Yes."

He speaks with a distinct accent.

"Where, sir?"

"47 West Fourth South Boston?"

"Yes, sir."

"I have a transfer voucher."

"Very good, sir."

I hand it to him, he examines it, stuffs it in his shirt pocket.

"Good, thank you, sir. Luggage?"

"No luggage."

"Okay, we go."

Riding in an electric car is a first for me... driverless electric vehicles had been all the rage before I left... sometimes they worked, often they didn't. I see the old lady was right, it snowed about an inch but the road is clear. The driver heads South on I-90 across Boston Harbor.

"Boston Harbor sir, very nice."

"Yes, it is."

As we cross over the harbor, I see a large electric billboard at the far end of the bridge. It displays a number over billion, but the total is continually decreasing

"Whoa, that's some billboard."

The driver's eyes dart to the rearview mirror again.

"Population total—going down."

"Oh, right."

Ah yes, over-population. Go forth and multiply... and boy did we ever.

"Returning home, sir?"

"Not really. Visited here before, but that was many years ago."

"Welcome back, sir."

"Mind if I ask where you're from?"

"Shri Lanka, Sir."

He taps his license mounted in a frame on the dashboard.

"My name is Rashmi."

"Rashmi."

"Yes."

"Been here long, Rashmi?"

"Five-years, sir."

"Have any trouble immigrating?"

"No, sir, government sponsored. All taxis run by Government. They chose the city I go."

"Do you like living in Boston?"

"Good when I arrive, not so much now."

"Why is that?"

"Much drugs and crime now, not safe. Is it so where you are coming from?"

Think quick, Billy, where are you from?

"San Francisco... it's bad out there too. So, drugs are the big problem?"

"Yes, here drugs, poverty, crime, disease. Many people die. Government say that is good, must reduce population."

I see an opening and seize it... maybe I can get an answer to what Costigan called the Pakistan-India event... that seems to be the pivot point for everything that followed.

"Damn those Pakistanis, screwed everything up."

Rashmi's brow crinkles, his eyes shoot to the review mirror.

"Yes, terrible, sir."

That's as far as he seems to want to go with that... can't press him further.

"I only see taxi's, where are all the private vehicles?"

"Curfew, only taxi's after nine."

"Oh, yeah right, forgot."

He exits to I-93 South and keeps shooting me looks in the review mirror like he wants to talk.

"What kind of work you do, sir?"

"Law enforcement."

"You are policeman?"

"Yeah."

"Oh, oh, very dangerous work."

"It can be, yes."

"You be safe."

"Thanks, I intend to."

We're on I-93 for only a couple of miles before we come to the exit for West 4th. Crossing over Silver Street, he stops on the right seven houses down, turns off his lights, but leaves his engine running and points to a two-story white clapboard tenement across the street. It's a typical two-story tenement so readily identified with older New England neighborhoods.

"Sir, this is it, don't be standing around."

He's acting a little uneasy, sitting pole-straight, peering out the window, his head swiveling from left to right like he's looking for something.

"Something wrong?"

"Don't be standing around, sir, not safe."

"Okay, thanks for the ride."

"You're welcome, sir. Good luck."

"To you too, Rashmi."

No sooner have I exited the car and closed the door, Rashmi turns on his lights and peels off, leaving me standing alone in the middle of the cold dark street.

"And a good evening to you too, Shri Lanka guy."

Must not be much traffic through here, the road is covered with a light dusting of snow. Staring up at the house, I can't help but wonder what I'll find inside. It has to be a thousand percent improvement over where I've been. The building is dark except for a flickering light in a first-floor window... someone must be watching television. There better be a TV in my place. 'My place', sounds odd to even think it. As I begin to cross the street, I hear footsteps moving fast over the snow. I look to my left, no one, then to my right... two shadowy figures are moving toward me fast... I take a quick step back.

"Hey."

There's no response... I strain to make out faces, but it's too dark.

"What do you want?"

"Whatever you can give, kind sir."

It's a man's voice, low and raspy, not demanding, more like pleading.

"I have nothing to give, back away."

"Anything will do kind sir, anything."

A light comes on over the front door of the tenement. I turn to it, then back to the two in front of me. The light casts just enough illumination to make out an elderly man and woman standing a few feet away, their faces gaunt, their eyes dark and sunken. I'm guessing they're in their late sixties. Their brown overcoats are frayed and dirty like they haven't been cleaned in a while. The man is unshaven... his thinning hair is white. The woman's hair is also white, her face gaunt, her expression plaintive. The door to the tenement swings open, I pivot to it... a short, balding man in loose-fitting blue jeans, house slippers, and a gray T-shirt rushes out, a cluster of keys jingling from his belt. In his right hand is what looks like a two-foot long riding crop. Moving quickly down the three cement steps to the sidewalk, he waves whatever that is in his hand high over his head and yells.

"Get your damn sick asses the hell away from that man! Go on, move it, or you'll get a taste of this!"

The two anorexic-looking elderly figures slink off into the dark night.

"Are you Russell?"

"Yeah."

"About damn time. I expected you earlier."

"The flight was delayed."

"Wonderful, just wonderful. You've kept me up way past my bedtime."

"Sorry, I had no control over the aircraft's mechanical problem."

"Yeah, well, get your ass in here before them street scum steals you blind. You're lucky there wasn't more of them. Come on, come on, it's cold, get in here."

"Who were they?"

"Street scum, whacked out on drugs most likely."

"I didn't get your name?"

He ignores me and steps inside... I'm barely in when he turns off the outside light, slams the door, and locks it. He hits a wall switch... a light comes on at the top of a flight of stairs. It's then I get my first good look at the guy. He's in his mid-sixties for sure, short, bald and overweight by twenty pounds. Before I can ask his name again, he's bounding up the stairs two at a time like a rabbit scampering for its burrow... impressive for a short, aging, fat man. He quicksteps down the hall to the only door on the right. I see light seeping from under the door across from this one... it smells like someone's cooking... whatever it is, it doesn't smell all that ap-

petizing. The mystery man removes a key from his ring, inserts it into the lock, swings the door open, steps inside and turns on a ceiling light in the middle of the room.

"Here is it, home sweet home."

Crossing the threshold, my nose is assaulted by a musty odor like the place hasn't been lived in for a while. He notices my sour expression.

"Open the window, it'll be fine."

The compact space sure isn't much to look at... a fading beige sofa, and a desk with a thirty-two-inch flat-screen TV perched on it. The only window overlooks the dark street below. To the left of the living room area is a wood dining table with two chairs beside a small kitchen with a refrigerator, a flat top electric stove, and a microwave sitting on the counter next to the sink. The guy points to the two doors just beyond and to the left of the dining table.

"Bathroom and closet to the left, bedroom to the right."

"No one mentioned what this was costing me."

"Five-hundred credits a month—includes utilities and cable."

"When's it due?"

"You short?"

"Until payday, yeah."

"Take care of it then."

This place is just short of a shit-hole and not worth rent to begin with. My salary better be a hell of a lot more generous than the credits I earned on Europa.

"I didn't catch your name."

"Didn't give it."

"Okay, how about now?"

Okay, that came off sounding snarky... if he's offended, he doesn't show it.

"Julius Sommers, house mother, and all-around nice guy. I own the place. Call me Jules."

I stick out my hand to shake his, but he doesn't offer it.

"What's your handle, William, Billy?"

"Billy."

"Billy—Billy Russell it is then. The apartment's been empty for a while."

"I would have never guessed."

He shoots me a narrow-eyed look like he's trying to decide if I was being a wise- ass, but then he grins.

"Good, a sense of humor, I like that. We're gonna' get along just fine. Now, everything you need is here: sheets, towels, cooking and eating utensils. There's no cleaning service, it's up to you to keep it up. There's a washer and dryer in the basement. If you need instructions on how to use them, let me know. As for TV, the government news channel is broadcast out of a studio in Marseilles, France via Menwith Hill Station, the old Royal Air Force base near Harrogate, North Yorkshire, England. Back in the old day's it provided communications and intelligence support services to the United Kingdom and United States[1]."

He laughs, the fat around his waist jiggles and the ring of keys on his belt jangle.

"That's more information than you need, but I'm ex-military and it's all about details, details, details."

"What branch?"

"United States Marines. You?"

"No, went into police work right out of college."

"Anyway, the government news channel pumps out bullshit propaganda twenty-four hours a day. The other news outlets, CNN, MSNBC, FOX are mostly soft news and documentaries now."

"Why is that?"

As soon as I ask, I wish I hadn't. He shoots me a questioning look.

"Government restrictions."

"Yes, right."

---

1.   https://en.wikipedia.org/wiki/United_States

"Channel thirteen is music 24/7. Most of the entertainment channels run way too many reruns, I don't watch them. Even the newer shows suck, like maybe those who actually knew how to write like adults have died replaced by fifth graders."

"It won't be a problem for me, I don't watch a lot of TV."

"Insert your debit card in that little slot just below the TV screen whenever you want to check your status."

My status? Huh, at the moment my status is no status. Dropping the envelope and the new toiletries pouch we received in Arizona on the sofa, I stroll to the kitchen, find a light switch, and flick it on.

"What about Internet?"

"No computer. You can buy one, of course, but we don't provide Internet service, so if you do buy one, it'll be a glorified word processor at best. Great if you want to keep a diary or write a book. The internet's a waste of time anyway, it'll poison your brain with more bullshit than a herd of bulls with diarrhea. Now for the good news. The frig is stocked to get you through for a few days, courtesy of your new employer. Coffee is in the cabinet above the sink next to a..."

He reaches into the cabinet and pulls out a bottle.

"... ta da... a bottle of good Bourbon, also courtesy of your employer."

"I was a gin man myself, Beefeaters on the rock, two olives, no vermouth. But the Bourbon will do just fine until I find a liquor store."

"There's one not far over on West Broadway—turn left on Broadway, you'll see it, big yellow sign. Now to business. I'm not privy to what qualified you for this penthouse suite, that's above my pay grade. All I know is you're on parole from wherever you were for whatever reason, and I'm to provide you housing. That's what the government pays me for. I don't ask questions beyond that. It's none of my business to begin with."

"I'm assigned to Precinct 513."

"It's an easy ten-minute walk from here. Out the front door, turn right, right again on Broadway, you'll find it a couple of blocks down on the left. Can't miss it, a two-story red brick building. Where's your suitcase?"

I wasn't about to have a heart-to-heart about where I've been, so I lie.

"The airline lost it."

"So much for that, you'll never see it again. You'll pass a clothing store on Broadway on your way to the precinct. Not a lot to choose from, but they won't rip you off. There's also a small grocery a couple of doors down from the clothing place. If you need me for anything, I live on the first floor, doors on the left at the bottom of the stairs. The apartment across from yours is also occupied."

"Someone was cooking over there."

"That's Conrad, strange guy, keeps to himself. Keep your door locked and stay off the streets after dark unless you're into drugs or have a death wish. What time is your check-in?"

"Ten in the morning."

He hands me the door key along with a second one.

"The longer one is for the front door. Never go out or in unless you lock it behind you. Sleep well."

He moves quickly to the door, stops and does a slow turn back, studies me for a second.

"Don't take offense, but nobody gets assigned to this building that doesn't have a story. If you ever feel the need to share yours, I'm all ears. If not, just tell me to screw off. That, usually, but not always, shuts me up."

I give him my best stoic stare... he tosses his head back and laughs.

"That's a screw off look if I ever saw one. You and me, we're gonna get along just fine."

And with that Jules, the energizer bunny, is gone. I decide then and there he's going to take some getting used to. Scanning the place again, I decide the accommodations are austere at best, but I have no business com-

plaining considering. Be thankful, Billy, be thankful. Time to celebrate your new-found freedom. I seem to recall something about a bottle of Bourbon hiding in a closet. I find it in the cabinet above the sink where Jules left it... it brings a smile of anticipation to my lips, my tongue, and my throat. Finding a glass, I pour a shot and down it in one gulp... it stings like hell, but I savor it like it's straight from the fountain of youth. Pouring a second shot, I raise the glass in a toast say out loud,

"To Europa, may a giant asteroid park itself there."

Down that second shot goes tasting even better than the first. So, what might there be in the frig? I see there isn't much... a package of hot dogs, baloney, Swiss cheese, a can of sliced pears, and a loaf of whole wheat bread. That's it. I slap a couple of slices of the baloney and cheese between two slices of bread and munch on it. Time to investigate... first the bathroom because I have to take a wiz. I swing the door open and immediately wish I hadn't. It's not much bigger than an oversized closet... a commode to the left, a rod on the wall next to it with several wire clothes hangers... so much for a closet. There's sink to the right and a small shower stall behind a powder-blue plastic curtain covered with red and white stars. I relieve myself and move on to door number two to see what awaits me there. The light switch is just inside on the right wall. It turns on a bare ceiling bulb dead center of a single bed, which is a foot from either side wall. That leaves three choices, crawl in from the bottom, slide along the wall sideways, or move the bed against one wall. That last one is not an option, I'm used to sleeping with both sides open. There's no night stand, no lamp, but there is a small window high up on the right wall... can't be more than two-feet by a foot and a half... why did they even bother? Off my clothes come, I turn off the light and sit on the edge of the bed staring into the darkness trying to come to grips with all that has happened since I vacated beautiful downtown Europa... it feels surreal. A thousand questions are bouncing around in my head... there's the little matter of a fifteen-year brain-gap that's in dire need of replenishing. For the time being, all I can do is remain vigilant, watch, observe, learn. I'm beginning a new life... no let's correct that... I'm picking up where the old one left off, so be thankful, run with it and make grapes into wine. Two quick shots of Bourbon when I haven't had a drink in over fifteen-years has made me a bit woozy. Used to be I could hold my own, but that was then, this is now. Falling back to the mattress, I close my eyes and try to come to grips with the frightening realization I've returned to a world I don't recognize, one that I may find difficultly merging with. I'm alone, there is no one to turn to... that leaves a God-awful empty feeling in my gut. I try conjuring up my wife and parent's faces again, but like yesterday, the day before, and all the days before that, I come up blank, and damn it, I don't understand why. It's like a shroud's been pulled over my memory... each time I try, I almost get there, but not quite. My mood darkens, I'm angry, why wouldn't I be in a foul mood? But there isn't a damn thing I can do about it so I lay back on the bed and drift off to sleep.

· · · ·

MY EYELIDS FLUTTER like a butterfly then open. It's midnight black, I can't see a damn thing. My legs are still dangling off the edge of the bed where I left them. I have no idea how long I've been out or where I am until the neurons in my brain decide to cooperate. Okay, got it, I'm in my new digs in South Boston, Massachusetts. I grope for the light switch, turn it on, light spills out the door and I frown.

"I need to find a good decorator."

Sliding off the bed and dragging myself into the living room, such as it is, I find the TV remote on the desk next to the initials SKL that a previous occupant scratched into the wooden surface. I examine the remote... electronics challenge me, always have, hope this isn't too complicated. It's a TV remote, Billy, how difficult can it be? The screen comes alive:

The screen comes alive:

Press 14-48 for entertainment channels,
10 for government news, 13 for music.
For status insert ID card and press 2.

Inserting my ID card into the slot, I press #2. The screen changes.

11349556 – Clearance verified.

TOUCH SCREEN & SELECT ONE

(1) Account Update

(2) User Profile

(3) General Information

(4) Cancel

Let's start with #2 and see what dirt they have on me.

• • • •

William Evan Russell

Age 43

Residence: 27 Ash Street, Boston, NH

Position: World Military Police, Unit 513,

Boston, New Hampshire

Weapons Restriction - None

Credits Available: 588.50

Restricted to M-5 Clearance

Press 0 to continue, 00 to cancel

AT LEAST I'M LISTED as a living, breathing member of the human race again, that's a major improvement. Removing the debit card, I press 0:

Select channels 10 for news, 14 through 48

For entertainment, 13 for music.

Roll the dice, try channel 18. A man is racing like the wind toward the camera. The music is hard driving and loud. Hot on his heels is another guy with a baseball bat in his right hand. In short order, the second guy catches up with the first and beats him senseless with the bat. The scene cuts to a closeup of the first man's bloodied head. More blows to his head and shoulders and one to his stomach… the guy crumbles to the ground, a bloody mess. Who the hell writes this stuff? Shades of the messy incident in the processing center back at Base-Arizona. Enough, roll the dice again, try channel thirteen for some music. Whoa, what' this... after all these many years Paul McCartney singing 'Hey Jude'... it brings a smile to my lips... damn if I don't remember the words. Singing along, I rescue the Bourbon from its dark hiding place, down another shot, crawl back into the sack while Mr. McCartney serenades me back to dreamland.

Chapter 9
Welcome to Purgatory

I**'m either sleeping or awake, I can't decide.** *Phantom images are moving fast bouncing around in my head like an errant bullet... they're vivid and they feel real... I'm working my ass off in one of the cold, damp mine shafts covered head to toe in dusty, smelly ore... sleeping in a steel box way too close to snoring, belching, farting inmates... eating the oatmeal that I hate just to stay alive... Quasi marching up and down the row of bunks threatening to zap anyone and everyone for the slightest infraction. Whoa, what the hell is this? Dierdre's standing at the foot of my bunk smiling warmly. Finally, finally, for the first time I see her face clearly... she's as beautiful as I remember. Her hand goes out to me, I reach for it and wrap it in mine, but I can't feel it. Stop it Billy, stop it, Deirdre's dead! Now I'm standing before the judge in the courtroom flanked by my parents and my attorney. The judge—a woman—is reading my sentence... twenty-years hard labor. I swallow hard, my dad gasps, mom collapses and they call a medic. Now someone's tugging on my left big toe. Damn it, who is it, what do they want?*

"Hey, wake up!"

Hard as I try, I can't open my eyelids, they feel glued shut.

"Come on, wake the hell up!"

Jesus, it's Quasi, I must be slow getting up this morning, he's going to zap me for sure. Wake up, wake up! My eyelids finally pop open like a soda can, sweat covers my face, I bound to a sitting position. Who the hell is the short, fat, balding guy at the foot of my bed?

"Wake up, already!"

It's Jules, the energizer bunny.

"What the hell are you doing here, Jules?"

"Didn't you say you had a 10:00 AM check-in?"

"Yeah, yeah, why?"

"Well, soldier, it's nine thirty-five."

"Holy crap!"

"Nothing holy about it, better hurry. And you left the music on all night—I turned it off."

"Thanks."

"You're welcome. Now get a move on, it's your first day in school, get your ass moving. And if some buggers approach you on the street, make it clear you're a cop, that'll send them sprinting for cover."

And with that Juley baby is gone. I skip shaving and showering... a questionable decision at best my first day on the job but there's no time. I wash my face, brush my teeth, and comb my hair. On my clothes go... I bolt out the door and take the stairs two at a time... Jules is standing at his open door.

"Don't dilly-dally on the way."

"What?"

"No sightseeing, get to the office."

Sightseeing? Is he kidding? I reach for my key to unlock the door.

"It's unlocked."

Out the door I go.

"You're welcome, Billy."

It's cold, but the sun, that glorious orb of warmth and light, is shining... for that I'm eternally grateful. I'm getting my first daylight look at 4th Street. Both sides are lined with old two-story tenements either painted white with gray trim or light gray with white trim. As I make my way toward Broadway, I pass three homeless people... at least I assume they are. We don't make eye contact. I cross over Silver Street and run into a man and a woman approaching me with outstretched hands. I swear it's the old couple from the night before, but I can't be certain. I tell them I'm a cop... they quickly back away like I have a communicable disease...... On the corner of 4th and Broadway is Sully's News Stand that also sells coffee, but there's no time... I smile at the guy behind the counter and move on. I pass the small clothing store on Broadway and peer in the window... I'll stop on my way home. With all that's happening, I almost forgot today's my birthday. Later I'll celebrate with new clothes and shots of Bourbon and a few of those hot dogs. Lucky me, I'm living large... or not...... The two-story red brick precinct is easy to spot on the corner of 'E' Street and Broadway. The prominent sign to the left of the double entry doors reads, 'World Military Regional Precinct 513'. *There's a dozen Boston city police vehicles and six unmarked Chevy Cruzes' bearing government plates in the adjoining parking lot next to a green unmarked military Humvee. I hesitate entering the building taking a moment to work up the courage to pass through to what is the next chapter of my life. A uniformed city cop comes out and sees me standing there.*

"You look a little lost."

"Ur, I'm reporting in."

"City or Drug Enforcement?"

"Enforcement."

"City cops on the first floor, drug troops on the second. You'll have to check in before they'll let you go up."

"Do you have the time?"

He glances at his watch.

"Ten-ten."

Shit-shit.

Descending the three cement steps, he offers me his hand.

"John Goulding."

I extend mine, and we shake.

"Billy Russell."

"Nice to meet you, Officer Russell. Where are you coming from?"

"San Francisco."

"Good luck with the new assignment. Tough as nails bunch up there."

"Oh?"

"Bad enough we deal with the small-time crap on the streets. Those guys upstairs deal with the big picture day in and day out. How was it out West?"

"They deal with the big picture day in and day out. Bad enough I have to deal with the small-time pushers and users on the streets. How was it out West?"

"Bad, really bad."

"It's bad here too. Well, good luck, I'm off to sweep clean the streets of South Boston."

"Good luck with that."

"I'll need all the luck I can get."

I climb the steps to the front door and pass through. The first floor is buzzing with activity. A uniformed lady cop behind the reception desk greets me.

"Yes, sir?"

"Good morning, I'm reporting in."

"For?"

"Drug Enforcement."

"Second floor. I'll need your ID before you can go up."

I hand it to her, she inserts into a slot on a device next to her computer.

"Okay, Officer Russell, second floor, third door on the right. Once they issue your badge you won't have to check in here anymore. Stairs are over there to your left. One day they might put in an elevator, but with budgets the way they are, don't hold your breath."

"Thank you."

On the second floor, the hall runs along windows that overlook Broadway, the offices are on the right. The sign on the first door reads...

'World Military Command, Precinct 13, Major Jesse Randolph, Commander'.

The small sign on the second door identifies a break room... the coffee smells good. The sign on the third door is drug enforcement.

'Narcotics Control, Lieutenant Frank Wilson, Director.'

I wish the hell I was at least clean shaven and not in these brown clothes... stop obsessing and get in there. Taking a deep breath through my nose and blowing it out, I take two nervous steps forward and enter. A woman is sitting at a horseshoe desk, her back to me... she's typing on her computer. The nameplate on the desk identifies her as 'Jade Miro'. Beyond, the room is one big open space with no windows. There're four desks that face out... a fifth is pushed up against the far-right back wall between two doors. Only one desk is occupied... the closest one... the man sitting there pays me no attention. The place is not much to write home about, but at least the walls are light beige and not cold, gray steel. The lady turns to me.

"Thought I heard someone come in. What can I do for you?"

Maybe it was my forced absence and enforced celibacy, maybe I'm as horny as one man can be after zero-physical contact with the fairer sex going on sixteen-years, but I can't help but notice the Asian lady staring at me is a bloody knockout, a full ten... flawless olive complexion, high cheekbones, full lips, expressive almond-shaped brown eyes that match her hair pulled back in a ponytail. Dierdre often wore hers in a ponytail.

"Sir, what can I do for you?"

The words escape her shapely mouth in a low, smooth, smoky tone... at least that's how it reaches my ears. Focus, Billy, focus.

"Yes, ah, sorry, I'm reporting in."

"Are you Russell?"

"That would be me."

She raises an eyebrow and glances at her watch.

"You're late."

Oh hell, first day and I've already been scolded the receptionist. Strike one.

"Yeah, sorry about that."

"Lieutenant Wilson demands promptness. I need your ID."

I dig it out of my pocket and hand it to her. She inserts it in a device next to her computer, verifies my status, and hands it back.

"After you pass muster with the effervescent Lieutenant, I'll check you in and get you up to speed. Beside promptness the Lieutenant demands his boys be clean shaven except for Victor's mustache."

"I was running a bit late, so I—"

"We've already established that."

Ouch! Strike two, this lady's tough. She extends a perfectly formed long-finger to her intercom.

"Lieutenant, Officer Russell's here."

A deep, gravelly voice resonates back.

"He's late."

Crap, strike three. The lovely Jade raises her right hand and points to a door to her right... I divert my eyes to her left hand... there's no rings. Easy Billy, put your tongue back in your mouth. Pretending I didn't see her nameplate, I say,

"Ur, I didn't get your name."

Her phone rings, she points to her nameplate as she answers.

"Drug Enforcement, please hold."

She motions to the open door off to her right.

"Through there. Come see me when the Lieutenant's done with you."

"Thank you."

First impression... as lovely a creature as she is, this lady's all business...... Wilson's office is small with a single window overlooking some houses. Two chairs face a dark wooden desk, the gold nameplate mounted on wood identifies the occupant as 'Frank R. Wilson.' I guess his age to be fifty-five plus, average height, receding salt and pepper hair, stout build, weathered face. A large map of New England hangs above a credenza on the wall behind him. No pictures, no mementoes, no awards.

"Come in, Russell, close the door. You're late."

"Sorry, I was whacked out from the trip and overslept. Won't happen again."

"No, it won't. And I expect you to show up clean shaven. No facial hair here except for Victor's damn mustache."

"Yes, sir."

So far, my first day is going straight down the commode. Wilson's up and coming around to greet me, thrusts out a beefy hand and shakes mine vigorously.

"Settled in okay?"

"The accommodations are a little raw, but it's fine. Thanks for the groceries and the booze."

"You're welcome, take a load off, have a seat."

As he strolls back to his chair, I notice what I hadn't when he first approached... he walks with a limp favoring his right leg.

"You go by William?"

"Billy."

"First things first, Billy. I know where you've been and why. That information stays with me and Major Randolph. The rule here is don't ask, don't tell. Everyone's history is their business. And never ever talk to anyone outside this office about what goes on here. Is that clear?"

"Yes, sir."

"Now then, under the terms of your release, you're on parole for one year starting today. At the end of that year, assuming all goes well, the government will reward you by expunging your record. Another condition of your early release from camp Europa is this is your life's work until you retire, die, or expire in the line of duty. I've only lost one officer, don't be the second."

I'll be doing this for the rest of my working life? Ah, yes, it's called job security.

"Now, my rules are simple. I expect you to be where and when you need to on time, keep your eyes and ears open, and trust no one outside this office... and never challenge my authority."

Wilson stops and studies me again and each time he does, he makes me nervous.

"Having served with the DRA, this must feel like a homecoming for you."

"Yes, sir, it's good to be back with the DEA."

"The DEA no longer exists, we're their replacement."

Before I can ask why the DEA no longer runs the show, he swivels in his chair and points to the wall mounted map.

"We're responsible for Maine, Vermont, New Hampshire, Massachusetts and Rhode Island, and Delaware. We're under the direct command of the military. We work hand and glove with them when—"

"Why the military?"

He shoots me an unmistakable look that says, 'don't interrupt me'.

"... when we go out on major busts. The regional military commander, Major Jesse Randolph—you passed his office down the hall—reports to the World Military Command in Marseilles. His office does the front-end work, identifying the bad guys and where we might find them. Together with a SWAT team, we go out and shut them down. Most of the time we leave small-time street stuff to the local cops. Oh, and, uh, just so you know, it was Major Randolph who sprung you. You can thank him in person, you have a face-to-face with him in thirty minutes."

So, I finally learn who was my savior. The question is, why? Better I don't ask.

"I'm more than grateful to the Major, but it's been fifteen-years since I did this."

His eyes narrow and he shoots me a stern look.

"In that time, did you ever lose confidence in yourself?"

"No, sir, never."

"Then you have your answer. All that counts now is your performance here. Got it?"

"Yes, sir."

"Call me Lieutenant, not sir. Major Randolph's a bit of a character and a little too gung-ho at times. Lord knows he has to be with the scum we deal with. The world is fighting the deadliest drug epidemic in its history. Heroin, cocaine, Fentanyl, Heroin mixed with Fentanyl, opium, crystal meth, any chemical combination that will send users to la-la land for a while... and often to their death. The crisis is so out of control, the government's bitching that it's hamstrung their ability to govern. They want it stopped. That's where we come in. Along with the other thirteen drug enforcement units around the world, our mandate is to shut down drug manufacturing and distribution sooner than later."

"How's the effort going?"

He sighs and shakes his head.

"So far, drug lords two, drug enforcement one."

"Why is that?"

"That's easy. It's the most lucrative cash industry on the face of the planet these days. Catch one, two more pop up."

Wilson pauses, stares at me long enough to make me even more uncomfortable.

"Terrible what happened to your wife. Tragic, just tragic. If it's any comfort, I would have done exactly what you did."

"And you would have paid the price I did."

"Was it worth it?"

"Up there living underground 24/7, fifteen years felt like fifty."

His eyes go to the ceiling and I know where he's going next, I wish he wouldn't, but he does.

"What was it like?"

"Um, where would I begin?"

He's waiting for more, but a shrug is all I give him.

"Okay, I understand, memory's still too fresh."

"Yes, considering I just got back yesterday."

"Someday you'll share details over a beer."

Like hell I will.

"Yeah, someday."

"Are you're up to speed on what our glorious civilization is up to these days?"

"No, I'm clueless. I assume it has something to do with the Pakistan-India event that was referenced during my processing, but when I asked about it, no explanation was offered."

Wilson shoots me a look like I'm a total idiot.

"Jesus, you really don't know?"

"We were in total isolation up there, Lieutenant."

"Surely you had access to some news?"

"Never, I'm starting with a blank page."

"Why the hell would they deny you news, especially about something like that?"

"It was their way of controlling body, soul and mind."

He falls silent, his head swivels to the window, he's thinking.

"We can travel to the frigging moon, Mars, even Europa, but we can't seem to get our act together at home base. Okay, here's the short answer. India and Pakistan got into another one of their border pissing matches—India blinked, Pakistan didn't. The goddamn fools shot a nuclear-tipped ICBM at New Delhi and—"

His words hit me like a sharp needle in the eye.

"What? When?"

"Eleven years ago. The missile was launched from a base in Multan in the Punjab Provence, three-hundred and fifty-five miles from New Delhi peaking at twenty-five-thousand feet before beginning its descent to its intended target."

My God, am I hearing right, a nuclear weapon? What the hell were they thinking? Wilson shakes his head in disgust and sighs.

"For reasons known only to those in the know, the bloody damn warhead exploded at three-thousand feet three point five miles short of New Delhi."

It's clear he finds it painful to recall the memory.

"Eighty-thousand men, women, and children on the ground died instantly and radiation fallout killed forty-eight thousand over the next year. Those that didn't die live in agony and disfiguration."

Wilson turns contemplative, his eyes stray to the window and linger there for several seconds before coming back to me, his stare intense, penetrating.

"And yet, not one damn country was willing to give up their arsenal of nuclear weapons. If there was ever a time to do it, that was it, but no, in all our infinite wisdom, we didn't. Fear consumed every living soul capable of comprehending the consequences if it ever happened again... people began hoarding supplies like doomsday was a foregone conclusion. Raw fear and a dose of stupidity brought us a world government because people bought into the idea that it could be the solution to all our problems. So far, it's feels like a terminal case of syphilis. Hardly a day goes by when that bunch in Marseilles doesn't break a norm or two. Theirs is a rich man's mentality—them first, everyone else second. Their wacky economic policies worked for them, not so much for the masses. Before you could say 'bomb', millions found themselves unemployed, government pensions and benefits frozen, the markets crashed and burned, consumer prices skyrocketed while currencies were being devalued daily. The end result was rampant poverty, crime, drugs, and disease. Suddenly, it was every man for himself, still is. What you see on the streets is just the tip of the iceberg. I'm not against the concept of a world government, I'm against the fools running it. Quote me on anything I just said and I'll deny it."

I can't imagine why every country on the face of the Earth would vote for a world government, let alone how the hell that even works.

"Is there push-back against this government?"

"There's conflicting information about a movement, but nothing concrete has been pinned down so far. It's a fool's errand to begin with, Marseilles controls the military, they'd crush an uprising before it could get off the ground. Anyway, the rest you'll learn for yourself. Our mission, mandated by the government, is to shut down the flow of drugs."

"If it's bad as you say, the courts must be jammed."

Wilson's eyelids narrow to thin slits like maybe I said something wrong.

"We kick ass, split heads, don't bother taking names. The courts have nothing to do with what we do."

"I'm not sure I understand."

"You will soon enough. Now, we have two teams of two here. You'll be partnered with Hank Drummond. A third man was recently authorized. I don't know why, but for some reason, his arrival has been delayed. When he does show up, he'll rotate between teams as back-up. Jade you met, she runs the administrative end and handles communications when we're on raids.

Whenever you're on the streets and you come across something that requires attention, you call for backup before acting. I don't want anyone killed because they took matters into their own hands without backup. You've been gone a hell of a long time, so take it slow, follow Hank around, watch how he handles things and learn. Think you still have what it takes?"

"I can hold my own."

"For your sake and ours, I'm counting on it."

Wilson pops up from his chair, comes around, pats me on the shoulder the way one does a loyal dog.

"Welcome aboard."

"Thanks."

"Jesus, Billy, your pale as an albino's ass, get some sun. Come meet the crew."

"Ah, Lieutenant, I hate to ask a favor right off but—"

"What is it?"

"My parents, they died in an auto accident after I left. I only learned of it yesterday."

"Jesus, they kept that from you too?"

"They kept everything from us."

"Oh hell, Billy, I'm sorry."

"I'd like to get a copy of the accident report from Providence?"

"Yeah, yeah, sure, I can take care of that."

He hands me a notepad and pen.

"Write down their names and last known address."

I jot down the information and hand him the pad. He tosses it on his desk.

"By the way, don't let Julie Summers rattle you."

"You know Jules?"

"Former Master Sergeant Julius Summers served under me in the Marines a hundred-years ago. Julie takes a bit of getting used to, sometimes takes too much personal interest in his house guests, but he's a damn good man, you can trust him. Okay, come on."

He limps his way to the open squad room and calls to the lone guy sitting at the first desk.

"Hank Drummond, meet Billy Russell, Rod's replacement."

Drummond is small in stature, lean and muscled with tight-cropped brown hair... I'd says he in his mid-forties. He sizes me up from side-to-side, top-to-bottom.

"Welcome to purgatory, Billy."

I hope he doesn't mean that literally. Wilson turns to the lovely Asian lady at the front desk.

"Jade you met, she runs the place."

The lovely Jade raises an eyebrow and says in her breathy voice,

"For once he's telling the truth."

"Where's Gustav and Victor?"

Drummond swivels in his chair and points to a door to the left of the desk at the back wall. The sign on the door reads 'Interrogation.'

"Okay, okay, you'll meet them later. Jade, get Billy up to speed."

He turns and limps back to his office. Drummond's on his feet, extends his hand, and we shake.

"Like I said, welcome to Purgatory."

"Should prove interesting."

"Yeah, interesting, that defines this place to a tee."

Jade waves me over.

"Let me have him, Hank. Billy, take a seat over here."

I gladly take a seat next to this lovely creature. From her bottom drawer, she retrieves a black leather holster with a Smith and Wesson in it, a badge, handcuffs, a cell phone, and places them on the desk.

"You wear your 9MM 45ACP on your belt. Your badge goes on the opposite side. Make sure both remain visible whenever you're out to keep street people from harassing you. Cops are the last humans they want to interact with. The office number is programmed into this cell phone. If you need to call in just press 'home'. Who are you listing as next of kin?"

There's a question I hadn't anticipated. With my parent's gone, there is no one.

"None."

She gives me a questioning look, then moves on.

"The first of each month your salary is automatically posted to your debit account: Three thousand credits, the equivalent of $3,000.00 dollars."

Whoa, I think I'm rich.

"If you're looking to get wealthy, you picked the wrong line of work. Today's the 28th, you're in luck, this Friday your first month gets posted. Don't spend it all in one place."

She points to a desk pushed up against the far back wall between the interrogation room and a door marked men's room.

"For now, that one's temporarily yours. You'll move next to Hank when the new guy shows up."

"Kind of like a test desk to see if I work out."

If she found that humorous, she doesn't show it.

"Your computer is limited to inter-office emails and case files."

"No internet?"

"Only mine and the Lieutenants."

"Why is that?"

She doesn't offer an explanation.

"You're not wearing a watch."

I roll my eyes and lie through my teeth.

"Yeah, that, I left it in the airport restroom."

"Which explains why you were late."

She's not going to let me forget, is she? From her middle drawer she retrieves a cheap-looking wristwatch with a faded brown leather strap.

"The guy that owned this won't be needing it any time soon. If you need anything, see me."

"Like what?'

"Like, whatever."

"Okay."

I slip the watch on and like a smitten schoolboy I sit and stare at her perfectly shaped face.

"Was there something else?"

"Ur, no, can't think of anything."

"Okay then, don't want to be late for your meet and greet with Major Randolph. When you get back, you can begin to build your temporary nest."

Chapter 10
The Military Rules the Roost

The military command's office *is about the same size as ours except there's no open area. Instead, there's two closed-in offices beyond the reception desk. Through the open doors, I see each is occupied by a man in military fatigues. To the left of the reception desk is another office, its door is closed. The lady at the reception desk is also wearing fatigues sporting four stripes on each arm. Her head comes up from whatever she's reading.*

"Can I help you, sir?"

"I have an appointment with Major Randolph."

"Your name?"

"Billy Russell."

"Yes, Officer Russell, I'm Staff Sergeant Maryanne Colby, the Major's administrative assistant. Welcome aboard."

"Thank you."

"The Major is expecting you."

She's on her intercom.

"Major, Officer Russell is here."

"Send him in."

"The door to my right, Officer Russell."

"Thank you."

When I enter, Major Jesse Randolph is standing in front of the map on the wall behind his desk... it's identical to the one in Wilson's office. On each shoulder of his combat fatigues are shiny gold oak leaf's. He's pushing sixty for sure, tall and slender, in good physical shape, a full head of light brown hair, eyes to match, with an uncompromising look that signals he's all business... most military officers are. His office is larger than Wilson's with a six-chair conference table in front of a window that, like Wilson's, overlooks houses. The left wall is lined with photographs and military awards. Without fanfare, Major Randolph greets me crisply.

"Russell, have a seat. I'm up to my ass in alligators this morning, so we'll make this short. Welcome aboard."

He sits in his chair, leans back, and studies me for a moment.

"I want to thank you, Major, for springing me from hell."

"I've heard horror stories about that place."

"I assure you, sir, none match the reality of actually being there."

"Hmm, well, that's behind you now. I arranged your transfer because I believed you could be a valuable asset in our fight against the drug wars."

I'm flattered, but suspicious... this guy knows zip about me other than I was a cop that was sent away for twenty years.

"The drug crisis is destroying society. If we don't get a handle on it and soon, they'll be no future societies. Over eighty-plus percent of the world's population is on something ever since that damn nuclear attack sent the world into the toilet. Here in New England it's as bad as anywhere, maybe worse. Thankfully, the government, in all its wisdom, has given us wide latitude in carrying out our mission. To put it bluntly, we kick ass, don't take names, get the job done."

Is he channeling Wilson, or is that the official slogan around here?

"Few offenders if any make it before a judge, or for that matter, to a jail cell."

I'm not exactly dense, I think I'm getting Randolph's message, and I'm not liking what I'm hearing.

"Questions, Russell?"

So, here's where you lie your ass off, Billy, because the truth is your full of questions.

"No, sir, can't think of any."

Okay, now blow some smoke up the Major's ass.

"I appreciate this opportunity. I assure you, sir, I will give it my all."

"We'll see how it works out. If you do things by *our* book, we'll have no problem."

If that doesn't put me on notice, then I'm one dense son of a bitch.

"There is one question, sir."

"Ask away."

"I wasn't going to ask, but... why was I chosen?"

"Is that important?"

"Well, sir, there were times I questioned if I would ever be useful again."

"I'll ask you a question. Did you ever lose confidence in yourself?"

That confirms it... he and Wilson have a script and they stick to it.

"No, sir, never, not once."

"Well then, you have your answer."

There follows one of those awkward pauses that drive me nuts... I never know who's to pick up the conversation... thankfully, he does.

"I'm, going to be straight up with you, Russell. I hand-pick men who delivered swift justice to someone who might have otherwise beat the system. Crimes by social standards maybe, but justice was well-served in each case. I put my requirements in the computer and your name came up."

"Really?"

"You did what you knew you had to do, but you must have known you'd pay a terrible personal price, but you still did it. Am I right?"

"Yes and no... fifteen-years in hell was a big price to pay."

"I'm betting if you could do it all over again, you wouldn't hesitate."

The good major is right on that score... I nod in agreement.

"Here you get to serve that same justice... only here it's legal. Understand?"

I understand all too well now that you've spelled it out in big red letters, Major. He's staring at me, waiting for me to confirm. So, what am I going to say, I'm not in? That'll ensure me a trip back to Europa or some equally uninviting hole in the ground. Smile, Billy Boy, tell him what he wants to hear.

"I'm in, Lieutenant, I'm in."

"Good, good."

He's up on his feet, coming around the desk with his right hand outstretched, we shake... his grip is strong.

"Welcome to the hunting party, Officer Russell."

Did he say hunting party? That's putting an interesting spin on it.

• • • •

WHEN I RETURN TO THE office, *Jade's banging away on her keyboard.*

"How'd go with Randolph?"

"I found the Major interesting."

"Hmm, first time I heard him described as interesting."

Without turning to me, she points to my temporary desk.

"Go build your nest."

I know when I've been properly dismissed, but before I can, Wilson calls to me from his office door.

"Billy, a moment please."

He hands me a sheet of paper.

"The accident report you asked for."

"That was quick, Lieutenant, thanks."

I fold the report and stuff it in my shirt pocket.

"Aren't you going to read it?"

"Later, maybe."

"All's well with you and the Major?"

"One-hundred percent."

"Good, good."

"Well, I'm off to build my nest."

"Your what?"

"My desk, Jade called it my nest."

"Ah, gotcha.'"

As I head to the back of the room and my desk, Hanks calls to me.

"How about I take you to lunch to celebrate your first day?"

"Sounds good, thanks."

I mosey back to my desk next to the men's room and sit. The accident report is burning a hole in my pocket... I want to read it, but I don't want to read it. Taking it out and unfolding it, I glance at it briefly, but decide this is not the time or place to read the details of my parent's death in a horrible auto accident. I stuff it back in my shirt pocket. Leaning back, I place my hands behind my head. I'm actually sitting here free of Quasi, cramped, smelly living quarters, dusty mines, and the constant din of mining machinery. It feels like a surreal dream... maybe I'll wake up and find out it is. My happy thoughts are interrupted by muffled voices coming from my left. Someone is shouting, but I can't make out what is being said. Then the distinct sound I recognize... someone's being whacked hard followed by a loud moan. I look to Hank, then at Jade, neither shows any interest. There it is again, only this time it sounds like someone bounced off the wall in the room next to me. Again, I look to Jade and Hank for a reaction... nothing. Too dumb to mind my own business, I rise and take the few steps to the interrogation room door and listen.

"Don't go there, Russell."

It's Hank calling to me.

"What's going on in there?"

"Business—mind yours."

"What kind of business?"

"The kind that's none of yours."

Leaning closer to the door, I hear a male voice and it sounds like he's cursing. There's another loud whack and a moan and a thump like a body hit the wall or the floor. I turn to Hank.

"Someone's being banged around in there."

Then comes my next stupid move... I reach for the doorknob.

"Billy!"

This time it's Jade, her strident tone a clear warning not to do what I'm about to do.

"What's going on in there?"

"Nothing that concerns you, get away from the door."

More sounds like someone's being whacked hard. Now Hank's on his feet coming my way.

"Hey, Russell, turn your hearing aid up, I told you it's business. Get away from the door."

But no, not me, I don't take good advice when it's offered. Now for my second stupid move... turning the doorknob, I swing the door open. Whoa, what have we here? The walls are padded for sound. No wonder I couldn't make out what was being said. A Hispanic-looking man is lying face-down on the floor, his hands are handcuffed behind him, and he's bleeding from the nose and mouth. There's a guy down on one knee beside him, fiftyish, black hair, trim body with a hard-looking stoic face that would scare ghosts on Halloween. In his right hand is a twelve-inch rubber club. He has a small tattoo of an Eagle just above his wrist. Another guy, tall and a bit heavy, with dark curly hair and a salt and pepper mustache, is leaning against the back wall with his arms folded across his chest. The one down on his knee snaps his head in my direction and bellows in a foreign language.

"Wer zum Teufel bist du?"

"What?"

The dude leaning against the wall spits out a translation.

"He wants to know who the fuck you are?"

Now he's closing the distance between us.

"Beat it."

He slams the door in my face. Hank is standing a few feet behind me and taps me on the shoulder.

"Hey, Billy. I tried telling you, man, it's business."

Now I'm really pissed... I don't appreciate having a door slammed in my face without at least a friendly hello or a hug.

"That man is handcuffed and he's bleeding."

"Get away from the damn door."

Before Hank can stop me, I swing the door open and step inside.

"Excuse me, but that man is handcuffed and bleeding badly."

The guy down on one knee waves the club and threatens me.

"Get your Lilly-white ass out of here."

"You should kiss my Lilly-white white ass and uncuff that man while you're at it."

He drops the club to the floor, stands and lunges, his right arm rising up, his fist coming at me fast like a deadly snake strike, and he sucker-punches me. WHACK! His knuckles crunch against the left side of my nose before I can get out of the way. The hit is hard enough to force me back two wobbly steps. My hands instinctively go to my face and I hear myself yell.

"Goddamn it!"

"Next time, jerk-off, mind your own business."

Slam! There goes the door again. Something wet is running from my nose to my upper lip... no doubt blood. I swing the door again... the guy that hit me is standing right there and yells.

"Jesus, man, are you stupid?"

"Not that I'm aware of."

He's about two inches shorter than me. My right-hand curls into a tight fist, my arm comes up and I swing, but he sees it coming and shifts to his right a half-second before I connect. My fist catches the left side of his head with enough force to knock him on his ass. The mustachioed one lunges with both arms extended hitting me squarely in the chest and knocking me to the floor. I land on my tailbone. Jesus Mother of God that hurt! A very angry Wilson comes limping out of his office and he's yelling.

"Hey, hey, hey! What's going on? What the hell are you two doing on the floor?"

"That man is handcuffed and bleeding and they're beating on him, for Christ's sake."

The guy I smacked struggles to his feet rubbing at the side of his head and fires a question to Wilson.

"Who the hell is this asshole?"

Wilson's brow crimps down hard and he folds his arms across his chest.

"Officer's Gustav Heinz, Officer Victor Augier, meet Rod's replacement, Officer Billy Russell. Now, don't you all feel just a wee-bit stupid?"

I make it to my feet and point to the man lying on the floor.

"Look at him, he's bleeding."

A very angry Wilson whips his head to me.

"And how is that your business?"

"I was just—"

"Be quiet."

He shakes a threatening finger at Heinz and Augier.

"Get that guy off the floor and out of here."

Now he's wagging that finger at me.

"And you, I thought I made it clear, everyone here minds their own business.

Your first day, Russell, and you're off to a shit-start."

You better sound contrite if you know what's good for you, Billy Boy.

"Sorry, I misunderstood the situation."

"Ya' think?"

Spinning around, Wilson tosses his hands up and mumbles.

"Sometimes I think I'm dealing with kindergarteners. Jade, take Officer Russell to the break room, get him a cup of strong coffee and educate him before he gets himself killed."

Jade is at my side with a handful of Kleenex.

"Hold these to your nose, clean up in the restroom."

Heinz and Augier drag off what's left of their prisoner... the man can't stand on his own, his feet are dragging on the floor. In the small restroom, I examine my nose, nothing feels broken, but it's turning black and blue.

"Dumb, really dumb, Billy."

A few splashes of cold water and I'm ready to go back to face the music. Jade's waiting.

"Come on macho man, the break room is down the hall. Cover the phones, Hank."

Hank shakes his head disapprovingly.

"Bring him back alive, Jade."

I better say something that sounds like an apology.

"My mistake, Hank, I overreacted."

"No, really, Officer Russell?"

"Yeah, really."

I follow a few steps behind Jade as we make our way to the break room. Despite my nose hurting like hell, my eyes zeros in on her shapely rear. How can I not admire how fetching she looks from this angle? She's about five-three with a trim figure that nicely fills out the black slacks she's wearing. My testosterone levels just peaked... got to get that under control before more trouble parks itself at my door. We enter the small break room.

"Sit. How do you take your coffee?'

"Black... with a little oatmeal."

"What?"

"Sorry, it's an inside joke, it's not that funny."

"Suit yourself."

I take a seat at one of the three tables while Jade fixes us coffee. She sets mine down and parks herself across from me and stares.

"You're staring?"

"Wondering what motivated you to do something that dumb?"

"Since when do you beat the hell out of a handcuffed and bloodied half-unconscious suspect?"

"Did Randolph and Wilson not give you the speech?"

"Yeah."

"Either you didn't listen, or you have a thick skull, which is it?"

"A little of both, I guess."

"Have we learned our lesson?"

"Now you're condescending?"

"Is it working?"

"Okay, okay, I may have crossed the line."

"Ah, the boy's come to his senses. Memorize this; In this job you don't win a prize for being Mr. Nice Guy. You'll either get with the program or you won't, and if you don't, you're of no use here, and Wilson will get rid of you before you can say 'my name is Billy Russell.' Log that thought in your memory bank."

She's on her feet, her sexy, expressive eyes trained on me like two bright seal beams.

"Take some advice, Officer Russell, keep your opinions to yourself, your eyes open, and learn. Come on, take your coffee."

If you want to stay in this lady's good graces, Billy Boy, convince her you have a working brain.

"What they were doing was wrong, but so was what I did."

She rolls her eyes and heads for the door.

"Come on."

I follow a few steps behind staring at those damn fetching legs, wondering what they look like out of those pants. I know what's on my mind. At her desk, she hands me a list of a four-digit numbers.

"You do remember how to use a computer?"

"I hunt and peck."

"Good enough. Click on the file labeled 'Cases.' In the search box, enter a case file number in the search box. And keep a hundred-yard distance from Heinz and Augier."

The lady does talk tough… I find it a turn on. On my way to my desk, I get a 'You screwed up' look from Hank.

Whatever you thinking, Hank, you'd be right. I fire up the computer, open the case file folder, and enter the first number in the search box. At the top of the page in all caps is… 'Investigation Complete Case closed'. The file documents the capture of a drug dealer by the name of Royal Flush… obviously bogus. His subsequent death is described as occurring during a shootout with a member of the unit who's not named. I close that one out and open the next file. With minor variation in the details, it reads pretty much the same as the first as if someone cut and pasted from one file to the next. The next three files follow the same pattern. The fourth file reports the suspect was apprehended and brought in alive for questioning. There's no documentation to indicate if the suspect was officially charged, tried, convicted, or sentenced. Information is limited to date arrested, charges filed, transcripts of an interrogation along with a signed confession. The next file is almost identical. What became of these two suspects? The lack of information is not lost on me... Wilson's and Randolph's description of how things are done here, what I witnessed in the interrogation room, and now these case files, is beginning to sink into my thick Scottish skull... I'm not the newest member of a drug enforcement unit, not even close. If I've got this right... and I pray I'm wrong... but everything I've heard so far, and all that I read in these files, points to my being the newest member of a government sanctioned assassination squad. If it looks like a duck, walks like a duck, quacks like a duck, it's a duck. Why did Wilson and Randolph skirt around the truth? Why not roll it out in plain English?

"Enjoying your first day?"

Wilson's standing behind me looking over my shoulder.

"Hey, Lieutenant, didn't see you there. Just going through old files to get up to speed."

He didn't come over to discuss these case files... why would he, he knows what's in them... probably made the entries himself. I smile and nod... the kind of smile and nod I learned on Europa that kept me out of trouble.

"Okay, first day, bad day, tomorrow will be better. Why don't you go home and ice that nose?"

"Good idea, thanks."

But he doesn't hear me, he's already on his way back to his office. I take a rain check on Hank's offer to join him for lunch. Heinz and Augier walk in as I'm leaving... they give me the evil eye. I can only guess what might have become of their bloodied suspect. As usual, I can't resist getting in the last word.

"That bruise on the side of your head, Officer Heinz, it's turning purple. You'll want to take care of that."

The German bastard smirks and gives me the finger. Jade's gives me a nasty, nasty look.

"Let it go, Officer Russell, let it go."

"See you in the morning, Officer Miro."

"In the morning, Officer Russell. Remember, lots of ice."

"Got it."

Chapter 11
Happy Birthday to Me

I *duck into the clothing store* on the way my back to my lavish penthouse suite. *The store is on par with Goodwill... most of what I find is clean but definitely recycled. With the help of the friendly sales lady, I scrounge through what's there in my size... I find two pairs of decent looking Khaki's, a blue shirt, a tan one, and seven pairs of underwear and socks hoping it all fits. The bill comes to sixty-two credits... I'm now down to five-twenty-six... at least the price was right. I'm living large with new clothes, some food in the fridge, and a bottle of decent booze. What more could an ex-con ask for on his forty-third birthday? Well, another line of work might be a step in the right direction...... I make it back to the house without incident, even though I pass several souls who stare with wanting if not threatening eyes. My badge and gun insure that they keep a safe distance...... Entering the apartment, I toss the new clothes on the sofa and head for the John. The mirror doesn't lie, I'm getting a first-class shiner around my left eye. And who's fault is that? All you had to do was mind your own business as Hank and Jade tried to tell you. Your first day was a disaster, Billy Boy. And you're talking to yourself—stop it. Grabbing some ice from the freezer, I wrap it in a washcloth and press it to my nose. In the living room... I use the term loosely... I flop on the sofa and kick off my shoes. Based on the job description and those case files, it's déjà vu all over again, only now it's me they're asking to zap suspects with a cattle prod... no, check that... with rubber clubs... but only when we bring them in alive. The question I'm struggling with is... will I do the nasty deed when my time comes... they will test me sooner than later to be certain they chose the right man for the job. How else will they confirm I'm on the team playing their game the way they want it played? There's a knock at the door. Without thinking, I respond.*

"It's open."

Jules sweeps in like a man on a mission... he's wearing the same baggy jeans as yesterday.

"What did I tell you about leaving your door unlocked?"

"I knew it was you, Jules."

"Bullshit—keep your door locked."

I slap my chest with an open hand.

"Mea culpa, mea-culpa."

Spying my nose and black eye, he moves in for a closer inspection.

"I heard you come in, wondered why so early on your first day. Now I know. What happened?"

"A slight difference of opinion."

"And the other guy?"

I shoot him my best 'screw off' look... he smacks his lips and snickers.

"Okay, okay."

"Washing machine busted?"

"What?"

"You're wearing the same clothes."

"So are you."

I point to my new wardrobe next to me.

"Yeah, but I got new ones."

"Score one for your team, Billy smart ass."

"Lieutenant Wilson sends his best."

"Ah yes, Frank. Send him my regards."

"You served under him in the Marines?"

"Yeah, back when I was young, thin, and fit, and there was still a United States Marine Corp. It was Frank who suggested I move here from Springfield and buy this place to house the likes of you."

"How did he come by his limp?"

"Ah, that. A terrorist group slaughtered thirty-seven men, women, and children in a village on the left bank of River Niger in Mali. Wilson commanded a Special Operations Capable unit, and I was his top dog. Along with a small UN combat squad, we tracked the extremists down.

Terrorists aren't interested in negotiations or their own survival, they show up and fight to the death if that's what it comes to. There was a too-close gun battle, Frank took two shots to his right hip. Two surgeries later his reward was that limp. The Marines offered him a desk job, but he turned it down and retired."

"Who won the fight?"

'We did... that day anyway."

Jules strolls to the refrigerator and opens it.

"You haven't touched anything."

"Baloney and cheese sandwich last night."

"Do you cook?"

"I'm a five-star Michelin chef. Hell-no I don't cook."

"You gotta eat, big boy."

"Don't you have a sick puppy that needs your attention?"

"My house guests, they're my puppies. I'll fix you a nice lunch. There's hot dogs in here, you like hot dogs?"

"Who doesn't like hot dogs?"

Searching through the cupboards, he finds a box of Mac and cheese, blows a sigh and mumbles.

"I can see you're going to be high-maintenance."

"Honestly, Jules, no need to do this."

"I'm inviting myself to lunch."

"Ah, there's a method to your madness."

I can't help but wonder why he's taken an interest in me... he doesn't know me, has no idea who I am or where I've been... so he says. Maybe his old war buddy Wilson shared my history with him. He unwraps the hot dogs, opens the box of Mac and cheese, fills a pot with water, and by God none of it remotely resembles oatmeal.

"Now, pay close attention. First, cut small slits in the dogs and zap them in the microwave for about two minutes, no more. When the Mac's ready, add the cheese, cut the dogs into one-inch pieces, mix it all up, and Bingo, dinner. Got it?"

I tap my temple.

"Indelibly etched forever."

"You have a smart mouth, young man."

"I've heard that as recently as this morning."

"Might that account for the black eye?"

I refuse to answer on the grounds I might reveal myself as a first-class idiot. While Jules finishes preparing the meal, I try to decide which new clothes I'll wear in the morning. The fact that I even have a choice makes me feel at least semi-human... almost. I chose the blue shirt to go with the newer-looking Khakis.

"Hey fashion king, food's ready, come eat."

"Too early for a shot of Bourbon to go with that?'

"Never too early."

Retrieving the bottle, I pour two shots and set one in front of him.

"My contribution to dinner."

I grin at the sight of the hotdog Mac and cheese concoction.

"What are you smiling about?"

"It's my birthday, and I'm eating mac and cheese and hotdogs."

"Well, now, if I had known it was your birthday, I would have bought filets. Happy Birthday, how old?"

"Forty-three."

"Wish I was forty-three."

After the slop served on glorious Europa, this meal, like those memorable airport burgers, is gourmet... I dig in with gusto.

"Slow down, you'll choke."

"Is there no one else you can piss off besides me?"

"Don't know anyone who seems to be in as much pain."

"The nose will heal."

"I wasn't referring to your nose."

"What then?"

"I sensed right off you're carrying heavy baggage. I have eyes, I can see."

"Feel free to close them.

That shuts him up, and we eat in silence, him stealing glances at me, me at him.

"How did it go with Wilson?"

"Time will tell."

"What's that mean?"

"It means ask me again in a month."

"Frank's a Marine through and through. Best to always play it straight with him. So, the question is... from where?"

"Where what?"

"Where were you before you arrived in our fair city."

"Why do you need to know?'

"Don't jerk me around, I know when something's burning in a man's soul. Come on, give it up."

"Jules, I, ah—"

"Come on, come on, you're almost there, you can do it."

I'm not about to confide in this pain in the ass landlord who I hardly know.

"I've been away, out of the loop for a while."

"It wasn't my intention to make you uncomfortable."

"Well, you have."

Change the subject, Billy Boy, before you find yourself crying the blues on Jules' shoulder.

"From what Wilson told me, the world's in a mess."

"And you're not aware of that?"

"Answer the question."

"Okay, try this on for size. In my twenty-two years in the Marines, I witnessed unbelievable pain, suffering, and atrocities. You can't believe the cruelty we humans are capable of until you've seen it up close and on occasion participated in. Pakistan's firing of a nuclear missile at India was the height of human cruelty. Thankfully, cooler heads prevailed and India didn't retaliate. But it was, as the saying goes, the straw that broke the Camel's back. Primeval fear kicked in... cold in your face fear that humanity was on the brink of nuclear annihilation. Unfortunately, the answer to stopping another event came in the form of a newly organized political party calling itself 'The People Populist Party', and we blindly bought their lies. What we got was a world government run by rich, white businessmen who lied and schemed their way to total dominance. Instead of unifying the world as promised, they divided it into the good, bad, and the ugly, labeling gays, blacks, Hispanics, Asian's, Jews and others as societies undesirables. The press was condemned as the enemy of the people, restrictions were placed on civil liberties, freedom of speech, and some religions. Countries retained their sovereignty as part of the bargain, but hand-picked generals really running the show in each country. In the United States, it's former U.S. Army General Albert Joseph Natali."

"So, why do people put up with this government if it's so oppressive?"

"Son, if I knew the answer, I'd be President for life instead of that narcissist French billionaire no one ever heard of before he became El Presidente' for life. His regime consists of like-minded billionaires who make no bones about their belief that white men are the rightful rulers of all others. In reality, they're nothing more than a bunch of autocrats helping themselves to the spoils. Enough, this conversation's depressing me."

I want to ask him so many questions swirling around in my head, but I don't.

"I gotta go, stuff to do."

"And stick me with the dirty dishes?"

"I cook, you clean."

Jules is on his feet heading...pauses there for a beat, and turns back.

"You're not like some of the others who have bunked here."

I don't know where he's going with this, but I don't appreciate being psychoanalyzed by anyone let alone someone I just met yesterday who I owe five-hundred bucks to.

"You don't know anything about me, Jules."

"I'm an excellent judge of character, Billy. I see a good and decent man in you."

"Score one for me."

He stuffs his hands in his pockets, takes three steps back into the room... his expression has turned somber.

"If you're looking for answers, dig beyond what you see on the surface. There's shit going on that pales in comparison."

"Like?"

"Like... like the camps."

"What camps?"

"Places where they send those undesirables I mentioned. It's the government's dirty little secret, except it's not so secret, it's just not openly talked about by anyone who wants to stay out of one of them."

"Where are these camps?"

He glances at his watch.

"I think I've said enough, maybe too much. Tune in the government channel, early news is coming on. Happy Birthday, kiddo."

Like a fart in a whirlwind, Jules is out the door. As crazy as a loon as he might be, I'm thankful someone was here to share my birthday. Although, given the assignment from hell... or purgatory, as Hank referred to it... this day is feeling anything but special. Now Jules goes and drops this secret camp crap on me. Why is he telling stuff like this to someone he's just met? Putting it out of my mind, I gather up the dishes, plunk them in the sink, pour a double shot of Bourbon, and turn on the TV to the government channel. A white flag with green edges and an Eagle in flight in the center fills the screen. Below the Eagle are the words, 'One World in Unity'... just like in the Redbook. Big, brassy, military music plays before a deep off-camera voice begins.

"From the World Broadcast center in Marseilles, France, this is the world news."

The flag is replaced with a graphic of the Earth's surface... the announcer continues.

"Population control and the substance abuse epidemic continue to top the news. During the past month, one-hundred and two-thousand world citizens died of drug related overdoses, a number higher than all those who died in car crashes and gun related deaths. In an effort to combat this crisis, the World Council in Marseilles has proposed the expansion of the number of worldwide drug enforcement units. A final vote is expected at next month's meeting. Another two-hundred twenty-seven thousand, five hundred and seventy-five world citizens passed away during the month of December. Combined with drug related deaths, the population total has been reduced to nine billion one-hundred million, moving the world closer to the government mandated goal of eight billion."

Holy shit, they're looking to reduce the population by over a billion people? Upbeat music begins, accompanied by animated characters dancing across the screen. Flashing text appears at the bottom... 'World Lotto Winners.' The animated characters are replaced by happy, smiling families as the announcer continues.

"Seven lucky families won this week's world lottery population estimate. Two were from the North American Continent, two from Africa, and three from Europe. Each will receive government subsidies for a period of one year. Congratulations to all the winners."

They have a lottery to see who correctly guesses how many people bit the dust? That's sick. The visual changes to a headshot. A graphic identifies him as Alexander Boucher.

"Commissioner Alexandre Boucher took to the floor of the World Council accusing fellow Commissioner Henry Dion of inflammatory rhetoric in his condemnation of the Government's population reduction policies. Mr. Dion has publicly spoken against such policies, labeling them as cruel and draconian."

A second photo is added in a split screen... Boucher on the left, a headshot of Commissioner Dion on the right.

"Noting that current world-wide polls support the government's policies as critical to mankind's survival, Commissioner Boucher labeled Commissioner Dion's comments seditious. If Mr. Dion's rhetoric continues, Boucher warned, he would personally propose leveling sanctions against Mr. Dion. Such a proposal would require a vote of fifty-one percent of Council members."

Hey, news guy, I have my own damn problems, so unless you have some good news to pass along, besides how many people died, forgive me if I turn a blind eye to the world's problems. Damn you, Billy, stop talking to the TV. I turn off the television and that's when I remember I haven't read the accident report. Taking it from my shirt pocket, I unfold it but hesitate. Do I really want to know the details? How will it resolve anything? No, I don't want to know how they died. I fold it, unfold it, and fold it again. Oh, for Christ's sake, Billy, read the damn thing and be done with it. Unfolding it for the fourth time, I scan the document. The report states that a fifty-eight-year old man driving a red pickup hit dad's car head on. A sobriety test confirmed his blood alcohol level to be twice that of the legal limit. At the bottom of the page are photos of both vehicles. The front end of Dad's car is pushed completely into the passenger section. Dear God, they never had a chance. The driver of the truck survived and was sentenced to ten years in prison for vehicular manslaughter... ten lousy years in exchange for my parent's lives. I want to track down the bastard in whatever prison he's in and do to him what I did to Dierdre's killer. Tear up the report, go ahead, Billy Boy, be done with it, put it behind you. I rip it up and fling the pieces to the floor, place my elbows on my knees, cup my face in my hands, and begin to cry.

Chapter 12
Reality Returns with a Vengeance

I tossed and turned all night... I'm not in the best of the moods this morning. The dirty dishes are still in the sink... I'll do them tonight. At least I have new clothes, maybe that'll improve my state of mind...... On my way to the office, I stop at Sully's News Stand, pick up the morning Boston Globe and a cup of black coffee. When I arrive in the office, Jade greets me with a silly smile.

"How's the nose?"

"Hurts."

"Nice blend of black and blue."

Now she's looking me up and down.

"What?"

"New clothes?"

"Yeah."

"They're a big improvement over brown. Lieutenant would like to see you. Heads up, Gustav and Victor are in there. Watch your tongue if you know what's good for you."

"Hang on to my newspaper until I get back."

I saunter into Wilson's office with a wide, friendly smile, pretending I have no idea what this meet and greet is about. Heinz is sitting, Augier's standing by the window. Wilson's got a long puss on, avoids eye contact, and points to the chair next to Gustav.

"Take a seat, Officer Russell."

Officer Russell? That's not a good sign. What happened to just plain 'Billy'. Go on, take a seat next to the good German Gustav and play nice.

"You three got off to a shit-start yesterday, today that ends."

I turn to Gustav, but he doesn't look at me... then words come out of my mouth that can only lead to more trouble.

"What became of that man after you dragged him off?"

That gets Gustav's attention... he turns to me and rolls his eyes.

"Schwachsinn! Since when has this been open for discussion?"

Whatever that first word was, it gets Wilson up out of his chair.

"Hold on, Gustav."

But no, Heinz won't let it go.

"If he's not a hundred-percent, maybe he's not for us."

But no, not me, I can't leave well enough alone.

"How many cops does it take to beat the crap out of one hand-cuffed suspect?"

Heinz leaps to his feet.

"Goddamn you, don't you dare question—"

Now Wilson's yelling and shaking a fist.

"Gustav, sit down! And you, Russell, no one gives a good fuck about your code of ethics."

Okay, okay, Billy, tell the nice Lieutenant you're sorry and live to fight another day.

"My faux pas, Lieutenant, I overreacted to something that was none of my business."

"Good, then it's settled. Gustav, Victor?"

Begrudgingly, the two both nod in agreement.

"Now all of you, get the hell out of my office. Billy, stay."

Wilson waits until Heinz and Augier leave... I sense an ass chewing is coming next.

"Close the door."

Damn, he's going to give it to me in spades.

"For a man who spent fifteen years digging ore, you're looking to toss away the only opportunity that's come your way."

"Sorry, Lieutenant."

"Sorry doesn't cut it. You don't get to change the rules, you carry them out without questioning them."

"I understand."

"Do you, do you really? I think not. There are serious consequences you haven't considered."

I hear it in his voice, I see it in his eyes... it's an unmistakable threat. He's short on details, but I get it.

"I'm giving you the benefit of the doubt this time, but you better damn well get up to speed quick."

"Understood."

"Let's hope so. And if you run into Major Randolph, do not tell him where you got that shiner. I don't want him thinking my crew fights each other. I like the new clothes by the way. Now go to work."

Having been chastised and dutifully warned, I make a quick exit out of there. Halfway back to my desk, Gustav calls to me.

"Wait a minute, Russell."

Oh crap, the German won't be denied his pound of flesh.

"What now?"

"If you can't buy into the solution, you are part of the problem."

"I thought we settled that back there?"

Now the damn fool makes the mistake of wrapping a hand around my left forearm.

"You sure you got the message?"

"Take your hand off me."

"Wenn ich fertig bin."

"What?"

"When I'm finished."

That's it, I've had it with this bastard. In a flash my right hand goes to his crotch... I have his balls in my hand squeezing just enough so it hurts. He moans, tries to back up, but I move with him. Victor is on me gripping my shoulders.

"Alright, alright, that's enough!"

I release his family jewels and back off.

"Explain to Officer Heinz he's never to put a hand on me."

Gustav sidesteps me, growls and stomps off to his desk, tossing off what I hope are his final words on the subject.

"Ich vertraue dir nicht."

Victor sidles up to me with a smile.

"He said he doesn't trust you."

"Okay, sure, I can live with that."

Hard to believe I had his nuts in my hand and he simply walked away. Just goes to prove it pays to squeeze a bully's nuts once in a while... this was one of those times. Hopefully, he knows not to screw with me a second time. I march toward the exit not sure of where I'm going, but feeling like I won a small victory and wink at the lovely Jade as I pass. She frowns and shakes her head with disapproval.

"Bravo, Billy... wonderful display of misplaced male testosterone."

"There's lots more where that came from."

"Where you going, macho man?"

"Break room for coffee."

"You're on the street with Hank in ten minutes."

"Be right back."

I quick-pace it down to the break room and pour a cup of coffee. Damn, I want a cigarette to go with it. Someone enters behind me mumbling.

"Coffee, I need coffee."

Oh crap, it's Major Randolph.

"Good morning, Major."

He spots my black and blue eye.

"Jesus, Russell, what happened to your face?"

"Ur... a bit of a tussle with a guy on the street a block from here."

"What about?"

"He wanted a handout, what else? When I explained I had nothing to give, he insisted I use my debit card to buy him food. When I refused, the fool rushed me. We did a little tug of war before I slapped handcuffs on him and hauled him into the city guys downstairs."

Jeez, even I believe that perfectly delivered lie. Randolph's got his coffee and heading for the door.

"Good work. Nasty bunch of bastards out there. Keep that nose iced."

"Yes, sir, I will."

Chapter 13
Hard Lessons to be Learned

H_ank and I are out patrolling the streets. Back only a few days and I find being out here depressing. The down-and-out walk aimlessly looking for handouts or drugs or are crouched in corners or alleys to stave off the cold. This is what it's come to, this is the new world order? It needs serious work._

"If you let Gustav and Victor get to you, you lose."

"Hank, for God's sake, what they did was inhumane."

"No one gives a damn about that dirt bag and neither should you."

"His mother might."

"Say that out loud to anyone but me and it'll bring you nothing but trouble."

"You saw how Gustav backed down when I grabbed his nuts. He's a bully, bullies need their nuts squeezed once in a while."

With an expression of scorn, Hank shakes his head and sends me a warning.

"Proceed at your own risk."

For the next two blocks, we ride in silence.

"When do I get assigned a car? I have no way of getting around."

"You don't. One vehicle per team, and I'm the senior member. If you need to get someplace, let me know, I'll take you."

"My very own private taxi."

"Limited taxi."

"Who was this guy Rod I replaced?"

"Sore subject. Why do you need to know?"

"I'm curious, always have been. It used to piss my father off to no end."

"I can understand why."

"Well, who was Rod and why have I replaced him?

"Alright, alright. Rod—Rod Holbrook—he was my partner. Turns out the bastard was in Scaglione's pocket."

"Who?"

"Dominick 'Scaggy' Scaglione, one of Boston's late drug lords of record. He had more hiding places than a squirrel and was always one step ahead of Randolph's men. The Major had Wilson assign Rod the task of tracking Skaggy through his various snitches. Unbeknownst to us, Randolph was setting Rod up—he'd been tipped off Rod might be on Skaggy's payroll. One morning we're told we're going to nab a suspect at Faneuil Hall here in Boston's North End between two and two-thirty that afternoon. We weren't told who, which was unusual. At two-ten, Scaggy comes out carrying a bag of fresh fish flanked by two of his goombahs. We were surprised when we realized who it was wondering why we hadn't been told beforehand. Rod turned white as a ghost. When we made our move, Scaggy spots Rod and goes bat-shit-nuts, whips out his gun and yells, 'Holbrook, you piece of shit, you sold me out, you're gonna'" fucking-die with me'. BANG, BANG. Rod goes down in the middle of the street before we dropped Scaggy and his two goons. Satisfied?"

There wasn't anything to be said beyond that, so I drop it and go back to staring out the window until my curiosity spikes again.

"Where do these people get money for drugs?"

"Are you kidding? They'd mug their grandmothers for a few bucks to get them. There's also a lot of cheap stuff out there."

"By cheap stuff you mean dangerous stuff."

"Yeah, dangerous enough to kill... and it kills a lot of them."

We drive on for ten-minutes without further comment when suddenly Hank's back goes straight, his head whips left, and his foot comes off the gas pedal.

"There, the alley on the left, a deal's going down!"

We passed the alley to fast... I didn't see what he saw.

"Damn, why don't they hang a sign on the sidewalk—'Drugs for Sale Here.'"

He makes a quick U-turn, cruises back slow stopping twenty-feet short of the alley's entrance. My first time up at bat and my hearts thumping before I even know what we're up against.

"There's three of them in the alley, one peddler, two buyers. Once we go in, it'll go down in a blink of an eye. Concentrate on the peddler, not the guys buying."

"Which is which?"

"Two of them are in suits, one's in jeans and a windbreaker, go for him."

"Aren't we supposed to call for backup?"

I come off sounding like a rookie cop on his first outing. Sixteen years ago, it would have been me giving instructions to one of the new kids just out of the academy.

"We'll handle this ourselves."

"Wilson made a point that we're supposed to call for backup."

"Jesus! Alright, alright, call Jade."

I hit 'home' on my cell phone. It rings three times before Jade answers.

"Billy, what's up?"

"Hank's spotted suspicious activity in an alley, we need backup."

"Gustav and Victor are here. Where are you?"

"Hank, where are we?"

"We're on Yonkers. Activity's in the alley between Winston and Thurman, Jade. Two buyers, one seller. Got that, Jade?"

"Got it, Hank. Heinz and Augier are on their way."

The line goes dead.

"Billy, check your weapon."

I reach for my Smith and Wesson... the first time in over fifteen years I've held a weapon with the intent of maybe using it... surprisingly, it feels good in my hand.

"These guys know the penalty for getting caught, they won't hesitate to knock you off in a flash so stay on your toes."

Before I can say anything, Hank's out the door moving fast toward the alley's entrance.

"Hey, wait a minute."

I scramble out trying to keep up with him, but my right foot dips into a rut in the sidewalk and I tumble head over heels and land on my back. Damn it! I bound to my feet hoping Hank didn't notice. He stops just short of the alley entrance and whispers.

"Stay the hell on your feet, will ya."

"What happened to waiting for backup?"

Hank's not listening, he's honed in what's going on in that alley.

"As soon as they see us, they'll make a break for it."

"Gustav and Victor are on their way, remember?"

He doesn't answer, he's springing up and down on his toes like a boxer, sucks in a breath and takes one long step into the alley's entrance, plants his feet wide apart, and raises his gun to eye level. Jesus, what the hell happened, I thought we were waiting for backup? Too late, Hank's calling to them.

"Afternoon, gentlemen, is this a private party?"

With my gun raised, I step out next to him. Halfway down the alley, two thirty-something guys dressed in business suits spin around toward us. The tall one in the black windbreaker pulls out a gun, grabs the suit closest to him in a choke hold using him as a shield.

"I'll blow his fucking brains out."

Hank raises his weapon a bit higher and aims.

"But then I get to remove yours."

The third guy, shaking like a vibrator, drops to his knees.

"Don't shoot, please, don't shoot!"

"On your stomach, hands behind your head!"

He does as Hank orders and lays face down, hands behind his head. The tall one is pressing his gun against the shaking hostage's temple.

"Please, please, I have a wife and two children."

The gunman presses his weapon harder.

"Shut the hell up."

We have a classic Mexican standoff going on here... somebody is going to get hurt or killed for sure.

"Hank?"

"Be quiet, Billy. Hey Batman, you know how this works, you off him, we off you. Put the gun down, live another day, behind bars, maybe, but at least you'll still be breathing."

"Who the hell are you kidding, I know how you pricks work."

Hank whispers to me out of the side of his mouth.

"His right leg, it's in the clear, my first shot will be just above his knee. He'll peel right, the hostage left and that's when you unload on him, shoot for his chest. Got it?"

"Got it."

"And for Christ's sake, don't miss."

Here comes the moment of truth. Raising my gun, I take aim at the hostage's chest... when he rolls left, I'll have a clear shot at the tall guy. Hank moves forward a couple of steps.

"Come on, put the gun down, man."

The guy tosses his head back and laughs.

"And I'm supposed to trust you?"

Hank whispers.

"Hell no, asshole."

He squeezes the trigger—click—BANG! The shot echoes like a double shotgun blast in this alley. The bullet strikes just above the gunman's right knee. A guttural cry escapes his throat, he rolls to his right, the hostage to his left just as Hank said he would. I fire, the bullet slams into the gunman's right shoulder. Damn, I missed. BANG, BANG, BANG... three rapid rounds from Hank's weapon strikes the guy squarely in the chest. With a stunned expression, his eyes wide, mouth agape, he stumbles back two steps and collapses to the ground... the hostage drops to his knees... it all happened in the blink of an eye. Angrily, Hank turns to me.

"Goddamn it, Billy, I told you not to miss."

Now Hank's hotfooting to the guy we shot checking for a pulse.

"He's toast."

I missed, I blew it. Hank looks to me and scowls, holsters his gun and turns his attention to the two men lying on the ground.

"Get up, come on, both of you, up on your feet."

One of them begins to speak, Hank waves him off.

"Don't say a goddamn word or you'll royally piss me off. Stand up."

Both men quickly rise to the feet.

"From the looks of those suits and expensive shoes, I'd guess you're a couple of high-level business guys, maybe bankers wishing they'd stayed the hell out of this alley."

"Lawyers, we're both lawyers."

"Dumb ones at that. Families?"

"Wife and kids, both of us."

"Whatta'" you think, Billy, should we give these brainless clowns a break?"

I'm not sure where Hank's going with this, so I go along.

"Sure, why not."

"There, you see, my partner's a generous guy. Today your lottery number comes up a winner. Now, get your dumb asses out of here before we change our mind. And do yourselves and us a favor, sign up for rehab."

The two men are ready to flee, but Hanks stops them.

"Remember what I said—rehab."

"Yes, sir."

"You have business cards?"

"Yes, sir."

"Give them to me so I can check up on your rehab progress.

Still shaking like frightened kids, they hand Hank their cards.

"Okay, beat it."

The men scamper out of the alley like cats being chased by angry dogs. Hank rips up their cards and tosses them.

"Why'd you let them go?"

"The only other option is to shoot them. If that was our mandate, we'd be knocking off users all day long like fish in a barrel. We want the makers and the peddlers, not the users."

"Got it."

"Good, at least you got something right."

Ouch, I had that coming. Tires screech out on the street and doors slam. Heinz and Augier come racing toward us. Hank casually points to the dead guy.

"You're a little late?"

Victor's shaking his head and grumbling.

"Tue aurais du attendre."

"Do you two slip in and out of foreign languages just to piss us off?"

"I said, you should have waited for us."

"Got the job done, didn't we?"

Then Hank does something I couldn't have anticipated.

"I hit the fool in the shoulder, Billy finished him off with three shots in the chest."

I'm stunned, I don't know what to say, so I say nothing. Gustav raises an eyebrow, looks over at the dead guy.

"That's what the government's paying him for. Right, Officer Russell?"

"Right you are, Officer, Heinz."

"Okay, see you cowboys back at the ranch. That's if you remember where it is."

Gustav laughs as he and Victor walk away. Hank whispers.

"Assholes."

He turns to me with a sour expression... I know I'm in for another ass chewing.

"And you, don't you ever miss again, at least not when you're with me."

"I got a little rattled, that's all, Hank."

"Next time don't be. Now we call the Body Snatchers."

"Who."

"The morgue guys."

He's on his cell phone, punching in the number.

"Morning Grace, this is Hank Drummond, 513. There's a dead one in the alley between Winston and Thurman off Yonkers. Yeah, yeah, that's the place. Pick him up before the dogs have him for lunch. Thanks, Grace, have a good one."

He stuffs his phone in his pocket and walks away.

"Coming?"

"To where?"

"Lunch, where else?"

Second day on the job and I've already participated in terminating a man's life. Hank, on the other hand, seems untroubled like it's all in a day's work... I suppose for him it is. Once the peddler took a hostage, we were left with one choice... end the threat. But I will never take the loss of any life casually under any circumstances, never did during my time in Providence, I won't start now.

. . . .

WE ENTER A SMALL DINER *on William J. Day Blvd along Boston Harbor across from the John F. Kennedy Presidential Library. I'm first through the door and head for a booth by the window, but Hanks waves me over to a booth.*

"Never sit by the window. Street people stare at you while you eat."

"Oh, hell, I can see how that would be upsetting."

"Yeah, smart ass, it is."

An unsmiling older, short, slightly portly woman, wearing an apron pockmarked with food stains, approaches.

"Hank."

"Hey Maggie, how're they hanging?"

She cups her sagging left breast.

"Better than your balls."

"And how would you know, Maggie dear?"

"Those naked pictures of yourself you on the Internet, I saved them to my desktop. Who's the new face?"

"Billy Russell, meet the most ill-tempered lady in Boston."

Whoa, what's going on with these two?

"Billy's my new partner."

"Jeez, I hope this one's better than Rod. Billy, be careful, Hank's a degenerate. What happened to your eye?"

"Walked into the bathroom door in the middle of the night."

"You heard about that new invention called lights?"

"Next time I'll know better."

"You two gonna" have the special?"

"Should I know what that is, Maggie?"

"Burger and fries, Billy, guaranteed safe for human consumption. Coffee?"

We both nod yes.

"Don't trash-talk me while I'm gone."

"You would deprive us of life's simple pleasures, Maggie?"

"The only thing simple, Hank, is you."

She waddles off with a smile. Apparently, these two take pleasure trading insults.

"Is this the regular routine between you two?"

"If I don't yank her chain, she gets depressed."

"By the way, thanks for what you did back there."

"My pleasure. I get my rocks off putting the screws to Gustav and Victor whenever the opportunity arises. You, on the other hand, get into a three-way brawl with them on your first day. What did you expect in return, hugs and kisses?"

"Okay, so I overreacted, but their prisoner was—"

"Jesus, Billy, you're thick headed. Don't you get it?"

"I get it, I get it."

"Do you?"

"Yes, damn it... we're not paid to bring them in alive."

Maggie returns with our coffee.

"Burgers and fries coming up."

Hank waits until she's out of earshot.

"The world's being run by thieves who stole it out from under the noses of an entire civilization. Take a look around, poverty, crime, drugs, that's what they've left us with. But, like it or not they're in control, they make the rules, leaving guys like you and me zero choices other than do what we're told."

"Guys like us?"

"Let's you and me get off on the right foot by laying our cards face up."

"Whatta'" mean?"

"We're both ex-cons, so was Rod."

"You don't know anything about me."

"Cut the shit, Billy, I said cards face up. I don't wanna know what you did, nor will I tell you what I did that earned us this plush assignment. But, because of what we did, we're exactly what Randolph was looking for—men willing to do the nasty deed to get out of prison and stay the hell out. Just keep reminding yourself, what we do is legal."

"Define legal."

"Whatever the government says it is."

"That doesn't make it morally right."

"You're preaching to the choir, Billy."

"Then you agree?"

"Yeah, but who the hell cares what I think?"

"What about Heinz and Augier?"

"Oh yeah, the joy boys. If you haven't figured it out, Heinz is a Kraut and Augier is French. They were here when Rod and I came aboard. Jade says they were sent directly from Central Security in Marseille. That's as much as I know, but I have my suspicions."

"Like what?"

"First, why would Central Security send two of their guys to play with the likes of us? Why not just find two more like us? I mean, hell, it's not like what we do is brain surgery, you know. We show up and we shoot people. And from time-to-time those two are missing in action for a day or two on special assignments for Randolph, so we're told."

So?"

"So, each time they're gone, someone bites the dust; a rogue journalist in London, another in Dallas, a U.S. network news anchor who in the middle of delivering the nightly news stands up, walks around to the camera and shouts profanities against the regime. The next day he nosedived off the balcony of his expensive twenty-second-floor New York condo. It was ruled a suicide... suicide my ass. Every time some high-profile type gets whacked, those two are on assignment for Randolph. I can't prove it, but if it looks like a duck, walks like a duck it's a—'

"Duck."

"Precisely."

Maggie returns with our food.

"Eat it up boys before the flies get at it."

Maggie waddles off... nothing further is said on the subject of Heinz and Augier.

"And then there's Jade."

"What about her, Hank?"

"Not so much her as you. Every time you're around her your dick's hanging out."

"It's that obvious?"

"Like the big flashing population billboard on Boston Harbor. I'm just passing along friendly advice before Wilson slaps you on the hand for messing around in the office. How's your living quarters?"

"Marginal at best, why?"

"Same place I stayed until my parole year was up."

"Ah, then you know uncle Jules."

"Oh yeah, how is the old bird?"

"Inquisitive as hell."

"Then he hasn't changed."

• • • •

BY MID-AFTERNOON WE'RE back in the office. *Gustav and Victor are there... I avoid interacting with them. With nothing urgent on the schedule, I scan more case files. They're all carbon copies of the one's I previously read... why bother...... Come closing time, I'm on my way out when Wilson calls to me.*

"Russell, a minute please?"

Oh crap, what now? He closes the door. Whenever the boss invites you to join him and closes the door, it's a bad omen.

"You lost your cherry today."

Go with the flow, Billy, say something that sounds reasonably like the truth.

"The guy was going to off a civilian. We didn't have much choice."

"Hank said you two worked well together. That's good, that's good."

Wilson's studying me like he's mulling over how to make a point.

"Even if the guy hadn't taken a hostage, would you have still done what you did?"

There it is, that's what he's called me in for... he wants to hear what he wants to hear or he'll book me steerage class back to Europa.

"I did what I had to do."

"I'll take that as a yes."

I smile and nod in agreement.

"Despite getting off to a bad start, you're going to do good work here."

If you call executing people good work, yeah, I'm your man, Lieutenant.

"Go home, relax, see you in the morning."

"See you in the morning."

Move, put one foot in front of the other, Billy, get out of here while you're ahead. Except for Jade, I find the squad room empty.

"Where is everybody?"

"Gone for the day. Give me a minute and I'll walk out with you."

She turns off her computer, grabs her coat and we're off. Out on the street, she motions to her left.

"I'm a couple of blocks in the opposite direction."

"You walk?"

"Every day when the weather is reasonable. I live close enough."

"Got time for a cup of coffee somewhere."

"Ah, not tonight, need to get home to feed the cat."

"Oh, you've got a cat. I'm allergic, my eyes water and I sneeze like hell."

"Sorry to hear that."

In the two short days I've been here, I'm inexplicably drawn to this lovely creature, this woman I know nothing about, this woman who knows nothing of my past... I'll be damned if I can explain it. Sure, she's a knockout, but there must be more going on beyond that, but I'll be damned if I can explain it.

"Be careful going home."

She tosses her head back and laughs, opens her coat revealing her belt-mounted revolver and badge.

"No one messes with Jade Miro. Till the morning, then."

"Till the morning."

Good night, Jade Miro, sleep tight, I'll be dreaming of you. My eyes stay with her until she disappears around a corner...... I follow her lead and open my jacket to make certain my badge is visible. Thankfully, I find Broadway absent any transients this night. I remember the only meat in the frig was those hotdogs and they're gone. Ducking in the grocery two doors down from the clothing store, I buy a ham steak, some hamburger, butter, and a couple of apples and I'm off...... As I turn onto 4th Street, a city squad car with its lights flashing is parked in front of the shit hole I call home. There's an EMS parked next to it and its rear doors are open. Two city cops stand at the foot of the steps smoking. Jules... Jesus, something's wrong with Jules. I quickstep the rest of the way. As I approach, I recognize John Goulding, the cop that greeted me outside headquarters.

"Hey, Officer Russell, how's it going?"

Careful Billy, don't let him know you live here.

"Hi, John, good to see you again. Pull a night shift?"

"Rotation, it was my turn. They send you over to check it out the guy who OD'd?"

"Lieutenant Wilson tracked me down on my cell. I live around the corner and he asked me to poke around. You guys seem to have it under control."

"Jesus, it's a mess up there. The guy lived like a pig."

He's talking about the second floor... it's not Jules, it's must be my neighbor across the hall.

"I'll just go up and take a look."

"You gonna" want a copy of our report?"

"No, no need to put you through extra work. You know his name?"

"The landlord identified him as Conrad Billings. Rented the place about three months ago. Funny, we ran a check, there's no record of a Conrad Billings anywhere. On the other hand, who gives a shit about some junkie who OD'd?"

"Right. Which apartment?"

"Second floor, door on the left."

"Thanks, have a good one."

"As soon as my shift is over, I'm gonna' have several good ones."

"Have one for me."

Two EMS guys appear at the door, struggling with a stretcher with a black body bag on it. I let them pass before heading upstairs where I find Jules standing in the hall by the open door to Billings' apartment.

"What's going on, Jules?"

"Ah, shit, I heard loud noises up here. By the time I came up to investigate, the noise had stopped. I knocked, but Conrad didn't answer, so I used my key and found him face down on the floor over there. It appears he tanked after partaking in a toxic mix of chemicals.

I peer in the apartment... the place is a pig sty... dishes piled in the sink, a plate of uneaten Chinese takeout on the table, dirty clothes strewn about on the sofa, a couple of broken dishes on the floor, and the place reeks. It wasn't food cooking that I smelled after all.

"Cops found enough coke, heroin, and Fentanyl to kill a herd of cows. I gotta' get somebody in here to clean this mess. Talk with you later."

"Yeah, later."

Another look into Conrad's apartment gives me a renewed appreciation for my own. I enter my place, put the food away, retrieve the Bourbon, and pour a shot and talk out loud to myself.

"This should interest you. I helped reduce the population by one human being today. Well, actually Hank did, I missed. I should find a shooting range and brush up. Oh, by the way, the guy across the hall OD'd and left the place looking worse than the city dump. One hell-of-a-great day, wouldn't you agree? I'm going to get very drunk, and there isn't a damn thing you can do about it, Billy Boy. One more point to be made... how many times have I told you to stop talking to yourself?"

Chapter 14
Will It Ever End?

My dream is running in an endless loop... we're in the alley...I miss the shot, rewind... we're in the alley... I miss the shot. This flashback, like all the others that plague me, lurks in the deep recesses of my brain that I can't un-see. I awake with a start and sit up. I'm sweating. If I go back to sleep it'll be a replay of the same. Maybe if I get up and take a wiz, I'll break the cycle. Feeling my way in the dark to my luxurious bathroom, I relieve myself without turning on the light... from the sound of it, I'm missing the bowl. A slight shift to the right, and bingo, water hits water. I'll clean the floor in the morning along with the dirty dishes in the sink. My cell phone is ringing, it startles me... I flinch and miss the damn bowl again. I don't know anyone outside the office, so who calling this time of the night? The phone, where did I leave it? Ah, under my pillow where I stashed it for the night. I dash back to the bedroom and find it.

"Yeah, hello, hello?"

"Billy, it's Hank."

"Jesus, what time is it?"

"Two-twenty."

"In the morning? It's still dark."

"It usually is at two-twenty. Be in front at four-forty-five—I'll pick you up."

"What the hell for?"

"Wilson called, game's on."

"What's that mean?"

"Just be out front."

The line goes dead, I flop back and groan. Damn, I'll never get back to sleep. I get up, make coffee, drink two cups, shave and shower, have another cup of coffee and two slices of toast slathered with the butter I bought.

• • • •

*AT FOUR-FORTY, TOTALLY **sleep deprived**, I'm standing out front in the dark… it's damn cold and there's snow flurries… can't wait for Spring to arrive. All I have is this brown Jacket issued when I departed the preferred vacation spot of the Cosmos… I should have bought a new one along with the other new clothes…… My eyes roam left to right, one or more street people might decide I'm a prime target at this hour of the morning. What would I do if one challenged me? I have a weapon, I could take care of it… unless they too had one, then it becomes a shootout, and if I missed like I did in the alley, I'm toast. Hank pulls up. I slip into the stripped-down version of the government issued Chevy Cruse. Nice man that he is, he hands me a cup of coffee.*

"You look like crap."

"That's because you woke me at two-twenty."

"Drink the coffee and be quiet."

"Where are we going?"

"Marshfield, thirty-two miles south of here."

"And the reason would be?"

"Randolph's guys located a factory. We're off to pay them a friendly visit."

We catch I-93 South, cross the Neponset River where Hank picks up route 3A all the way down to route 139 to Ocean Street to an abandoned two-story warehouse in an open field about a quarter-mile past Caldwell Lumber. Hank turns his headlights off as we approach. Jade, Gustav, and Victor are there along with the two guys in military fatigues I remember seeing in Randolph's office on my one and only visit there. Wilson and Randolph are off by themselves next to the green unmarked Humvee. There's also an EMS unit and six men in black uniforms milling around a large black box van… the white lettering on the side identifies it as SWAT from the World Law Enforcement.

"Whoa, looks serious."

"These get togethers always are, Billy."

Jade and Randolph's lady, Maryanne, have their arms wrapped around M4A1 automatic rifles... they're wearing flak jackets and ear-mounted communication devices... Jade looks like a sexy, kick-ass super-hero in one of those computer-driven female action films I remember from way back when. Focus, Billy, focus.

"Morning Jade, Maryanne. You two look smashing in those outfits."

Jade frowns and rolls her eyes.

"Hank, Darling, flattery will get you nowhere. Lieutenant's looking for you two."

I smile big at Jade, too big and too obvious.

"Good morning, how's your cat?"

"Just fine, thanks."

As we walk off, I ask Hank what to me is seems like an obvious observation.

"Hank, if the ladies only handle communications and don't engage in the action, what's with the outfits and the weapons?"

"Randolph's orders just in case."

"In case of what?"

"In case they have to use them, I guess."

We pass Heinz and Augier. They too are suited up with flak jackets, communications devices, and M4 rifles. Heinz shoots me one of his better poisonous looks, but it's Augier who rags on me.

"Hey, it's Officer Russell, the straight-shootin' cowboy."

"Give it a rest, Victor."

"Just giving credit where credits due, Officer Russell."

"Thank you, Officer Augier. Now give it a rest."

Over by the Humvee, Wilson's deep in conversation with Major Randolph. Under their flak jackets, they're both decked out in camouflage military fatigues looking every bit the anxious soldiers. Randolph greets us.

"Gentlemen, welcome to the hunting party."

Must be his favorite metaphor... he says it with a little too much brava-do for my liking, like maybe this is what he lives for, this is what gets his juices flowing. Not sure how I'm supposed to respond... I smile and nod.

"Okay, now that's everyone's here, let's crank up the action. Frank, send Hank, Gustav and Victor to cover the back. Officer Russell, since this is your first hunting party, you'll go in the front door with us."

One of Randolph guys comes over with flak jackets communication devices, and M4 rifles.

"Here you go, boys. Officer Russell?"

"That's me."

"I'm Staff Sergeant Tom Carlton. The tall Master Sergeant over there is Olie Olsen. Welcome to the hunting party."

Yes, he works for Randolph alright. I make no mention I've never fired an M4. How difficult can it be? Lock and load, aim, pull the trigger...... Victor's voice comes over our headsets.

"Jade, we're in position in the rear."

"Copy that, Victor."

Randolph's prancing around like a race horse waiting for the starting bell.

"Same routine as always. Sergeant Olsen will open the doors, then SWAT clears the way. Once we get the all-clear, we go in and take care of what's left of the bad guys."

They obviously have this routine down pat. From the back of the Humvee, Sergeant Olsen takes out a small shoulder-mounted rocket launcher. Well, now, boys and girls, this looks serious after all. Olsen and Carlton join the SWAT team by the box van.

"Do we know how many are in there?"

Randolph smiles wide.

"I see lights peeking out the second floor, Frank. Let's go see how many are home."

The good Major spit that out with an air of confidence... or was it arrogance... I can't be sure. Standing tall, he points his rifle's laser mounted beam on Sergeant Olsen's chest. Olsen does the same back acknowledging the signal. With the SWAT team in tow, they trek toward the fading white warehouse to a position that affords them a direct shot at the double sliding wooden doors. We wait, seconds tick off until Olsen gives us a heads up.

"Fire in the hole!"

Then comes a bright flash, a loud boom that causes me to recoil followed by a whooshing sound as the projectile streaks from the launcher and slams into the doors. The resulting explosion sheds the doors into hundreds of small pieces, leaving only a gaping hole. A ball of orange-red flames snakes up the side of the building briefly lighting up the area before dissipating into thick swirls of gray and black smoke. The SWAT team is on the move toward the gaping hole. Almost immediately, they're met by a hail of gunfire coming from inside. They're scattering left and right while returning fire. All we can do is watch as a full-on gunfight continues for a couple of minutes before two members of the SWAT team make it through the opening to the inside. We can hear shots being fired inside for another thirty-seconds before all goes silent. Then a call comes from the SWAT leader.

"First floor is secure, Major, three bad guys down. Activity on the second level, making our way up."

"Your men okay?"

"Everyone accounted for, sir."

Several tense minutes pass, more gunfire is heard... now it's coming from the second floor. Randolph's pacing, waiting, waiting, before the call finally comes.

"Building secure, Major."

Randolph face breaks out in a broad smile.

"Damn, those guys are good, they never fail me."

Raising his right arm high over his head, he thrusts it forward like he's leading the charge in some long-forgotten battle.

"Follow me!"

Randolph, Wilson and me race the distance to the shattered doors. Inside, the smell of the smoldering door frame and gunpowder lingers.

A SWAT member stands at the foot of stairs leading to the second floor. At his feet, two men lay face down, blood pooling on the floor from their wounds. SWAT's team leader is at the top of the stairs... a third body lies at his feet.

"Up here, Major."

"On our way."

Wilson makes the call to Jade and Maryanne.

"Ladies, we're in, on our way to the second floor."

"Copy that, Lieutenant."

We reach the second floor the smell of gunpowder remains strong. The SWAT leader motions to the end of the hall.

"Last door on the left, sir."

Randolph's leading the way down the dimly lit hallway. Wilson's in front of me... he stops half-way and peers into a small room on the right... he gasps. I look over his shoulder... there's a man's bloodied body propped in a hap-hazard position against the back wall. Part of the left side of his face is missing... the wall's spattered with blood... it's a horrific sight. At the end of the hall, we enter a large open room. Immediately to our left, two four by eight plywood sheets rest atop saw horses. Neat mounds of white powder are stacked on each. A few feet away a SWAT member stands over two white guys down on their knees, their hands handcuffed behind them. Neither man looks older than thirty. The SWAT leader motions to the tables.

"There's plenty there to supply half the city with cocaine for a week."

"Good work."

"Thanks, Major, as always, it's been fun, we're out of here."

"Until the next hunting party."

"Until the next hunting party, Sir."

SWAT, Olsen, and Carlton leave, which I find strange. Randolph steps to the first table, dips a finger in one of the mounds and rubs it on his gums.

"Coke."

He repeats the process at the next table.

"Cornstarch."

He moves to a slightly darker colored pile at the end of the second table.

"Might this be Fentanyl?"

He does a slow turn to the two handcuffed men.

"Nasty, boys, nasty. Alright, let's get on with it. Who wants to go first?"

Neither man answers.

"Come on, come on, boys, we're all friends here."

No response from either man.

"Perhaps you need an incentive."

Randolph's approaches the nearest of the two men, stares at him for a beat, then swift-kicks him with such force we can hear ribs crack. The man cries out and tips to his right falling to the dusty wooden floor with a loud thump. His partner cringes and looks away.

"If I ask a question, I expect an answer. Russell, pull him to his knees."

Slipping my hands under his armpits, I lift the young man to his knees... he moans in pain, his head comes up, his eyelids half-closed.

"Let's try this again. What's your name?"

"Mick the Mouse."

"You mean Mick the Rat."

Randolph kicks him again in the same spot... Jeez, that has to hurt like hell. Wailing in pain, the guy falls to the floor again. Now Randolph turns to the second guy.

"You, what do you have to say for yourself?"

"Nothing."

"Russell, lift the other one again."

I do as he asks, the guy groans... he's hurting bad. Randolph looks to Wilson.

"Lieutenant, a little assistance please."

Wilson sets his M4 down and takes out his pistol, crouches down and looks the first guy in the eyes. Something tells me they've played the scene out before.

"Best to answer the Major."

The man grimaces and looks away... Wilson jams the barrel of his pistol into the guy's crotch... the guy cries out in pain. Damn, that's gotta hurt.

"Talk to the Major."

"Alright, alright, first we make a deal first."

Randolph takes a step closer and squats and gets within inches of the man's face.

"Do either of us look like your parish priest? Better talk to me before the Lieutenant's trigger finger slips."

"It's not us you want, man, give us a break."

"Then tell us who it is we do want."

"We don't know."

Randolph's head swivels to the second man.

"What about you?"

"He's telling the truth, we don't know. Someone shows up at the end of the week with envelopes, we get paid, we go home."

"Is he the guy we want?"

"No, some young black kid brings the envelopes."

Wilson jabs his pistol further into the man's groin.

"Jesus, man, wait, wait!"

The other guy whips his head around and bellows.

"Anthony, shut the hell up!"

In a flash, Wilson swings his arm up and across. His gun connects to the left side of the man's head breaking the skin and drawing blood. Randolph sniggers.

"Gee, that must have stung like hell. Be quiet, I'll get to you when I finish with your friend Anthony."

What the hell is going on here? This isn't an interrogation, this is sadistic torture... and Randolph seems to be enjoying it. Hank, Gustav, and Victor make their entrance.

"You're just in time for the grand finale, fellas."

"Whatta" we got here, Major?"

"More scum, Victor, more scum."

Wilson pushes his gun further into Anthony's crotch and rolls the barrel over his testicles... Anthony cringes and turns his head away.

"Want to keep them, do ya?"

"Jesus, man stop!"

"Hurts, doesn't it, huh?

This is getting tough to watch. The second guy snarls at Anthony again.

"Keep your damn trap shut!"

Randolph slaps him hard across the face with an open hand.

"Shh, I told you to be quiet. Now, Anthony, might the name Matias Diego Alvera strike a bell?"

Wilson pulls his gun back a few inches. Anthony's breathing hard, looks to Wilson, his eyes pleading.

"My ribs, man, they're broken."

"Then answer the Major's question."

"Yes, yes, okay."

Randolph's face lights up like a kid who got an 'A" in math class.

"Say his name."

"Alvera."

"His whole name."

"Matias Diego Alvera."

"Louder."

"Matias Diego Alvera!"

"Where might we find the ever-charming Mr. Alvera?"

"I don't know, honest."

"You work for him and you don't know?"

"On my dead mother's soul, I'm telling the truth, man."

Like a hunter stalking his prey, Randolph begins circling Anthony.

"Let's try this one last time. Where is Mr. Alvera?"

"I told you, we do our work, get paid, and that's all we know. Jesus, man, I'm telling the truth."

"You have a wife and kids, Anthony?"

"No."

Randolph circles behind the second man.

"And you?"

"No."

"So, maybe Alvera sees you both as expendable and replaceable."

The man's head snaps up and he yelps.

"I don't give a good fuck what you think!"

Randolph moves around front of the men and with his hand makes a 'gimme' sign to Wilson and Wilson hands Randolph his pistol. Randolph crouches in front of Anthony and pushes the gun muzzle into his crotch. Anthony winches.

"I hope you weren't planning on having kids."

Anthony's face turns ashen-white and his mouth flaps open.

"Wait!"

BANG!

Oh my God, Randolph shot him! Anthony screams, falls back and rolls twice before stopping, his body jerking erratically... blood's squirting from his crotch like a broken hose. Never have I witnessed anything so cruel, so barbaric, so calculated. Randolph's begins circling rises the second man.

"How about you, planning on a family?"

"You're a fucking crazed animal."

"Because I have to deal with swine like you, Anthony, and your dead friends scattered between here and the front door. Now, one last time. Where will I find Matias Diego Alvera?"

"Honest to God, man, I don't know."

"No God would claim you, pig."

The guy spits... Saliva lands on Randolph's left shoe.

"Okay, that's it, games up, we're out of here."

Randolph approaches Wilson's and speaks low... I'm close enough to hear.

"Frank, have Gustav and Victor finish up here. Leave the bodies, Olsen will give the local fire department a courtesy call before he and Carlton torch the place."

"How about the drugs?"

"Leave them."

I don't need a road map to know what Gustav and Victor are about to do. Hanks taps my arm and motions to the door... together we leave...... In the hall, Randolph, Wilson, Olsen, and Carlton are huddled in conversation. As Hank and I pass, Randolph places a hand on my arm.

"That's how we get the job done, Billy."

I'm sick to my stomach from what I've witnessed here. But what am I going to say... it'll be a cold day in hell before I do what you just did, Major, or what Gustav and Victor are about to do? Best not to speak, just give him your practiced 'yes' nod. They'll be another raid, more men down on their knees, their hands cuffed behind them, and it'll be your turn, Billy... count on it...... Hank and I move down the hallway, the others follow... and then it happens... single shot rings out and I flinch like somebody pinched me really hard.

"Jesus!"

"Billy, keep your voice down."

We're almost to the bottom of the stairs when three rapid shots ring out causing all of us to freeze. Wilson's head snaps up.

"Those came from outside!"

Hank's on the move, dashing ahead... I'm right on his heels with the others close behind me. Outside is a sight no one ever thought they'd see... Maryanne is lying on the ground on her back... her hands are gripping her upper right thigh and she's rolling from side to side moaning. Both the EMS men reach her. Jade's standing only a few feet away... smoke's seeping from the barrel of her M4. It slips from her hands to the ground. She raises her right arm and points to the right corner of the warehouse. A man is lying face down, a pistol inches away from his right hand.

"He came out of a side door, fired one shot and hit Maryanne before I put two in him."

One of the EMS medics hollers.

"The shot went clean through the fleshy part of the right thigh, she'll be okay."

Randolph, Olsen, and Carlton rush to Maryanne. My attention is on Jade... she's as white as a ghost and looks like she's going to faint... she drops to a sitting position, places her head in her hands, and begins to cry. I rush to her side and put an arm around her.

"Olsen, drag that bastard inside with the others."

"We're on it, Major."

Olsen and Carlton each grab one of the dead guy's legs and drag him into the warehouse. As soon as Gustav and Victor are clear, the building is set ablaze... it only takes a short time before the flames leap quickly through the dry wooden structure. It's a scene capped with utter madness.

• • • •

WE RIDE BACK IN SILENCE until we reach I-93 North. I want to shout and scream at the atrocities that were committed back there... I wait for Hank and Jade to bring up, but neither does. Jade's in the back seat, staring vacantly out the window with her arms wrapped tightly around her chest.

"Jade, are you okay?"

She lowers her arms to her lap and looks to me... she's fighting back tears.

"Yeah, I'm fine."

"You don't look fine."

"I'll be okay, Billy, really."

Hank's eyes go to the review mirror.

"You did what you had to, Jade."

"If you say so."

"I say so... you had no choice."

I want to console her, to tell her it's okay, that in taking a life she saved Maryanne's and very possibly hers. But there are no words, not now, maybe never. I lean across the seat and whisper to Hank.

"Why did everyone but Gustav and Victor leave?"

Jade overhears me and offers an explanation.

"I'll answer that—Plausible deniability."

"Plausible what?"

"Randolph, Wilson, SWAT, Olsen, Carlton—even the EMS guys—wouldn't be held responsible for what they didn't see or participate in. If it ever became public how suspects are regularly executed, you guys would be tried as rogue cops."

"But the government sanctions what we do."

"From your lips to God's ear."

"But everyone in that room witnessed what Randolph did. How could he deny—"

Hank cuts me off.

"This is not a healthy conversation to have, so zip it."

"Okay, what about Alvera, what's his background?"

Again, it's Jade, who answers.

"His cartel controlled the flow of drugs in and out of Guatemala. But the Guatemalan judicial police were fast closing in on him. His time was coming to an end. Enter the new World government. Their economic failures were the fuel behind the worldwide rise in drug use, especially in America."

"Why especially in America?"

"The U.S. was the world's greatest economic engine, had been for a solid decade; Americans were doing well and living well. That all ended when the economy crashed and jobs began to rapidly vaporize, especially in the ranks of the middle class—they were crucial if the economic engine was to remain running at full speed. The loss of so many jobs was followed by a meteoric rise in drug addiction and drug related deaths."

"But if there was no money?"

"Cheap drugs, dangerous drugs. You saw how they were cutting the stuff back there—make it cheap, sell it cheap, sell lots of it, and the money keeps rolling in. Hell, people spend money on their drugs before they do food. Alvera saw an opportunity and seized it. He fled Guatemala and regrouped here on the East Coast. Within a year, he controlled the flow of drugs throughout New England by eliminating his competition Mafia style."

"Hey, how difficult can it be to find one man?"

That causes Hank to laugh.

"What, I said something funny."

"They don't call him 'Ghost Dog' for nothing.

Chapter 15
Like a Whipped Dog

When we return, *Randolph's office is dark, and so is ours.*
"Everyone must have stayed behind for the grand finale and cheer while the warehouse went up in flames with seven bodies being incinerated."

"Put it behind you, Billy, or it'll send you nuts. Either of you want a lift home? Jade?"

"Yes."

"How about you, Billy."

"Thanks, Hanks, I wanna walk."

"Suit yourself."

• • • •

WHEN I HIT THE STREET, it's twilight, that time of day when the sun dips below the horizon and the light is soft and diffused. Like a whipped dog, I walk ploddingly down Broadway, hands in my pockets, shoulders slumped. My mind is clouded, my mood dark and edgy. If anyone approaches me this night, they do so at their own risk. I can't help replaying the torture and gangland-style executions I was witness to this dark day. How can such inhuman behavior be justified under any circumstances? I have to find a way out, I must find a way out, I can't continue to be a party to this lunacy...... Oh hell, what now, there's a city police vehicle ahead and its lights are flashing. Looks like two city cops are rousting a couple of floaters. One of the cops is poking one of the men with his nightstick.

"I told you to get your sorry ass away from of here."

"Where, where do you want us to go, Officer?"

"That's not my problem, now move it."

He whacks the guy with his nightstick... the man howls and slithers off with his companion. The second cop shines his flashlight on me.

"Hey you, come over here."

He lowers the light to my badge and gun.

"Oh, sorry, didn't see your badge, officer—"

"Russell... Precinct 513."

"Bad idea to be walking these streets."

"I live close by, just wanted some fresh air."

"Do us both a favor, get home."

"Yup, going there now. Goodnight, Officer."

Thankfully, I make it the rest of the way without running into anyone else. I climb the stairs slower than usual and stop and stare at the door across from mine. Who was Conrad Billings, what was his crime? Not that any of it makes a plug-nickel difference, but I wonder......Unlocking my door, I hesitate before crossing the threshold... I'll be alone with my thoughts and my anguish. Turning on the light, I cross to the kitchen... the dirty dishes are still in the sink. Retrieving that precious bottle of Bourbon, I pour a shot and down it in one gulp. There's a knock at the door, I flinch... I wait for a second knock, it doesn't come. I clear my throat to let whoever is there know someone's in here. The doorknob's turning, I whip out my gun... the door swings open... Jesus, it's Jules. At the sight of my gun, he freezes.

"Whoa, put that thing away!"

"Christ, I could have shot you, Jules."

"Sorry, I thought I heard you say come in."

"I coughed."

"Learn to keep your door locked."

Jules taps the peephole in the door.

"And in case you haven't figured this out, it's here for a reason. There's sub-humans out there that would kill you for a Saltine."

"I can only assume you're here for a reason."

He strolls to the sofa and sits.

"You look like you lost your best friend."

"It's been a long day."

He spies the Bourdon bottle on the kitchen counter.

"It's not good to drink alone."

"That's a myth perpetrated by those who want a drink."

Damn, the bottle's almost empty. Begrudgingly, I pour him a shot and another for me. He raises his glass in a toast.

"Success in your new job."

Ha, would he say that if you knew what we really did at Unit 513... or does he already know? I play along, down the shot, and sit next to him. He Pulls out a pack of cigarettes and extends it to me.

"I quit."

"Suit yourself. Mind if I do?"

"Go for it."

Lighting the cig, he takes a long drag and holds it before exhaling. White smoke rises up around his head like an errant cloud... some of it drifts my way. Damn it, I want one bad.

"Toss one over."

"So much for willpower."

"Screw willpower."

I light the damn thing, inhale deeply and hold it in like maybe the toxins will clear my brain. Yes, I do miss them... I miss them a lot.

"So, the reason for my visit. Around eleven this morning, this Godzilla of a human comes by, flashes an official government badge, and introduces himself as your parole officer, says he's checking up on you. Never had that happen before."

"What did he want?"

"To confirm you reported for your work assignment and if you were behaving yourself. Hell, he could have just checked with Wilson and saved himself a trip. Anyway, I told him you were Mother Teresa in a male body. You're not in trouble already?"

"I haven't been back long enough."

"Government agents are all over like fleas, keeping tabs on all sorts of people, so be careful. You could pass one on the street and never know it."

Jules downs the rest of his drink and snuffs the cigarette out in his glass.

"That's not an ashtray."

"Then get one. Okay, gotta run."

"Leave me a couple of cigarettes."

God love him, he passes me three.

"Keep an eye in the back of your head my friend, somebody's checking you out. I see the dishes are still dirty."

"Goodnight, Jules."

"Yeah, yeah, I'm going."

And with that, my friendly energizer bunny is out the door. Locking it behind him, I make a beeline for the booze and pour another shot... the last one... the bottle's empty... I need to find a liquor store. I down the Bourbon and light another cigarette remembering again that today I watched in absolute horror as Randolph violated every moral principle that defines us as human. Define human, Billy Boy. You can't because it keeps changing. With the cigarette dangling from my lips, I drag myself to the kitchen and wash the damn dishes.

• • • •

THE NEXT MORNING, I risk flirting with Jade as soon as I walk in the door. She's reading something and doesn't acknowledge me. Putting the events of yesterday on the back burner, I make my first mistake of the day.

"And here I thought the sun only shined outside."

She looks up and gives me a forced-smile that says 'go away, don't mess with me this morning. No sooner do I settle at my new desk between Hank and Gustav—I've been promoted, I guess— Gustav rags on me.

"A shame you didn't stay for the grand finale, Russell."

My life would be easier if my new desk wasn't next to his.

"Call it what it was, Gustav... an execution."

"And for good reason."

"And that would be?"

"There's more of them than us."

"Oh shit, Gustav, why didn't I think of that?"

"You're not going to make it here."

"I seem to recall you telling me that once before?"

"Consider it a reminder."

He turns his back to me... hopefully, that's the end of his harassment for the day. I need another cup of coffee to calm me so I head for the door, but Jade stops me.

"You two sound like schoolboys."

"One of us is, one of us isn't."

"I'm having trouble telling which is which, Billy."

"The short one is, the taller one isn't. You look like you could use a cup of coffee. I'm headed that way, in case you'd like to join me."

She smiles warmly... probably sorry she blew me off when I came in.

"Maybe in a couple of minutes."

I know she's coming, I could see it in her eyes, those beautiful flashing, almond-shaped eyes. She incapable of resisting my animal magnetism. Right, keep telling yourself these foolish lies and they'll have you committed to a nice country home for egomaniacs. Oh good, the break room is empty... I fix a cup of coffee and take a seat. A couple of minutes later, Jade waltzes in.

"I would have fixed you one, but I don't how you like it."

"Light cream, one sweetener."

She fixes her coffee and sits across from me.

"You're bummed out."

"Is that a question. Sir Billy?"

"You're bummed out over yesterday."

"Who wouldn't be? Neither I or Maryanne believed we'd ever have to use our weapons. It just wasn't something we thought about. Yesterday proved us wrong."

"How is Maryanne?"

"She's lucky, it was just a flesh wound, she'll be out of the hospital tomorrow."

"And you, Jade, how are you doing?"

"I'm fine, Billy, stop asking already."

"I don't want to belabor the subject, but what happened yesterday was just plain inhumane. Randolph should be stripped of his membership in the human race... not just him, all of us, we're all complicit."

"We can't lose faith in the future, Billy. If we do, humanity ceases to exist."

"Maybe we already have and haven't yet realized it. Maybe we're a computer game, a hologram, or something worse, and we haven't yet realized it."

She's up on her feet, coffee in hand.

"You have a weird sense of humor. I better get back."

"You just got here."

"Things to do, Officer Russell."

"Alright, I'll be along in a minute."

She reaches the door, turns back, hesitates, then tosses me a smile.

"It's going to get better, Billy."

"Yeah, well, sooner than later would be good."

"It will, I promise."

"Don't make promises you can't keep."

"Keep the faith buckaroo."

"Buckaroo?"

. . . .

FRIDAY PROVES TO BE *a dud of a day with nothing much happening. Unless we're out shooting someone in an alley, knocking off seven* *men and leaving them in a burning warehouse, there isn't much else to do around here. We mostly mark time until we're called upon to execute gangland style more of the bad guys. I've flat-out stopped reading old case files... it's a waste of time unless I enjoy fiction. Some good news finally brightens my day when Jade announces it's the first of the month and three thousand credits were electronically deposited to my account. I'm damn rich... question is how to spend at least some of it. I'll begin by paying Jules the first month's rent. ...... At noon, Hank and I head out for lunch and we invite Jade to go along, but she has an errand to run, so she says.*

"It's payday, Hank, lunch is on me."

"Big spender, let's go someplace expensive."

"McDonald's comes to mind."

Tomorrow is Saturday, we're off for the weekend. Must be something I can do to amuse myself. This is Boston after all, it's not like they roll up the sidewalks on the weekend. When's the last time I had a weekend to blow on nothing but me? Over lunch, Hank comes to my rescue.

"How are you spending your first weekend in town?"

"Well, my toenails need trimming."

"I have a better idea. Ever been to the Kennedy Library?"

"No, never."

"Want to go?"

"Sure, why not."

"I'll pick you up around ten. There's to be no talk of the office. We get enough of that bullshit during the week."

"It's a deal."

At closing time, Wilson comes out of his hole long enough to remind us we're on call 24/7.

"Enjoy your weekend everyone. Just remember to keep your cell phones on in case something comes up."

On the way out, I ask Jade how she plans to spend her weekend. If she doesn't come up with a good excuse, I'll invite her to join Hank and me.

"Jade, Hank and I are going to the Kennedy Library tomorrow, want to join us?"

"I've been there, would love to go again, just not tomorrow, too much to accomplish over the weekend."

Shot down again.

• • • •

SATURDAY MORNING, I pay Jules for a month's rent...... Hank picks me up exactly at ten and we're off to the Kennedy Library. It turns out to be the best two hours I've spent since getting back. Following the tour, Hank takes me to his favorite North End Italian restaurant called Arico's run by Carmela and Vincenzo Arico. It's a small place with twelve tables and a bar. Carmela and Vincenzo run the kitchen, their daughter Angelina the floor service... a real family affair. On this Saturday, the restaurant is half-empty.

"I come here pretty regularly."

"I got that impression when Carmela hugged you at the door."

"They're good people, and the food is the best."

Hanks insists on ordering for us... Spaghetti and jumbo shrimp in Angelina's fresh tomato sauce.

"Trust me, you'll love it. Angelina sauté's fresh tomatoes, fresh basil, a touch of garlic, and red wine all simmered in the best imported olive oil. At the end, she adds jumbo shrimp. Simple, but I promise you'll think you died and gone to heaven... or at least to Italy."

"My late wife was Italian... daughter of Sicilian immigrants, actually. How about you, Hank, were you married?"

"Yeah, for a time, anyway. Following my court-martial, I was imprisoned at Leavenworth. After two visits, my wife—June—decides she wasn't gonna" wait for me to get out, and filed for divorce. I have no idea what became of her, nor do I care. Okay, your turn."

"Ur, not today, Hank. Maybe one day soon."

"Okay, fair enough."

Carmela arrives with our food. Boy, was Hank ever right... turns out to be one of the best meals I ever had... but then again, I've been eating a lot of oatmeal in recent years... anything and everything is an improvement.

"So, tell me, Hank, do you have a life outside the office?"

"I play for the Bruins and perform with the Boston Pops. If you must know, I've been involved with a nice lady for a few years. To keep your sanity, I recommend you do the same—just not Jade."

"That's not going to happen. Jade's on my radar screen and I intend for her to stay there."

"God, you must love pain, because that's what Wilson's gonna" send your way when he finds out."

"Wilson's got nothing to do with this. Jade's a big girl, I'm a big boy. We make our own decision."

"And if we functioned in a normal world, that would be true. But we don't, we are indentured servants. They won't allow a coupling between you and Jade. Make note of that."

• • • •

AT THREE, HANK DROPS me off *at the house. I wave as he pulls away, then turn to go into the house just as Jules is coming out flanked by two men in dark suits. He handcuffed and he looks terrified.*

"Billy, find Wilson."

"What's going on?"

I step in front of them blocking their path... one of the men gives me a stern look and tries to brush me aside.

"Don't make a scene, Billy, just find Wilson, tell him they're taking me in."

"To where?

One of the goons puts a hand on my chest.

"Step aside, sir."

"What's going on, where are you taking him?"

"I asked you nicely to step aside. I won't ask again."

"Billy, just call Wilson, please."

Reluctantly, I let them pass. They place Jules in the back seat of their black. He presses his face to the window and mouths Wilson's name as they pull away. Jesus, what's going on? What am I supposed to do, it's Saturday, how will I find Wilson... don't know where he lives, nor do I have his phone number...... I rush upstairs... I haven't a clue what I'm gonna" do next. Jade, I'll call Jade. Damn, I don't have her personal cell number either. Try the office number. I hit 'home' on my cell phone, it's ringing... once, twice, three times. I'm surprised when Jade answers.

"Billy, what's up?"

"Thank God you're in the office."

"No, I'm home. On Weekends, the office number is transferred to my cell."

"Can you contact Wilson?"

"Well, yeah, why?"

"Tell him his friend Jules was just taken away."

"Taken where, where, by whom?"

"I was entering the house when he and two guys in suits were coming out. He was handcuffed."

"Handcuffed?"

"Yeah, looked like he was being arrested."

"Arrested for what?"

"I don't know, Jules kept telling me to find Wilson."

"Alright, alright, I'll call him."

"Tell him Jules looked pretty panicked."

"I'll find him."

"Let me know what happens."

· · · ·

THE REST OF THE AFTERNOON *slips by with no word from Jade. I should call her back... no, wait for her to call. Later, with still no word* *from Jade, I crawl into bed, pull the covers over my head to shut out the world... I'm drifting off when my cell rings... it's Jade.*

"I finally found Wilson, he said he'd take care of it immediately."

"If you hear from him again, call me."

"I will."

But she never calls back, so I assume she's doesn't hear from Wilson again.

· · · ·

SUNDAY MORNING, I DRESS and rush downstairs *and knock on Jules' door. No answer. I hardly know the guy, and I fear for him. In my short time here, he ingratiated himself into my life in the best way. I shower and go for a walk around the block... no one on the street bothers me... good because I left my badge and gun in the apartment...... When I return, I knock on Jules' door again... still no answer. Skipping lunch, I nap for a couple of hours. At six, I'm up, slip downstairs and knock on Jules' door... still no answer. I remember there's a frozen dinner of penne pasta and roasted vegetable in the freezer that Jade must have left with my welcome supply of food... I zap it in the microwave... it's not half bad. I skip the news, it's too depressing, so I channel surf and only find more bad TV... I opt for some early sleep. A short time later I'm awakened by someone knocking on my door. With gun in hand, I make my way and peer through the peep hole... it's Jules. I unlock the door and swing it open.*

"Thank God you're back. What the hell happened?"

He looks crestfallen.

"Please don't tell me you're out of booze."

"I am."

Moving sluggishly across the room, he sits on the sofa and lights a cigarette.

"Want one?"

"Sure. Where were you, who were those men?"

"Whoa, slow down, I just got back, give me a minute to breathe."

He passes me a cigarette... he's sucking on his one puff after another like he's afraid someone's going to take it from him.

"Thank goodness for these."

I put some water in a glass and we use it as an ashtray.

"Well?"

"Thanks to you, Wilson found me."

"No, it was Jade who found him."

"Then I owe the lady a debt of gratitude."

"So?"

"I was arrested by the misanthropic Police."

"The who?"

"Real name, Défenseurs de la société, French for 'Defenders of Society.' The sons of bitches round up undesirables the government deems unfit to live among normal society. Huh, they fucked up normal society, how would they know what's normal and what's not? Thank God Wilson found me in time."

Jules looks away... he takes in a deep breath... it comes out as a long sigh.

"What crime did you commit?"

"None by my standards."

He lowers his head and stares at the floor, when his eyes come back to me, there's tears rolling down his cheeks.

"By their standards, my sexual orientation."

"Oh Jules, I'm sorry."

"They were going to take me to one of those camps I told you about. Before they could, it was Wilson to the rescue, God love him."

He douses the cigarette in the glass and is up on his feet wiping away the tears.

"I wanted to let you know I was back... I'm gonna" get some rest."

"Good idea. Come back later if you need to talk."

"Thank you. How about I pick up a pizza around six-thirty?"

"Okay, go, get some rest."

· · · ·

*AT SIX-THIRTY, TRUE **to his word,** Jules shows up with a large cheese and pepperoni pizza and a six-pack of beer. He looks a bit worse for wear for his ordeal.*

"I hope you like pepperoni pizza."

"Love it, and the beer too."

We settle at the table and begin eating. I expect him to unload about what happened, but he doesn't, so I don't bring it up until he does. When I can't stand it anymore, I do what I always say I'm not going to do.

"It was announced on the news that pigs can't fly after all."

"Is that your way of asking me?"

"A little humor always helps."

"Someone outed me. If not for Wilson, I'd be in one of those camps I told you about."

"Do you know where?"

"Nope, no idea."

He's up on his feet... he acts nervous.

"Thanks for the company, Billy, I really appreciate it. Three beers went straight to my head. I'm gonna" lay down again."

"Okay, I'm here if you need me."

"I know, and I appreciate it."

He makes his way to the door, stops, turns back, his face is drawn.

"They're bad people, Billy... every one of them, bad people."

"I know, Jules, I know."

Chapter 16
Life's a Bowl of Cherry Pits

O*n my way-out Monday morning, I check on Jules. He answers the door in his robe. He looks like hell, but assures me he's fine.*

"Billy, I appreciate your concern, I'm fine, go to work, save the world for the rest of us."

"I'll do my best, but I make no promises."

My next stop is Sully's for a cup of his dark roast brew... an improvement over the office break room coffee. When I arrive at the precinct, I find Hank sitting alone.

"Where is everyone?"

"Jade's down the hall visiting the ladies' room, Wilson's in his office, Gustav and Victor are off on an assignment for Randolph... so Wilson says."

I approach him and whisper.

"If your theory's correct, someone's gonna" end up dead."

"Yes, news at eleven."

Wilson sticks his head out and calls me in and closes the door.

"Thanks for what you did for Jules."

"Thank goodness Jade knew how to reach you."

"I spoke with Jules late last night, told him I called in a favor... they won't bother him again. You know, he's like family to me."

"And a good friend to me, Lieutenant. Will that be all?"

"Yes, and thanks again. And, ah, keep an eye on him, will ya."

"I will."

• • • •

THE NEXT THREE DAYS are quiet... *no firm leads coming from Randolph's office means no imminent raids. And no Gustav and Victor in the office is a blessing, despite the fact that someone out there just might*

lose their life. Wilson holds a meeting with us each day to review poten-
tial leads Randolph, Olsen, and Carlton are working. Why we need to be
briefed is a mystery since all we have to do is show up and shoot some peo-
ple, call the Body Snatchers, and it's done... next. When the new guy shows
up, I'll suggest we put him in charge of all future executions... that'll be my
contribution to streamlining the operation. Whenever I'm in the office, I
flirt with Jade every opportunity I get. Now and again she graces me with
a smile, which only encourages me. I suggested again we meet for that cup
of coffee outside the office, but she gives me the same excuse... she has to get
home to feed her damn cat. I'm betting she doesn't even have a cat... it's an
excuse to keep me at bay. On the other hand, she's yet to tell me to screw
off, to cease and desist. Until she does, I remain her pursuer...... Hank and
I spend time patrolling the streets to ease the boredom. Several times, we
spot stuff going down, but nothing Hank wants to deal with.

"Let the uniform guys deal with the small stuff."

Suits me fine.

· · · ·

THURSDAY MORNING, GUSTAV and Victor return. *Not a word*
out of either of them where they might have been and Hank and I don't
dare ask...... At the end of the day, I join Hank for dinner at a Mexican
joint around the corner from the office on Athens Street. We order and
Hank kicks off the conversation.

"An ex-member of South Africa's Parliament was assassinated in Jo-
hannesburg Tuesday."

"What was his sin?"

"Publicly accusing the regime's honchos of draining the government trough for personal gain. Gustav and Victor were gone for three
days, enough time to have assassinated the man and be back this morning. Where I come from, two and two always adds up to four."

"We could simply ask if they did it."

"Bad joke, Billy. We don't ask, we don't nose around, we do nothing."

When we leave, Hanks offers to give me a lift home, but I refuse. Dangerous as these streets can be, I prefer to walk, helps clear the cobwebs...... The sun is kissing the far Western horizon as I make my way along Broadway. Three homeless souls approach me seeking handouts. When I expose my badge, they quickly slink away like I have a communicable disease...... As I make my way along Broadway, I hear a commotion in a narrow alley next to the clothing store. Two male voices are taking turns threatening someone. Now a third voice... it's a man and he's pleading for them to stop. I whip out my gun and cautiously enter the alley. It's dark, hard to see, but I make out two men standing over a man on the ground and they're taking turns kicking him.

"Hey, what's going on?"

I might as well have been talking to myself because they ignore me... I raise my weapon and take aim.

"I'm a cop, there's a gun trained on you."

Now, I have their attention. The two men standing do a slow turn in my direction, the guy on the ground pops to his feet and yells to me.

"Thank God you came by, they would have killed me!"

One of the men says something to the other that I can't hear. Next thing I know, they're off running like rabbits toward the far end of the alley and disappear around the corner. Now the victim is backing away... he looks like he's going to make a run for it too.

"Hey, where are you going? Are you alright?"

"Fine, fine, I don't want any trouble with the police."

And with that, he's running in the same direction as the other two. Screw it, if he's that dumb and doesn't want help, the hell with him. Holstering my gun, I hightail it out of the alley, walking at a quickened pace to 4th Street. I'm within thirty-feet of home when someone calls my name.

"Mr. Russell?"

Jesus, is there a full moon... what now? My head spins in the direction of the voice. There's a man is sitting in a shiny black Lexus across from the house. He waves at me from his open window and slips out. Whoa, he's a big one, over six feet and at least two hundred and fifty pounds with broad linebacker shoulders. He's strolling casually toward me like he's in no hurry and doing his best not to look threatening. Is this the guy that Jules told me was nosing around asking questions? A second man exits the front passenger seat and leans against the car... now I'm on full alert.

"Mr. Russell?"

He's within fifteen feet of me, I can make out his round, beefy face, no real distinguishing features other than he's big all over and he's smiling and that unnerves me. My hand wraps around my pistol grip.

"Do I know you?"

"My name is Norman."

"I don't know any Norman."

His right-hand rises up... I catch a glint of steel.

"I'm armed, Mr. Russell."

Jesus, who the hell is this guy?

"Please, sir, with your index finger and thumb, pass me your weapon. Do as I ask and no harm will come to you."

"What do you want?"

"Please, sir, your weapon, hand it to me."

My hand tightens on the Smith and Wesson... I hesitate... a shootout on this darkened street would be suicide for one or both of us... and there's that other one by the car... I have to assume he's armed too. I do as he asks and remove my revolver and hand it to him.

"Thank you, now please walk to the car."

"Look, whoever you are, I have nothing of value."

"We're not here to rob you, please walk to the car."

I've been here for all of eleven days and already I'm being kidnapped by who the hell knows who these men are or what they want with me. As I reach the vehicle, the second guy comes around... this one's short and wiry, thin face with dark eyes behind thick, dark-framed glasses. He's holding something black in his right hand and extends it to me.

"Mr. Russell, please place this hood over your head."

"A hood? What for?"

Big Norman places his hand on my arm.

"We mean you no harm, Mr. Russell, please place the hood over your head."

"Look, you must have me mixed up with someone else."

"No, sir. Now, if you will please do as we ask, we can be on our way."

The skinny one hands me the hood... I balk.

"I'm not putting that on."

"Please sir, place the hood over your head."

"I don't think so."

Norman raises the gun... now it's pointing at my head.

"Please, don't make this difficult."

"I'm a cop and—"

"We know who you are."

Easy, Billy Boy, you're not holding the cards here, put the hood over your head and hope the hell they're telling the truth that they mean you no harm. The skinny one takes my arm. I slip the hood on.

"I'll guide you into the back seat, watch your head."

The interior of the car smells like new expensive leather.

"Slide over, sir."

He gets in next to me.

"If you will cooperate, I won't tie your hands."

"And if I don't?"

Neither man answers.

• • • •

WE'VE BEEN TRAVELING *for about twenty-minutes with four short stops along the way... I'm guessing for traffic lights. When we stop a fifth time, Norman turns off the engine... we must be at our destination. Mr.*

Skinny helps me from the back seat, takes my arm and guides me a short distance... we stop. One of them, I'm guessing Norman, is messing with a door key... a door opens and we enter a building... a dusty odor assaults my nose.

"Can't afford the high-rent district?"

It's Norman that answers.

"I beg your pardon, sir."

"Forget it."

We walk about twenty steps, make a left turn, walk another ten or so steps and make a right... a few steps further we stop and I'm eased into a chair. For a few seconds, it's dead silent.

"Tell me, Norman, was it you nosing around asking questions about me?"

"It was, yes."

Then, footsteps... a third person has joined the party. The hood's removed and a bright light hits me hard, my hand goes to my eyes.

"What's with the light?"

No one answers. I blink until my eyes adjust enough to see someone standing in the shadows beyond this bloody light.

"Thank you for coming, Mr. Russell."

Whoever he is, he has a distinct upper-class, very proper, British accent.

"I came at gunpoint with a hood over my head. Who are you?"

"My name is Gideon. I apologize, under the circumstance, I understand your ire. I assure you, you are in no danger."

"I'll take you at your word. It's late, I'm tired, get to the point."

Well, that came out sounding like one of my better threats. Not a time to be a smart ass, Billy Boy, be cool, there's three of them and one of you.

"The light, it's blinding me."

"I apologize again. At this point in our relationship, it's necessary."

"We don't have a relationship. Turn the damn thing off."

There's several seconds of silence... I guess he's thinking about it.

"Norman, turn it off, please."

"Are you sure, sir?"

"Yes, yes, turn it off."

"But sir—"

"It's fine Norman, turn it off."

That was easy, maybe too easy. If points were given for politeness, these guys win hands down. Norman turns off the light, I blink, trying to refocus yet again. When I do, I do a quick scan of the room... looks to be a stockroom, unlabeled cardboard boxes are piled high along the back wall behind this sixty-plus looking Gideon character. He's dressed in an expensive-looking tailored dark gray suit, off-white shirt, two-tone blue striped tie and matching vest... I smell money. His full head of white hair is neatly Combed crowning a friendly, grandfatherly, smiling face... that's unnerving.

"Would you like anything, Mr. Russell, water, perhaps?"

"A Cappuccino would be nice."

The mysterious Gideon raises an eyebrow, a signal he doesn't appreciate my humor. He's pacing now, five steps one way, five steps back. I steal a look over my shoulder at Norman... he pays me no attention... his eyes are locked on Gideon like a well-trained service dog.

"There is no cause for alarm, we are all friends here."

"Then let's shake, call it a night, and have Norman take me home."

"All in good time, Mr. Russell."

He's pacing again like he's thinking... he stops and stares at me deliberately, cautiously.

"To the point. We hope to enlist your support."

"Me? For what?"

"You possess expertise that would prove useful."

"I'm not exactly the cerebral type... be a bit more explicit. Which expertise is that?"

The corner of his mouth curls into a smug grin.

"Are you settled in? Any difficulty assimilating since your return from Europa?"

What? How does he know that?

"Where did you get that information?"

"We are not without resources."

"So, it would it seem. Look, Mr. Gideon—"

"Please, just Gideon."

"Okay, Gideon. We've obviously never met, you know nothing about me so—"

"On the contrary, Mr. Russell, we know everything about you. Your record as a narcotics officer in Providence, it was quite impressive: First year out of the academy chosen rookie of the year, year three promoted to sergeant well on your way to becoming a Lieutenant one day. You were on the fast-track until that fateful day in that fateful closet."

Dear Mother of God, who is this guy... how does he know what he knows?

"Okay, okay, you've made your point. Know this... I left my hell behind, I'm not looking to enter another one."

"You're still in hell, Mr. Russell, just a different location."

From his breast pocket, he retrieves a long, fat cigar, pinches off the end before striking his lighter, and rolling the tip over the flame until it glows red.

"Forgive me, would you care for one?"

"Let's skip the pleasantries and get to the reason you had me brought here."

"Yes, to the point then. I represent an organization that will bring down this hideous government."

"Really? And how to you propose to do that?"

"I can well understand your skepticism at such a bold pronouncement."

"Ya' think?"

"Do you know the meaning of term Volte-face?"

"Can't say that I do, nor do I care."

"It is French meaning a reversal in policy, a change in direction... a rather benign moniker for a Byzantine task dedicated to ending the pestilence of tyranny by men holding an entire civilization hostage, men who embrace white nationalism and xenophobia, who espouse dangerous and inflammatory views contrary to the basic principles of morality and do not hesitate to employ thuggery to achieve their vainglorious goals. It is a painful reminder that the worst of humanity can emerge when we let our guard down."

"Look, I have no idea what you're talking, but whatever it is, it doesn't involve me."

"If we hope to reclaim what has been stolen from us, it requires the participation of everyone, Mr. Russell. When the full force of Volteface is unleashed, it will bring about a revolution that will purge these 'Latet anguis in Herba' from the face of the Earth."

"The what?"

"Latet anguis in Herba', Roman for 'Snakes in the grass.'

I have no clue what this man is talking about, or how it could possibly involve me in any way... I just want out of here. He's rolling that cigar slowly over his lips and pacing again. I open my mouth to protest my kidnapping, but he plows on.

"Allow me an abridged version of what you missed during your forced absence. Instead of dealing with life's challenges head on, far too many citizens preferred to ah... to sleep in. I don't mean physically, but cerebral. It was a generation that grew up connected to social media and 24-hour news. They were so connected, much of what flowed became unimportant, especially regarding politics. They were a generation far more interested in seeking position and monetary gain, leaving them vulnerable to men who recognized opportunity and how to seize it when the inevitable downturn began."

He makes a smacking sound with his lips and shakes his head with disapproval.

"To further complicate world order, a shift to a global economy allowed the powerful and wealthy to further enriched themselves while systematically leaving the working class behind."

"You're not telling me anything I don't know. That slide was well under way before I left."

I've listened to enough of this bullshit. Popping to on my feet, I turn to leave.

"Thanks for the history lesson, I'm out of here."

"Please sit down, Mr. Russell."

"This one-sided gab Fest is over. Norman, be a good man and take me home."

Norman's baseball-mitt-sized left hand is on my shoulder pressing me down to the chair. Gideon's pacing again and puffing on that damn cigar... the air's getting thick with smoke.

"Now then, if I may continue. Pakistan's iniquitous attack on India was the red line in the sand, a spiritual awakening of sorts, at least for those who could comprehend. That horrifically evil event, along with mother's nature's fury, rising waters, mass migrations, extreme heat and droughts, the rise in terrorism, and changing demographics, left the world teetering on the brink of certain disaster. People turned to praying when they should have gotten up from their knees and admitted their apathy was the root cause of what was happening. Unfortunately, we humans only see symptoms, never the solutions. Like the caged gerbil, we go around and around meeting ourselves at the end of every turn only to repeat the cycle. Is any of this resonating, Mr. Russell?"

"If you think you're going to change the world, Gideon, you're whistling in the wind. It's always been this way, always will be. People settle into their comfort zones, then rise up and demand change only when they realize they've been screwed."

"Yes, Mr. Russell, that is true. This time they chose to place their fate in the hands of men whose only interest was to bolster their own positions. Wealthy, powerful men moved quickly to assemble a secret coalition of like-minded political and military leaders from around the world. Their plan was quite simple. If they addressed middle class grievances with populist solutions, the masses would respond favorably. With the financial backing and leadership of a French billionaire, this secret cabal set in motion a scheme that culminated in the most brazenly conceived bloodless coup ever attempted; the complete political takeover of the entire world."

"How do you go about convincing over nine billion people and one-hundred and ninety-six countries that a takeover of the world is good for them?"

"By winning elections. A new world political party was formed; The Peoples Cooperative Populist Party. How could the suffering masses not fall in love with that? Candidates from all industrialized nations began running for high office under the Populist Party banner winning elections in country after country. Once enough were in positions of power, they put forth the concept of a one-world government. There was immediate push-back from the intelligentsia who condemned the idea as ridiculously unworkable. What the intelligentsia had failed to recognize, by then the cabal had gained the support of citizens around the world who had bought their promise to restore equal opportunities for all. Over the objections of most all governments, these so-called Populists forced a world-wide vote: Seventy-two percent voted in favor quite unaware of the demons they were about to unleash. A World Council, consisting of thirty-seven white men was created: One seat for each of the industrialized nations... all chosen from the ranks of those loyal to this French billionaire's vision of how the world should be ruled. This Council was tasked with forming a world government. The lurking serpent behind the movement, Jean Lumiere Laurent, President and controlling shareholder of MAXMinerai, was—"

That stops me cold.

"MAXMinerai!"

"Yes, yes, Mr. Russell, your former employer."

"Holy Christ."

"Laurent was proclaimed President for life, not by public election, but by unanimous proclamation by the New World Council, which was to also function as Laurent's Cabinet. The newly formed government set up shop in the heart of Marseilles in sight of MAXMinerai Corporation. Wealthy white men, most of whom controlled the world's largest corporations, had successfully turned the globe into their private businesses."

"This is unbelievable!"

"As history notes, every oppressor begins by disarming its citizenry. The new government set about streamlining the world's military forces into a single unit under their command. There was push-back, of course, but Laurent had the support of enough generals to pull it off. One of his closest allies, French General Andre Couture, was installed as the Supreme Military Commander of world forces."

"What about privately held guns? America alone had over three hundred million out there."

"Banned and collected. Anyone found with one was immediately jailed. There was an upside of course. With a single world military, wars between nations were effectively eradicated. With most of the world's personally held weapons gone, violence and killings dropped dramatically. Next, the regime gathered and dismantled all nuclear weapons. As you might imagine, that proved wildly popular with the masses who feared a repeat of the Pakistan-India disaster. Countries maintained their sovereignty, but would be heavily taxed by Marseilles for services rendered. Each country was to be overseen by one of Laurent's hand-picked generals. Here in America it is former U.S. Army General Albert Joseph Natali. The mechanics of how it all works is complicated... a conversation for another day perhaps."

Gideon drags on the cigar, inhale's deeply and holds it in, savoring the carcinogens that one day will bless him with lung disease that did in poor Leon Grover.

"Once firmly in control, Laurent and the New World Council began governing as autocrats; they would make the rules, no discussion, no debate, no vote. Minorities, the oppressed, and those of color were treated as second class citizens. Gays, lesbians, Transgenders, and dissenters were rounded up and sent to government retraining camps; Shades of Nazi Germany as well as what was taking place in modern day China around two thousand ten."

Jesus! The camps that Jules referred to.

"But alas, Laurent and his henchmen proved vulnerable to the same human shortcomings as everyone. Their self-serving inept economic policies led to a stunning economic collapse of the global economy."

"Okay, okay, I got it. What does this have to do with me?"

"Do you know who Commissioner Henry Dion is?"

"I heard his name on the news. Sounds like he's out of favor with the Marseilles gang."

"Once a highly successful Boston trial attorney, Henry was an early supporter of the world government concept. After all, he reasoned, all else had failed, why not this. He ran for the United States Senate as a Populist candidate and won. When the new government formed, he was given the U.S. seat on the World Council. However, it wasn't long before Henry and four other Council members began to question the regime's oppressive restraints. They rightly concluded that Laurent was, in fact, an autocratic, melomaniac, corporate charlatan playing a human chess game to satisfy their narcissistic appetites. Henry and his cohorts vowed to bring down this tyrannical regime. Henry chose to be the one who would speak out publicly, the one who created the Volteface movement. Today, millions upon millions stand ready to act with him."

"What are they going to fight with, stick and pitchforks?"

"Are you familiar with the term 'Black Swan Event?'"

"Can't say that I am."

"This criminal regime has committed a litany of sins. It would only take the discovery and exposure of one to turn the public against them. Henry is in possession of documentation of one of their greatest sins. It will cause a Black Swan Event... a metaphor describing an incident that leaves an indelible mark. This one will bring about the largest uprising in the history of our civilization."

"That's a pretty tall order. What is it that Dion has?"

He doesn't respond to the question... he looks away and keeps sucking on that cigar.

"Following the event, Henry and others will require sentinels for a short time while the masses rise up."

"Ah, so now we get to my expertise. Well, let me break the news to you gently, Gideon. These sentinels will be participating in a suicide mission."

No response from Gideon... he's pacing again.

"Look, I'm just a cop strapped to a job I didn't seek. The last thing I need is to become involved with—"

He stops pacing and angrily wags at finger at me.

"Do not tell me you were jumping for joy by what greeted you upon your return. Do not tell me you were not appalled by the brutal beating of a handcuffed man on your first day, or the man you helped kill in that alley, or the cold-blooded execution of seven dead men left to be cremated in a burning warehouse. Because if you do, Mr. Russell, I will be forced to label you a liar."

Christ, where does this man get his information? I'll toss him an out and see where it goes.

"Have you considered that when I leave here, I'll simply turn you in and blow up whatever plans you have?"

There, I gave him an opening, but surprisingly he doesn't take the bait, he doesn't even acknowledge my threat.

"Do you know who George Orwell was, Mr. Russell?"

"I'm not totally illiterate, I read '1984.'"

"May I quote his insightful words?"

"Would it make a difference if I said no?"

That wisecrack finally gets a smile out of him.

"Mr. Orwell wrote these insightful words. "'For if leisure and security were enjoyed by all alike, the great mass of human beings who are normally stupefied by poverty would become literate and would learn to think for themselves; and when once they had done this, they would sooner or later realize that the privileged minority had no function, and they would sweep it away. In the long run, a hierarchical society was only possible on a basis of poverty and ignorance.' At its core the Volte-face movement is not a political one, but a human one that will define mankind for as long as we inhabit this Earth. With the support of the people, we will sweep away this tyrannical government and restore democracy and the rule of law across the entire globe. That is all I can share with you now, Mr. Russell. Whatever your decision, it will be respected. In return, I trust you will not betray us. Norman will give you my direct phone number."

"What am I supposed to do with it?"

"It is our hope in the coming days, when you have searched your soul, you will offer your assistance. If and when you do, identify yourself only as 556."

He knows that was my number on Europa. I can't help but smile at the irony.

"If you decide to call, I will provide you further instructions. Thank you for coming, Mr. Russell."

In a cloud of cigar smoke, Gideon abruptly makes an exit. Norman hands me a slip of paper. Without looking at it, I stuff it in my shirt pocket and promptly forget about it.

"We'll take you home now, Mr. Russell."

"Norman, does your friend here have a name?"

"It's Jason."

"Jason, do I get to keep the hood?"

"If you like, Mr. Russell, I have others."

"Ah, you bought a six-pack."

"A dozen, actually."

At least Jason has a sense of humor. Score one for him. Now I need to work on Norman. Hey, Billy Boy, stop with the jokes, there nothing funny about what just took place here. Nothing at all.

I **ask Normal to drop me off** *at the newsstand... don't want Jules questioning where I've been. As he and Jason pull away in their shiny black Lexus, Norman smiles and waves as if we've become best buds. Humor him, wave back... hopefully I'll never see them again...... What am I supposed to make of this night's inexplicable meet and greet with Gideon the proper Englishman? Wasn't Europa enough agony for one lifetime? No sooner am I back on terra-firma, I'm hijacked by some nut-job dissident group with the whimsical name Volte-face that believes they can save the world from a bunch of rich autocrats, and in some cockamamie way, me, the son of Amelia and Alistair Russell, is willing to place his ass on the line for them. If there's one thing I know, nobody's going to save the human race, not in a million years... we're in possession of a gene that renders us self-destructive. It we weren't, we'd stop repeating the same dumb mistakes over and over again from generation to generation...... On my way to the house, I spot a couple huddled in a doorway. Damned if it isn't the same one's I met my first night here. As I approach, the back away.*

"Don't want any trouble, officer."

"I'm not going to harass you. How long have you been on the streets?"

The old man looks at the women like he can't remember... she answers.

"About eight months now."

"You have no place to go, no family?"

"No, sir, we've lost everything."

"How do you eat how do you take care of yourselves?"

Neither answers... they look frightened.

"Tomorrow morning I'll be walking this way around seven-thirty. If you're here, follow me to the grocery store over on Broadway and I'll get you something to eat. You know where the store is?"

"Yes, sir."

"Are you on drugs?"

No answer... they huddle closer to one another.

"You're not in trouble, just tell me."

"No, sir, drugs cost money, we have no money."

"Are you married?"

"We are."

"Okay, I have to go now. If you're here in the morning, I promise to get you food."

They're staring at me through soulful eyes... no doubt wondering who this crazy man is that's offered his help.

"Goodnight."

"Goodnight, Officer."

I amble down the street feeling good about my encounter with the old couple. Climbing the steps to the front door, I unlock it and step inside, but before I can turn on the light at the top of the stairs, Jules opens his door and steps out.

"Thought I heard you come in."

"Jesus, you scared the crap out of me."

I switch on the light... Jules is in his robe.

"Where have you been?"

"I didn't know I needed your permission to go out after dark."

"I told you, it's dangerous. And you've kept your company waiting."

"Company?"

"The female type—showed up ten minutes ago."

"What are you talking about?"

"The lady cop, Jade, the one who stocked the frig... the one who saved my life. I thanked her for finding Wilson and let her in."

My eyes shoot to the top of the stairs... my heart skips a beat... I try to act cool.

"Oh, yeah, Jade."

"She's a looker, that one."

"Yeah, that she is. She mentioned she might bring some files over."

"I didn't see any files, just a brown paper bag."

"Okay, thanks."

"You're welcome. And stop walking the damn streets alone at night."

"You're okay now, right?"

"Stop asking me that. Go, don't keep the lady waiting."

I wait for Jules to close his door before taking the stairs two at a time. I'm half way up when the obvious hits me... if Jade is the one who stocked the frig, maybe she knows what only Wilson and Randolph are supposed to know regarding my past. Okay, play it cool, don't bring it up unless she does...... When I open the door, she's draped on one end of the sofa looking like one of those supermodels in a magazine ad for an expensive woman's cologne. She's decked out in tan slacks that fit her body like a glove. A light blue shirt hangs loosely over her waist. Next to her neatly folded on the sofa is a black waist-length leather coat and a small brown paper bag. She doesn't smile, just stares with those beautiful eyes.

"Been out bowling?"

"Just a walk to get some fresh air."

"Find any?"

"What brings you to my lavish penthouse pad?"

She scans the room... her expression clearly says she disapproves.

"Needs work."

"You're being kind. Want something? All I have is water and coffee. I don't recommend the water.

She reaches into the paper bag and pulls out a bottle of Bourbon.

"I assume the first one didn't last."

"You assume correctly. Is that from you or Wilson?"

"Me."

"What did I do to deserve this kind gesture?"

She just smiles. Okay, what the hell is happening here? I'm getting mixed signals. I hang my jacket on the back of one of the kitchen chairs, grab a couple of glasses, join her on the sofa and pour shots for both of us. She raises her glass in a toast.

"To better times."

"To better times... and soon."

She downs the shot in one gulp and holds out the glass, I pour her another. Then I hear myself bring up the very subject I said I wouldn't.

"You know, don't you?"

"Know what, Billy?"

"Where I've been and why?"

"I, ah—"

"Careful, no lying while you're drinking."

"I keep the office records, remember."

"Well now, there's no putting that Jack back in the box, so we'll let it go at that and move on."

"Now you're angry."

"No, curious why you didn't let me know right off."

She shrugs and diverts her eyes.

"Besides the booze, you had a reason for coming."

"Don't look a gift horse in the mouth."

"That's a cliché."

"I'm full of them."

"Come on, Jade, out with it. What brought you here?"

"Maybe I see a wounded warrior that needs a lifeline before he gets into serious trouble."

"Wounded warrior, interesting way to put it. Trust me, I can take care of myself."

"So far you haven't demonstrated that."

"The business with Gustav and Victor will blow over. That's why you came, isn't it... to warn me?"

"They are the last two on the planet you want to be on the wrong side of, Billy. They take their work seriously and—"

"Work? Is that what it's called? Oh wait, I forgot, we provide a valuable service to population control by executing people."

"I'm just saying, they don't take kindly to anyone calling them out."

"Is that what I did?"

"Jesus, you're thick headed."

After listening to long-winded Gideon, I'm anxious to hear someone else's take on the world.

"Let's switch gears."

"To what?"

"Fifteen lost years... maybe you can fill in some blank spots. Let's start with what brought the world to where it is."

"That could take a while."

"I have time if you do."

She leans back, crosses those lovely legs, takes a long, slow breath.

"Well... as the saying goes, we have met the enemy, and he is us. The Pakistan debacle forced us to confront what we should have known; that in the space of a few hours, mankind could through stupidity bequeath the planet to the bugs and animals. That realization, albeit it a bit late, forced the world into survival mode."

"What I see on the streets is not survival, it's more desperation."

"That's because people—all of us—want things to be better than they are without having to work too hard for it. Take us American's, for example. We became far too complacent in our belief that our country would always be a safe haven in a dangerous world simply because we believed in American exceptionalism. When that turned out not to be so, and other voices came along singing a convincing song, we jumped on board without engaging our brains. You wanted change people, okay, you got it, now live with it."

"That big flashing billboard on Boston Harbor, what's the policies behind it?"

"God knows we need population control, but not the way it's being carried out. It's a slash and burn policy... there's no morality, no empathy behind it. The elderly, the terminally ill, AIDS and other communicable disease victims, they're all rounded up and moved to camps with others deemed unfit to live among society and left to die. If this government could get away with mass executions, they would and be done with it."

"What do you know about these camps?"

"That's a tightly controlled secret. I know they exist, no more. I don't know anyone who does."

"Children, I don't see any."

"That's because it's against the law to have children."

"You're joking."

"No, no joke. It's zero births until further notice. If a woman becomes pregnant, by law, she must get an abortion at a government run facility. And if one slips through, mom, dad and baby are seized."

"My God. What happens to them?"

"Don't know."

"What about this Commissioner—what's his name—Henry Dion? I saw something about him on the news."

"Dion speaks to power, one of the few that dares. But his rhetoric has brought him nothing but trouble. In times past, what Laurent's government is doing would have gotten them all booted out of office in disgrace, maybe even jailed.

"And the Henry Dion's of this world? Are they alone in their opposition?"

"There's rumors of a movement, but it's just rumors."

Having just spent more time than I cared to with Gideon, Norman, and Jason, I fish around to see if she knows more.

"If an opposition movement does exist, you think it will surface?"

"First of all, I don't know that one exists. Second, if it does there's a problem; people limit their thinking to today, tomorrow, maybe a week out at best. Who knows what they'll do if and when some organized group surfaces?"

I want to share with her my meeting with Gideon, but I don't dare. A few beats pass before she gets to what I suspect is the real reason for this visit.

"Randolph and Wilson are going to test you, Billy. They need to know you're one-hundred percent embedded in the program and ready to do the job. If you're not—"

Now she goes silent again and looks away.

"Or what?"

She doesn't answer... or by her silence, did she?

"I'll cross that bridge when I come to it, Jade."

"Choose your bridges carefully or trouble will find you."

"Trouble found me fifteen years ago, and because of what I did it changed the plot of my life. I was punished for my crime, and rightly so, but I feel no remorse for what I believed I did, for what I felt I had to do. But now for the bad news; I've served one prison sentence, and now I've been given another."

She holds out her glass, I pour her another shot... she's going to drink me under the table.

"You know all about me, yet I know nothing about you. Where does Jade Miro fit in this picture?"

"What would you like to know?"

"Whatever you care to share."

"Quick answer, I'm the daughter of a Hawaiian mother and a Japanese father. I have an older brother, an architect, he lives in Seattle."

"And his baby sister became a cop."

"Not exactly. I graduated college with a degree in psychology. The Boston Police Department had an opening for one. I applied and was hired to diagnose and treat cops suffering from psychological stress issues."

"Why the switch to this unit? It isn't exactly your line of work."

"Police work is one of the most stressful jobs a man or women can choose as a career. So many of them burn out. After five years, their stress became mine—I couldn't do it anymore. When this job opened up. It was still law enforcement, which is where I wanted to stay, but without the stress. Anyway, Wilson liked my resume and hired me. It's been almost a year now."

"Were you aware of what the unit did when you signed on?"

"Hell no. I only knew it was drug enforcement and that interested me since the drug epidemic had become so widespread and dangerous. I only became aware of their true mission after I was on the job."

"And you stayed on?"

"Were you given a choice once you were on-board?"

"Point made."

"Neither was I, neither was Hank or Rod."

"And Gustav and Victor?"

"Different animals all together straight from Marseilles. That's why I'm telling you to stay clear of them."

"You're what, Jade, thirty-six, thirty-seven? No rings on your finger, no husband or boyfriend waiting at home?"

"Jeez, Billy, could you be more direct? Okay, if you must know, I was married to a Boston cop, it didn't work out. After five years he went his way, I went mine. And I'm thirty-eight."

She glances at her watch and feigns a sigh.

"Show and tell is over, I have to go."

"To feed your cat?"

Her head bobs back and she laughs.

"I don't have a cat. Let's leave it at that. Oh, one last question before I go if you don't mind."

"What?"

"Space, what was it like?"

"I saw none of it going over, coming back we had a portal."

"And?"

"If I told you it was a mind blower, that wouldn't come close to explaining what was a truly spiritual experience."

"Wow. Another time you have to tell me more."

She's up and slipping on her coat. As she reaches the door, she turns back.

"What we do and what the government's solution is to the drug epidemic is against God's laws, but legal by theirs. As sick as that is, keep it in mind."

"I will."

"Goodnight, Billy, see you in the morning. And mums the word I was here."

"My lips are sealed. Thanks for the booze. Till the morning, then."

Chapter 18
An Eye Opener

*T**he following morning,** I bound out of bed with a renewed enthusiasm reliving every questionable moment with Gideon, and every delicious moment with Jade. I shower, shave, have two cups of coffee, toast, and remind myself not to show Jade too much attention. That's going to be difficult... I'm ready to shower her with words that I haven't used in over fifteen years. Slow down, Billy, don't smother her or you'll spook her......*
With a spring in my step, I'm down the stairs and out the door. Jules is standing on the sidewalk, his riding crop in hand, looking like he's ready to kill.

"Good morning, why the long puss?"

"Look over there, some lowlife pissed on my steps."

Sure enough, I had walked over a puddle of yellow liquid without seeing it.

"Maybe it was a dog?"

"I saw the slug who did it from my window. By the time I got out here the son of a bitch was gone."

"It'll wash off."

"Thanks smart-ass, maybe you'll do it for me."

"Don't hold your breath."

"I heard the lady leave last night."

"So?"

"Strike out, did we?"

"I told you, Jules, she was here on official office business."

"Yeah, and I was a two-star general in the Marines."

"Goodbye, Jules, nice to see you're back to your old self."

As I head up Fourth toward Broadway, I hear Jules yelling at the top of his voice.

"Okay, you sons of bitches, the next one I see hanging around my stoop, I'm gonna" shoot their ass!"

I'm looking for the old couple, but they're nowhere in sight. Okay, I made the offer, that's the best I can do. I skip my coffee stop at Sully's and move on down Broadway when I spot them huddled two doors down from by the grocery store.

"Good morning."

"Good morning, sir."

"Billy's the name, what's yours?"

"I'm Harold, this is Catherine."

"I don't suppose they let you in the store."

"No, sir, not unless we can prove we have credits to spend."

"Okay, wait here."

Dipping in the store, I buy two loaves of sliced bread, a pound of sliced ham, a pound of sliced Swiss cheese, four apples, and two one-gallon jugs of water. Makes me feel damn good that I can afford it. Outside, I hand over the food to Harold and Catherine.

"Be careful, don't let anyone steal this from you."

"We have a place we can go where no one will bother us."

"Good, go there."

With a friendly smile, I bid them a goodbye and begin to leave when Harold calls to me.

"Mr. Billy."

"Yes, Harold?"

"Thank you, sir."

"You're welcome, stay safe."

• • • •

*JADE GREETS ME WITH **a smile,** not a good morning smile, but 'I'm glad I visited you' smile... or is it just the way I'm reading it? Okay, put your ego on hold and say something nice.*

"Lovely morning, Jade."

"It could be warmer."

"It will be."

"When?"

"In a couple of months."

"You're full of witticisms this morning, Officer Russell."

Before my flirting gets out of hand, Lieutenant Wilson pops his head out his door. He looks excited about something.

"Everybody in my office."

Gustav and Victor have taken the two chairs, so I stand by the window next to Hank. Gustav glances in my direction, smirks and looks away. Wilson lights a cigarette... first time I've seen him smoke... I want one really bad.

"Major Randolph thinks he's got a solid lead on Alvera's location."

Victor raises his hand.

"Finally, where?"

"He won't say until it's confirmed. You know how bad the Major wants the grand prize, so do I, so should you, so no screw ups if and when this comes down. Okay, until we hear more, out on the streets, make it a productive day, bust some heads. If you don't hear from me sooner, be back by four in case Randolph has an update."

· · · ·

HANK AND I SPEND THE morning *cruising the extreme South end of South Boston, Gustav and Augier the North end. It's unusually quiet, no action this morning that draws our attention. Around noon, we end up at Maggie's place for lunch.*

"What's the routine today?"

"Watch and learn, Billy, watch and learn."

As soon as we settle into a booth, Maggie comes over with a long face like maybe she's in less than a good mood.

"Hey Maggie baby, heard you won the Miss Bitchy Boston contest."

"Not today, Hank, I'm in a shit-mood. Special today is Southwestern Chili with garlic toast."

"You mean you turned yesterday's rancid hamburger into today's special?"

"Hank, your sphincter muscle is showing."

"Whoa, a big word, Maggie. I'm may have to take your dictionary away."

Maggie waddles off mumbling to herself.

"She loves it."

"I don't know, Hank, today she seems upset."

"Trust me, it's an act, watch when she comes back."

"So, what else do I need to know about this Alvera guy?"

"He's Randolph's nemesis for sure. Olie Olsen let it slip the Major's up for a promotion with The International Drug Council in Marseilles. Shutting Alvera down could be the clincher he needs to snag the job."

"After what he did to those men in that warehouse, he should be locked away in an insane asylum."

"Never say that out loud if you hope to see another sunrise."

Maggie's back with our coffee, looking more pissed off than before.

"So, Hank, the word on the street is you're into boys."

Hank whips his head to me and feigns anger.

"Damn it you, Billy, you been blabbing again?"

"I'm sorry, Hank, it slipped."

"Okay, you two, enough, you want the chili or what?"

"I'll give it a try."

"You, Billy?"

"Sure."

As she waddles off again, I call after her.

"Hey Maggie, how about you and I go on a date?"

No comeback from Maggie other than a loud grunt.

"Speaking of hooking up, I'm surprised Wilson hasn't kicked your ass, he's very protective of Jade."

"I think Jade's old enough to make her own decisions."

"Okay, don't say I didn't warn you when Wilson—"

Maggie's back with the chili.

"Enjoy, I made this myself at three this morning."

"Maggie, Maggie, the last time you were up at that hour, there was a full moon and you were running with wolves."

"Whoa, Hank, that's a good one."

Off she goes smiling again.

"One day you're going to say something that really pisses her off and that'll be the end of that."

"And that's the day hell freezes over."

We dig into the chili, it turns out to be pretty damn good.

"I haven't figured out Wilson yet."

"Do you need to, Billy?"

"I don't know, I get the feeling something's going on there."

"Like?"

"Like maybe he's caught in the same trap we are."

"Don't be fooled because he acts semi-human sometimes. He's Randolph's man through and through. Both of them have ice in their veins."

• • • •

***WE'RE BACK IN THE OFFICE** at three-forty-five... Wilson calls everyone in.*

"Okay, it's game on. Alvera's camping out in an oceanfront house in Old Orchard Beach, Maine."

"Maine? What the hell's he doing up there?"

"As opposed to where, Victor?"

"I don't know, Lieutenant, Hawaii maybe? And it's Saturday, do we get paid overtime?"

"If you can stop with the jokes... one of Alvera's lieutenant's cut a deal with Randolph to save his sorry ass, so the information's solid. Olie

Olsen is coordinating the meet-up time with SWAT and their EMS unit for one tomorrow behind the Blue Wave resort on Seaside Avenue."

Victor pops to his feet like somebody lit a firecracker under his ass.

"We're doing this in broad daylight? Jesus, man, we'll lose the element of surprise."

"Feel free to tell the Major when you see him. You and Gustav ride with me. Billy, Jade, with Hank. That's it."

Gustav is grumbling under his breath as he heads for the door.

"In broad daylight. Damn it!"

When I return home that evening, *I check in on Jules again, whether he likes it or not. A few seconds go by before I hear him moving behind the door.*

"That you, Billy?"

"Yeah."

The door opens slowly, Jules is in his robe.

"My peephole is too high, I have to get it lowered one of these days."

"Just checking up on you."

"It's over, they won't bother me again. If they do, Wilson will have their asses, end of story, now stop mothering me. Wanna come in for a drink, I got a bottle of good Whiskey?"

"Never turn down good Whiskey."

My first time in his apartment. It's not the Ritz, but it's not shabby either. Until this minute I had no idea he occupied the entire first floor.

"Upstairs was the same when I bought the place. I had it divided into two apartments. Sit, be comfortable, got a present for you."

He shuffles off to the kitchen and returns with two bottles and two glasses. One of the bottles is Bourbon.

"I think I drank the last of yours."

"Thanks, Jules, that wasn't necessary."

"My appreciation for what you did."

He tosses me a cigarette. I have to buy a pack, that's all there is to it. He pours us both shots of the Whiskey and sits across from me. I can tell he wants to talk.

"You don't owe me an explanation, Jules."

"No, I don't, but I want to. From an early age, I knew who I was, but I kept it from everyone, even my parents and my sister—she was five years older than me. She died four years ago from liver cancer."

"Sorry."

"In high school, I dated the ladies on occasion to keep up appearances. I joined the Marines right out of school, and for twenty-two years, no one knew... no one other than those I became involved with. Well, Wilson knew, but he never judged me, not once. When those two cretins took me away, I was scared, really scared. I know where they take people like me."

He talks at length of growing up in Jackson, New Hampshire, a resort area east of the White Mountains National Forest, population nine-hundred and sixty. There he enjoyed a happy childhood with loving parents, but lived in fear that one day his secret would come out.

"Okay, that's it, that's my story."

And then I do what I had not intended... what's remained a black mark on my soul all these years. I confide to him my story, all of it, leaving nothing out. It proves to be a cleansing, one that's been too long coming. By the time I finish, we've shared our secrets and consumed way too much Whiskey, and we're both in tears.

Chapter 19
The Test That Wasn't

A s we follow Wilson's car up I-95 North the next morning, I'm apprehensive about this day. It's just a feeling, one I can't explain, but feel in my gut. Hank's driving, I'm in the passenger seat, Jade's in the back. A light snow is dusting the trees and countryside in a blanket of white powder. Jade explains how the area has had little snow so far this year, something to do with climate change that's brought a warmer than usual Winter to the Eastern Seaboard. She sounds like an encyclopedia...... Wilson exits on I-195 East... as we enter Old Orchard Beach it becomes Temple Avenue. We turn left on Seaside Avenue, which parallels the Atlantic Ocean. Sergeant Carlton in standing by the roadside next to the oceanfront resort's sign which says the place is closed for the season. Carlton points to a parking area in the rear of the complex. Randolph and Olsen are waiting for us by the Humvee.

"Good morning, lovely day for a hunting party."

That one's getting old, Major, try something a bit less unprofessional.

"Our boy is at 400 River Sands Drive at the end of the Peninsula. It's a big white two-story place facing the ocean."

"What about neighbors?"

"Summer residents, gone until Spring."

"That's a break. Where's SWAT and the EMS?"

Randolph's look turns crusty.

"Damn fools got the arrival time wrong by an hour."

Wilson looks like he's ready to blow a gasket.

"An hour? How the hell do you get the friggin' arrival time wrong?"

Randolph blows a hard breath and checks his watch.

"Jade, check SWAT's ETA."

All eyes are on Jade as she calls. She listens, rolls her eyes, and hangs up.

"SWAT leader says they're forty-five minutes out."

Randolph makes a fist and punches the air.

"Damn it, damn it, we can't wait all bloody day."

Now he's pacing, shoulders forward, eyes to the ground. He stops and stares at the ocean for several beats.

"We'll move into position."

"That's against protocol, wait for SWAT."

"I say what the hell protocol is, Frank."

"But with SWAT we—"

"I have Alvera's cell number. While we're waiting for SWAT to show, we'll let him know we're here before he discovers we are and tries to make a run for it. This one I want alive. We'll parade him all over the news, let the world know we're doing our job shutting these guys down."

Hanks leans close and whispers.

"He means show off his shit for the brass in Marseilles."

"Surely, he's got men with him, Jesse. What if they start a fight before SWAT arrives?"

"Then we'll give them one back, Frank. Sergeant Olsen, we're moving up."

"Yes, sir."

Wilson makes the mistake of placing a hand on Randolph's arm.

"Jesse, there's a reason why we use SWAT."

"Take your hand off my arm."

"I'm just saying—"

Randolph jerks his arm away.

"Don't ever do that again, Frank."

"I'm just concerned for everyone's safety."

"Leave that to me."

This is not going well and it's snowing again and the temperature is dropping and I'm thinking the odds are stacked against us. Sergeant Carlton's busy handing out Kevlar vests, M4 rifles, and communications head-

set. *The Major's pacing and constantly looking at his watch and it's making the rest of us pretty damn nervous.*

"Alright, here's what we're going to do. We'll move to the house on foot behind the Humvee and—"

"Jesse, that doesn't give us much protection. My people can't—"

Randolph spins around to Wilson and gets in his face.

"My people, Frank—not yours. And it's Major, not Jesse. Load up, let's go."

What the hell's happening here? Randolph is acting way too edgy and anxious for the one who's supposed to be in charge of what could prove to be a dangerous operation...... We get back in our vehicles and follow the Humvee up Seaside Avenue to Jones Creek Drive, right on Avenue Five to the end of Pillsbury Drive where we park just short of where River Sands Drive begins. Randolph hops out of the Humvee and gathers everyone around him.

"The house is the third in on the left. Victor, Gustav, make your way around the back of the place. Anybody comes out the back door, drop them."

As Victor and Gustav move out, Jade approaches Hank and me and speaks in a hushed tone.

"We've never done this without SWAT."

"Thank God it's off season, not a single soul in sight."

"Doesn't make me feel safer, Hank."

"The alternative is to bend over and kiss our asses goodbye."

If Hank meant that as a joke, it was a bad one. Olsen is driving the Humvee, Carlton is in the passenger seat. Randolph's machismo is on full display... he's going to walk with Wilson, Hank, Jade and me on the right side of the Humvee as we make our way up to the house and hope the hell this Alvera or one of his goons doesn't spot us. With trepidation and weapons at the ready, we move beside the Humvee looking like a band of terrorists. The call comes from Gustav confirming he and Victor are in position in some tall bushes behind the house. Olsen stops the Humvee direct-

ly across the street from Alvera's place. Randolph opens the side door to the Humvee and climbs in.

"I'm going to make phone contact."

Wilson frowns and looks at his watch.

"Where the hell's SWAT?"

Hank and Jade I exchange uneasy glances, waiting and wondering what's going on inside the Humvee. Seven minutes pass before the door opens and Randolph slips out.

"I made contact."

"And?"

"He said I should take a flying fuck."

"You said you wanted him alive. I agree with you, it'll be a PR coup. You should keep negotiating with him."

"I did, Lieutenant, he's not interested."

"He's nuts if he thinks he can fight his way out of this."

Randolph glowers and turns away and paces the length of the Humvee twice, glancing at his watch at least three times. Five minutes pass... he's on the phone again.

"Alvera, damn it, answer your bloody damn phone."

He paces as he waits for Alvera to answer. After a minute, he terminates the call... this is not looking good... Wilson's right, we should wait for SWAT. The look on Randolph face tells me he's not dealing with this well.

"Screw him, if that's the game he wants to play, then game on."

Interesting that he uses 'I' instead of 'we.' He yanks open the Humvee side door.

"Olsen, Carlton, get out here, tear gas the windows on the first and second floors."

"Without SWAT, sir?"

"Did I stutter, Sergeants Olsen?"

"No, sir."

"Then get it done."

"Yes, sir.

Randolph's acting irrational, he's throwing caution to the wind and that'll only get one or more of us killed. Sergeant Carlton retrieves two tear gas guns from the rear of the Humvee and hands one to Olsen. Two minutes later, they send tear gas canisters through all six of the first and second floor windows. We wait. Five-minutes go by, then seven, ten. Randolph pacing, his cell phone in hand, waiting, waiting. He's dialing the phone again.

"Alvera, you son of a bitch, answer your phone."

"SWAT should be here anytime."

But Randolph's not listening to Wilson.

"Olsen, open the front door."

"Yes, sir."

I look to Wilson for a reaction... he washes a hand over his face and mumbles.

"Jesus!"

With the launcher up on his shoulder, Olsen takes aim and fires, the shell traveling faster than my eye can follow. KABOOM! The door and surrounding frame explode, sending hundreds of small pieces of wood flying in all directions. Bright red and orange flames snake up the front of the house to the second floor and into the sky as black smoke.

"Jade, let Gustav and Victor know we're going in."

"I think the blast might have given it away."

"What?"

"Yes, sir, calling them now."

This is a bad repeat of the warehouse bust a few days ago... an ill-thought-out one at that.

"Jade, stay behind the Humvee."

"Okay, Lieutenant. The second I hear from SWAT, I'll let you know."

"Too late for that."

Randolph's prancing around and barking orders at Olsen and Carlton.

"Olsen, you and Carlton, lead the way."

"Sir?"

"Go, damn it, we're right behind you."

The next thing we know, with no idea what resistance we'll encounter, we're all rushing across the street behind Olsen and Carlton like a high school football team unsure of who has the ball. Just as Olsen and Carlton reach the sidewalk, there's a burst of gunfire, but it's not directed at us. Wilson freezes and yells to Randolph.

"Where's that coming from?"

"Keep running, damn it, keep running!"

We make it across the street, scramble through some low hedges, and huddle against the building. There's more gunfire... sounds like it's coming from the second floor now. Olsen sprints up the five steps to the small front porch, hesitates, then peeks through the mangled hole that used to be the door. The gunfire stops. Now Olsen's dashing through with Carlton right behind. Several heart-stopping seconds later, Olsen appears at the door.

"Sir, two down in the living room."

"What?"

"Two down on the first floor, sir."

"Who the hell shot them?"

"Don't know, sir."

"Alright, alright, we're coming in."

Cautiously, we file into the house... there on the living room floor two men lay in pools of blood.

"What the hell? Who shot them?"

Olsen whispers to Randolph.

"Don't know, sir. More shots were fired upstairs."

"What in the hell is going on?"

We're all stunned when a familiar voice comes over our headsets.

"All clear up here. Down the hall, master bedroom, last door on the right, Major."

Jesus, it's Victor.

"Victor, for Christ's sake, what's happening, where are you?"

"Second floor, come on up, Major."

"What?"

"Come up."

Randolph pushes past Olsen and Carlton and bounds up the stairs yelling.

"Come, on!"

On the second floor two dead bodies lay in our path... they're shot up pretty bad... we step over them and file into the bedroom at the end of the hall. To everyone's astonishment, Victor and Gustav are standing over a man down on his knees, his hands cuffed behind him. Gustav's smiling wide like the cat that snagged the mouse. The look on Randolph's face is one of confusion.

"Gustav, what in the hell happened here?"

"When we heard the explosion, we made our way in through the back door, Major. Damn, if we didn't catch them all by surprise. While his men fought the good fight, Mr. Alvera here crawled in that closet over there."

"Both of you could have been killed."

"But we weren't, Major."

"Good work. Just don't be playing cowboys, wait for the damn team."

"Like we waited for SWAT?"

"You want to get in a pissing match with me?"

"We got the job done, didn't we, Major?"

Jade's anxious voice comes over the headsets just in time to head off a verbal donnybrook between Gustav and Randolph.

"Lieutenant, what's going on?"

"We're in, it's over."

"Everyone okay?"

"Yes."

"Alvera?"

"Got him."

"Alive?"

"Yes."

So, this is the infamous Alvera's. He's in his late sixties, dark complexion with deep-set eyes, salt and pepper receding hair, and a white mustache and goatee. With a devilish grin, Randolph drops his M4 to the floor, takes out his Smith and Wesson, and approaches Alvera.

"Damn if you don't look just like your photos."

Alvera studies Randolph for a few seconds before responding in a barely audible voice.

"Este mierda y muere."

"Hmm, anyone speak Spanish?"

Carlton raises a hand.

"He said eat shit and die, sir."

"Hmm, really now?"

Randolph moves close to Alvera, swings his arm, and strikes him on the side of his head with his pistol. Alvera moans and tumbles to the floor... blood's seeping from his left ear. It's Déjà vu all over again, a repeat of the torture scene that played out only days ago.

"Get the pig up."

Hank's closest... he lifts Alvera to his knees. Randolph squats and gets in Alvera's face.

"Matias Diego Alvera, do you know who I am?"

Alvera's mouth twists into a crooked smile.

"Major Jesse 'Fuck-Face' Randolph."

Randolph switches his gun in his left hand, and with his open right hand, slaps Alvera hard across the face. The Guatemalan's head whips right then slowly swivel's back.

"Jesse, easy, we'll want to parade him around on the news."

"Shut the fuck up, Frank."

Making eye contact with Randolph, Alvera spits in his face. Randolph smiles and wipes away the spittle.

"We got us a real fighter here, one who cowers in a closet while his men go down in flames."

Alvera closes his eyes and turns away.

"You believe in God, Mr. Alvera?"

Slowly, Alvera's eyes open.

"I believe in me, Senor Cerdo."

Carlton stifles a laugh.

"Ah, sir, he called you a pig."

Randolph tosses his head back and laughs.

"Okay, here's how this going to work, Amigo. I'm going to provide you with paper and pen and you're going to write down the location of your poison mills, your top lieutenants, and the names of every one of your street peddlers."

"Ur, that's easy. My headquarters is Cinderella's Castle, my associates the Seven Dwarfs."

"Didn't I promised we'd take you in alive if you cooperated?"

"Stop jerking me off, I know how you pinchazos work."

"It doesn't have to be that way. You'll be in prison, sure, but at least you'll be alive. All you have to do is put pen to paper."

Alvera grins, spits on the floor.

"There, you have my answer. It's been one hell of a run while it lasted. One that will go on long after me. You can take that to the bank, Cara de mierda, Randolph."

"Sir, he said—"

"I think I got it, Sergeant."

I can't decide who's nuttier here, Alvera or Randolph. I think they're both in serious need of Jade's psych services. Randolph rises up and begins circling Alvera with his pistol pointed at his head. No one says a word. I look to the others... Carlton and Olsen exchange nervous glances. With a twisted grin, Randolph's eyes come to me. Oh crap, there it is, Billy Boy, that look, that evil smile... today's the day... he's gonna" hand to you the grand prize of prizes, the biggest drug lord on the East Coast of the United

States is yours to whack. Randolph just stands there smiling and staring at me... what's he waiting for? Alvera closes his eyes, lowers his head, and offers up what he thinks are his final words.

"You should all rot in hell."

Randolph mouths twists into a grin.

"Maybe we will."

Randolph's eyelids narrow to slits, his eyes laser-locked on the back of Alvera's head, his face twisted into a fiendish grin. He moves the pistol to within a couple of inches of Alvera's skull. His eyes come up to me... a cold chill runs up my spine... this is it, he's gonna" hand me that damn pistol any second and I'll be forced to make a decision. Wilson senses something's wrong.

"Jesse!"

Randolph ignores him calls to me.

"Officer Russell?"

I wait for the other shoe to drop that will force me to make that decision I've been dreading.

"Yes, Major."

"Today is your lucky goddamn day."

Wilson eyes widen... he sees what the rest of us have missed... he takes a quick step toward Randolph.

"Jesse!"

Randolph ignores him, his eyes never leaving mine for a second... and then he does what none of us saw coming, but Wilson did. He squeezes the trigger. My God! I recoil as Alvera's head explodes spattering blood on my legs and shoes... Alvera body slams forward to the floor. Randolph's gun hand is shaking. I turn to the others... they look as horrified as I do. Wilson turns and looks away. Olsen moves quickly to Randolph's side.

"Sir?"

Randolph doesn't respond... He's staring at Alvera's dead body, he looks dazed and confused like he doesn't realize what he did.

"Sir, let me have your weapon."

Olsen removes the gun from Randolph's still shaking hand.

"Sir, it's time to go."

"What?"

"It's time to go."

Olsen passes the weapon to Carlton, places an arm around Randolph's waist, and leads him out. No one says a word.

. . . .

THE SWAT TEAM AND EMS unit *show up as Olsen is easing an unresponsive Major Randolph into the back seat of the Humvee. A very confused-looking SWAT leader approaches Wilson who's huddling with Heinz and Augier.*

"What happened here, what's wrong with the Major?"

"You guys are a dollar short and a day late."

"What?"

"There's five bodies in there. Get rid of them."

"That's not our job, Lieutenant."

"Today it is."

"What do you want us to do with them?"

"Take them back, turn them over to the morgue, bury them in the backyard if you want, I don't give a shit."

"But—"

"Shut the fuck up and do it."

. . . .

THE HORROR OF WHAT happened *in Old Orchard Beach lingers with us as we ride back in dazed silence. Finally, from the back seat, Jade speaks.*

"I'm thankful I wasn't there to see it."

"God, did you see the lunatic expression on his face when he pulled the trigger."

"He never once took his eyes from me, Hank, not once. What was that all about?"

"Only his shrink knows for sure?"

I'm furious, confused, disgusted, and sick to my stomach.

"When he shot that guy's testicles off, I wanted to beat him with my bare hands. Today... today I wanted to beat him with my bare hands right there in front of everybody. I feel dirty and ashamed for having witnessed it."

"Let it go, Billy. If you dwell on it, it'll drive you nuts."

"Can't let it go, Hank, not now, not tomorrow, not ever."

Chapter 20
All is Not Lost

*H*ank gave Jade a lift home*... I opted to walk as usual... I've been walking aimlessly now for almost an hour trying to pull myself together, trying to clear my head of the moment Randolph pulled that trigger. I can't, it keeps replaying over and over in my head. When I finally return to the house, I'm barely through the front door when Jules pops out of his apartment.*

"I heard you come in."

His eyes go to my bloodstained Kaki's.

"What happened to you?"

"Nose bleed."

"Come on, what happened?"

"Not now, Jules."

He places a hand on my forearm and gently squeezes.

"Okay, okay, but if you need to talk it out, I'm here."

"Thanks."

"Why don't you give the lady a key? I have extras."

"What?"

"That lady cop, she's upstairs."

My eyes widen and shoot to the top of the stairs.

"Boy, she's a looker. I'm telling you, Billy, you hit the jackpot."

"Yeah. Goodnight, Jules."

"Goodnight, Billy. Get out of those clothes."

When I open the door, there's Jade's sitting on the sofa looking as beautiful as when I first set eyes on her. Her right leg is slung over those black slacks she wore when we first met, a gray long-sleeve sweater covers her top, her black leather coat draped by her side.

"I thought Hank took you home?"

"He did... I'm here now."

"If you came to cheer me up, please don't."

"I'm as angry at what happened as you are, Billy."

I remove my jacket and toss it on the chair.

"I was standing just a few feet away."

"You need to get out of those clothes."

"You want coffee?"

"Bourbon. But first, soak those pants or the blood will stain."

"Alright, give me a minute."

I change into my UPS brown outfit and leave the trousers soaking in the bathroom sink.

"Is there a washing machine in the building?"

"In the basement."

"Let them soak overnight, wash them tomorrow."

I grab the Bourbon and a couple of glasses and pour us both a shot

"If you're here in your capacity as a former psychologist to restore my failing state of mind, forget it."

"After what went down today, I needed company, thought you might too."

"I do."

"By the way, I don't have a cat."

"Why did you tell me you did?"

"Because you've been circling me from day one and I wasn't sure what was going on."

"And now?"

"I wasn't offended by your attention. It just took me a while to—"

She leaves the sentence hanging and it's stringing me out like a rubber band.

"Say what you mean and mean what you say."

"I always do."

She takes a deep breath and exhales slowly.

"I told you, my marriage didn't go all that well. So, maybe I'm a bit skittish when it comes to getting involved again, you know."

"Are you planning to go through life always being skittish?"

She laughs in that smoky, silky voice.

"It sounds silly when you say it."

Now comes one of those silent moments that drive me nuts.

I hope you don't mind, I took a tour of your bachelor pad."

"That must have taken all of thirty seconds."

"Well, it is a bit small, and it does need work."

"That's an understatement."

She looks away and goes silent again. Something's on her mind... I wish she'd get to it. Her eyes come back to me.

"You said to say what I mean and mean what I say."

"I find it to be the best policy."

"That bed in there, it looks small. Is there room for two?"

What? That's it, the green light to go past go. Now would be a perfect time to dig deep into the recesses of my memory bank and recall just how this is done. Come on, Billy, it's like riding a bike... so they say. No more chit-chat, no more idle flirting, either this is it, or it's not.

"Am I reading this correctly?"

"I thought I made clear."

"Just checking."

"Stop checking and kiss me before I get cold feet."

I slide across the sofa, take her in my arms and kiss her gently... her arms go around me. The kiss advances from gentle to intense until she breaks it off, rises to her feet, pulls the sweater over her head, and drops it to the sofa. Off my shoes come, then my shirt... I drop it to the floor. We're moving to the bedroom, body to body like a carefully rehearsed ballet. She makes it to the bed first and lays on her back... she's beautiful, everything I imagined and more when I first followed her down that hallway to the break room. Off my pants come then my shorts. She speaks to me in that smoky, silken voice.

"Don't rush it."

Count on it, beautiful, count on it, let's make this last into the afterlife. What happens next must be what's like to travel on the wings of an angel to a glorious heaven, wherever the hell that might be. I slip into the bed next to her. I'm not sure where to put my hands first, I want to touch every part of her... slow down, Billy Boy, slow down. I kiss her without touching... it's a long kiss, one of those wet, open-mouth kisses that go on forever. My whole body's aflame with primal desire. My right hand is on the move... to her shoulder, her waist, up to her firm right breast. Blood rushes to my head and I'm dizzy... dizzy with passion, floating, floating, ascending on a white puffy cloud on my way to that heaven.

• • • •

A HALF-HOUR LATER WE **lay quietly** *wrapped tightly in each other's arms. In the past thirty-minutes, I experienced what it took fifteen long years to reclaim. I feel whole again... good sex will do that. Wrong, this was not good sex, this was skyrocketing sex with fireworks and loud music with strings and horns and crashing cymbals and a chorus of heavenly voices. She was into me one-hundred percent, this was not a mercy mission... I know that, I felt that...... And yet, she knows nothing of my life other than what's in my file. I want her to know, I want to get it out once and for all... to put it behind me forever.*

"Her name was Diedre."

"What?"

"My late wife, her name was Diedre."

"Billy, you don't have to tell me this."

"I want to, I need to. It's the only way I'll be able to box it up and bury it for good."

She places a hand on mine and squeezes gently.

"I met Diedre on a blind date. It was arranged by a friend of mine—he was dating a friend of hers. After a whirlwind nine months, we were married."

I swallowed hard... my eyes welling up.

"She died of strangulation... the coroner said most likely while the creep was—"

"Oh God, Billy, I'm sorry."

"Two fingerprints on the headboard... that's how they identified him. None of what followed would have occurred if one of my fellow officer friends hadn't heard it from a friend of his on Boston's homicide squad. He thought he was doing me a favor by telling me. In fact, he was. The night before they were set to make an arrest, I paid the creep a visit. I had motive, so I know I'd be the prime suspect, and I was. But I was careful, I had worn gloves and got rid of my clothes. But then there were my damn shoes. I had cleaned them and tossed them in a closet. When they searched the house, they found them. There was a single drop of his blood on the heel of the right shoe—one damn drop."

Even though I had poured my heart out to Jules, it still plagued me. I pray Jade understands why I had to say it out loud, to bring the closure I've been so desperately seeking for fifteen long years. Her hand is still wrapped around mine... she squeezes it gently. We lay in each other's arms quietly for a long time.

"Stay the night."

"Maybe next time."

"Will there be a next time?"

"I hope there is, Billy, I do."

A short time later we're standing by the door in an embrace sharing one hell of a great kiss. When we break, I look into her eyes.

"Forgive my insecurity, but what's happening here?"

"Something good, I hope. Let's take it slow, see where it leads us. Okay?"

"Okay, beautiful."

She plants a quick kiss on my lips.

"Sleep well, Billy Russell."

"Tonight, I will, Jade Miro... thanks to you, despite what I won't be able get out of my head. After what Randolph did today, I'm going to have a hard time showing up."

"I understand. It's that way with me too."

I wanted so badly for her to stay, to hold her in my arms through the night and every night from this day on. How do I explain my deep, emotional desire for this woman when we've only known one another for a just short time? I don't, let it remain a mystery... just get on with making it work...... I'm too damn wired to sleep now... maybe if I watch some television for a while. I tune to the government channel to see what the thugs in Marseilles might be up to... the news is already in progress. The announcer is droning on... no, he's bragging... about how many citizens bit the dust and what a wonderful thing that is for all of humanity. Damn, if he doesn't sound like he's hosting a game show.

"At this accelerated rate the mandated goal of eight billion could very well be met sooner than anticipated."

Yeah, man, keep those cremation incinerators working 24/7.

"In other news, a major storm is sweeping across North Africa and—

He stops mid-sentence... his hand goes to his right ear and he listens. Whatever he's hearing in his earpiece changes the expression on his face.

"I'm being informed by control there has been a skirmish at a small anti-government rally in central Paris. We go live now to World News correspondent Alexander Charbonneau."

The shot cuts to a deserted park before switching to the reporter.

"I'm standing in Square Suzanne Buisson at 7 bis rue Girardon in front of the reflection pool beneath the statue of Saint Denis. A short time ago World Council Commissioner Henry Dion stood on this very spot addressing a small gathering."

Whoa, what, Henry Dion?

"Several men in the crowd began to jeer Mr. Dion for his continued attacks against the very government in which he serves. A scuffle broke out between the instigators and Dion supporters. Several people received minor injuries before the police arrived. No arrests were made. Mr. Dion is reported to be unharmed."

Gideon, Gideon, you need to get your guy better security. Screw this crap, they're all out of their frigging minds. I'm going to bed, shut out the world and try to wipe from my memory the cold-blooded, cruel execution I witnessed this day. I head for the bedroom, undress and lay down. Jade's scent lingers... I miss her already. A sudden rush of emotion comes over me. Let it come, Billy, let it come. Burying my face in the pillow, I cry until sleep rescues me.

Chapter 21
The Past Returns

*I **toss and turn**, my brain's juxtaposing a good dream with a bad one... Jade's warm body next to mine... Alvera's head explodes a few feet away spraying blood on me... Jade kissing me goodnight. It goes on for what feels like the entire night... or has it been mere seconds?...... I'm up by seven thirty. While I'm taking my morning wiz, I noticed the bloodstained pants still soaking in the bathroom sink. It's Sunday, a perfect day to wash some clothes...... As soon as I've had my second cup of coffee, shower and dress, rinse the pants, grab some other stuff that needs washing, I hustle down to Jules' door. He greets me with a wide smile.*

"Good morning. I trust you slept well."

"I did."

"And well you should have considering your company."

"Mind your own business, old man. Show me how to use the washer dryer."

"Mind your own business, old man. Show me how to use the washer and dryer."

"I've been wondering how long you were going to get around to washing clothes."

"Recycling is a wonderful thing."

"Not when it's underwear."

"Are you going to chew on my ass or show me how to use the machines?"

"Where's your soap?"

"Soap?"

"You need detergent."

"I don't have any."

"Come on, come on, you can use mine."

The basement is a cave of a place, dark and musty with a half-dozen boxes piled up in one corner.

"They're full of military stuff. Don't know why I keep it."

He gives me a quick tutorial on the workings of the washer... in the clothes go.

"They'll be finished in an hour. Call me and we'll do the dryer."

A half-hour later, we're putting the clean clothes in the dryer. Jules explained in detail how to use both machines, but none of it sticks... it'll take a second lesson for sure... maybe a third...... The sojourn to Jules' basement turns out to be the highlight of my otherwise uneventful, boring Sunday, the rest of which I spend watching badly written, badly directed, and badly performed episodes of bad TV series. I want to call Jade, but I neglected to get her number. It's the weekend... I could call the office and it'll ring on her cell. No, don't bother her. Nothing left to do but take a nap. It's six-fifteen when I finally awake... my mood is in the shitter... for the love of me, I can't get Randolph's cold-blooded, maniacal killing of Alvera out of my head. The man needs serious psychiatric help. Okay, I need human company and Jules is closest. When he answers his door, he's in his robe.

"It's only six-twenty-three, going to bed?"

"What's wrong with being comfortable? What's up?"

"I'm cooking."

"So?"

"I feel like company."

"What's on the menu?"

"Ham steak."

"Where did you get a ham steak?"

"At the grocery store like everyone else. But you can't come in your robe. And, bring that extra key. Fifteen minutes."

I'm in the middle of frying the ham when Jules shows up waving a key chain with two keys dangling from it.

"Here you go, lucky boy."

"Thanks."

"You're here less than a month and you snare a fox. What does the lady see in you?"

"Good looks, charm, charisma, I smell good, and—"

"You're overselling it. That ham smells good. First dinner invite I received from a tenant."

"Sit, it's almost ready."

"You want something, Billy, what is it?"

"Nothing, I just felt like company."

"Something eating at you."

"Stop already or I'll send you home."

"Oh, while I'm thinking about it, you have a new neighbor across the hall. Moved in this afternoon."

"In that filthy rat trap?"

"I had it cleaned, it's fine."

"Does whoever it is have a name?"

"Yeah, yeah, it's ah—"

He gets this blank look on his face.

"Shit, I can't remember."

"First signs of dementia, Jules."

"It'll come to me."

"Want a shot of Bourbon? It might help your failing memory."

"Bourbon is known to do that."

"Food's ready. Ham steak, a can of cut carrots, brown bread, and all the water you can drink."

"All the water what?

"Never mind, let's eat."

Halfway through the meal, Jules sits up straight like someone stuck a pin in his ass.

"Henley."

"What about it?"

"The new guy across the hall, his name is Henley."

"Henley?"

"His first name is—wait, it's coming to me. Chris, Christopher Henley."

Jesus, what? I try to hold back my excitement... can it really be Chris?

"Let's hope this one keeps the place clean. I'm gonna" begin holding weekly inspections with you guys."

"Where's he from?"

"I never know, never ask, it's none of my business. Seems like a nice enough guy, though."

Now I can't wait for Jules to leave so I can march across the hall and find out for sure. A half-hour later, Jules yawns and decides to leave.

"Time for bed. Thanks for the meal and the Bourbon."

"You're going to leave me with dirty dishes again?"

"Of course. My very best to the Asian lady."

"Jade."

"Yes, Jade. You're one lucky son-of-a-bitch."

"Get moving before I kick your old ass out."

"Feel free to feed me anytime, young man."

I listen at the door as Jules descends the stairs. As soon as I hear his door close, I'm in the hall. The TV in the next apartment is on... I knock, but there's no answer... I knock again. The TV goes off and a voice bellows.

"Who the hell is banging on my door?"

Can it really be? That's Chris's voice.

"Your neighbor, asshole."

"Who you calling an asshole?"

The door swings open, and low and behold, it's Chris Henley in the flesh. The look on his face when he sees me is pure gold.

"Hot damn, if it isn't Billy Russell! What the hell are you doing here?"

"I could ask you the same."

We laugh and fly into each other's arms like long lost brothers.

"Come on, come on, I live four steps away."

"What? Where?"

"Across the hall through that open door. Come."

*Grabbing his arm, I all but drag him across the hall into my place...
he sniffs the air.*

"Whoa, this smells better than mine."

I can't help but laugh.

"What's funny?"

"Your former occupant of your place, but that's a story for another time. Jeez Chris, what happened, I thought we'd meet up on the bus... you never showed? What're you doing in this building?"

"Whoa, slow down, where to begin? I mean, talk about your royal screw-ups. I'm not in processing five minutes before the guy discovers a paperwork fuck-up. My assignment check-in date was wrong. It wasn't the following day, it's tomorrow."

"Tomorrow?"

"I was booked on Europa-1, not Europa-2."

"But the Commandant's orders said Otherwise."

"The screwup was with the written orders he received."

"Jeez, Chris, now that I think of it, every bunk on Europa-2 was taken."

"That should have been your first clue. Anyway, what does the brain trust do to cover up? They bunked me on Base-Arizona until it was time for Europa-1 to leave. I arrived here this afternoon."

"What did you do all that time on the base?"

He laughs and slaps his knee.

"I was free to roam at will. Hooked up with a gorgeous, sex-starved, unattached staff sergeant who worked in base administration. Best couple of weeks I've spent since Gloria Delgado."

"Who?"

"Gloria Delgado, we swapped virginities in our senior year."

"Lucky you, lucky Gloria. How about a drink?"

"Love one."

"Sit, be comfortable."

He's examining sofa and comments.

"How come this one looks cleaner than mine?"

I retrieve the Bourbon from its hiding place, grab a couple of glasses, and join Chris on the sofa. His eyes go to the bottle... a quizzical look comes over his face.

"Where did you get that Bourbon?"

"A gift from the office, why?"

"Because I got one too, same brand."

"From who?"

"Jules said some lady from the office came by and left it along with the food in the fridge."

"Wait a minute. Where are you assigned?"

"Military Drug Enforcement, Unit 513."

"Holy shit!"

I'm up on my feet crossing the few steps to the kitchen and reaching into the cabinet where I keep my gun and badge. I retrieve the badge, march back, and hold it in front of his face... his eyes bloom like golf balls when he sees it.

"You're assigned 513?"

"Yep."

"Holy crap!"

"That's putting it mildly. I mean, what are the chances? Okay, tell me what it was that got you sent to Europa?"

"Why?"

"Just tell me."

"Why do you need to know?"

"Trust me, it'll all become clear."

"Hey, what's with the interrogation, Billy?"

"Answer the damn question."

He hesitates... he looks pissed that I'm pressing him.

"I was a career Marine."

"Yeah... and?"

"I told you, man, I don't like talking about it?"

"It'll all become clear, trust me."

"Okay already, I was with a sniper unit."

"This is like pulling teeth. Just tell me, already."

"I took out a couple of Afghanis dudes who weren't on the kill list."

"By accident?"

"I never shot anyone by accident, Billy."

"Then what?"

"Both these guys were paid informants for our side. I'd seen them around Command a couple of times, so I knew who they were. One day I'm on a hill overlooking the village of Farah in Eastern Afghanistan with my spotter, Brad Stone. A man, women, and two young girls are being dragged out of their house. I recognize who's doing it, it's the two informants. A shouting match takes place between them and the father. They smack him around a little, then cold-bloodily execute the whole family right there in the street. Screw it, I said, these two animals are toast. Brad warns me not to do it. I'm in easy range, I don't need him to line me up. I took two shots, one for each prick, sending them to their heavenly reward. Brad, that son of a bitch, fearing for his own ass, reports me to Command. My reward for offing them without permission was a court martial and a trip to Europa. Your turn."

I tell him why I did what I did to that little creep in the closet... how I made him suffer first.

"I will never regret what I did, Chris, not for a second."

"Me neither. Now, here we are, free again and—"

"Maybe not so free."

"Whatta" mean?"

In as much detail as I can, I fill him in on the Pakistan-India episode, the worldwide fear that followed, the creation of a world government... everything that I know about the crazy world we've returned to...... What I don't mention is my secret meeting with Gideon, Norman, and Jason.

"Jesus, Billy, this is getting weird."

"Do you know what we do at 513?"

"Is this a trick question?"

"Before I tell you the kicker, you're going to need this."

I pour him another shot and proceed to explain in vivid detail the unit's government sanctioned mission and the two raids I've been on that ended in cold-blooded executions.

"I haven't killed anyone—not yet—but my time's coming as will yours."

"No way, I don't want any part of this."

"You don't have a choice, pal. When you report in tomorrow, you'll be briefed by Lieutenant Frank Wilson, he's our boss. Then you'll meet Major Jesse Randolph, he's everybody's boss and personally chose you and me for this job. Neither of them is going to tell you straight-out what I just told you. Play along, the truth will raise its ugly head soon enough. Above all, we can't let Wilson or Randolph know of our relationship."

"If this Randolph picked us, he knows."

"Maybe, maybe not. If he brings it up, say we bunked in separate bays and never crossed paths."

"I don't know, Billy, it would be easy enough to check."

"Why would he? It's the chance we take."

"Jesus, out of the frying pan and into the fire."

"Tell me about, pal."

"Hey, were you still there when they had that shooting in the processing area?"

"Ah, yeah. I was there."

"I was still being processed, I didn't see what happened."

"Just as well, my friend. I was there."

I relate how I became involved in the shooting incident.

"Lucky you didn't get shot."

"It was close, it was damn close."

At nine-forty-five, a little tipsy from the booze, Chris gives me a hug, and returns to his apartment... such as it is. Tomorrow should prove to be an interesting day.

Chapter 22
What's Normal, What's Not

Monday morning, *I look out my only front window and the sun is shining... that's a plus. I finish my second cup of coffee... I'm ready to meet Hank who's picking me up. On my way out, I knock on Chris's door.*

"Morning, Billy."

"Sleep Okay?

"Considering where I previously slept, this was heaven."

"Lieutenant Wilson has a hissy-fit when anyone's late, so don't be. Okay with the directions?"

"Jules filled me in, sounds like a short walk. Can't say I'm looking forward to this."

"I remind you, we haven't been given a choice. Now, if anyone bothers you on the street, tell them you're a cop—scatters them like flies. There's a clothing store on Broadway. I'll take you by there tonight if you want."

"Good, I need to ditch this brown crap."

"Remember, we've never met."

"Say, what did you say your name was again?"

Minutes later, I'm on the sidewalk waiting for Hank to arrive. A couple of homeless souls look like they're gonna" approach, but see my badge and scurry away in the opposite direction. Another poor soul, talking to himself like he's high on something or other stumbles toward me, sees the badge and backs off. I experience this daily and it's heartbreaking... it has to change... it must change. I'm a disappointed that Harold and Catherine are nowhere in sight... I hope they're okay...... At seven-forty-five, Hank arrives.

"Morning, Hank."

"Get any sleep last night?"

"Like an unborn in the womb."

"You're okay then?"

I just nod... I don't have a burning desire to relive what took place in Old Orchard Beach. But, as usual, I hear my mouth doing just the opposite.

"So much for plausible deniability. If what Randolph did was ever become public, he's royally screwed."

"It won't, Gustav or Victor will see to that. If any of us was to blab..."

He places a finger close to my temple.

"... Pop, pop... your history."

"Yeah, yeah, I got it."

"Wilson called when I was leaving my apartment. He wants us to cruise around for a while."

"Why, so we can wave at all the happy street people? Drive."

We're traveling West on Broadway when something catches Hank's attention.

"Hello."

"What?"

"One of my snitches. The little shit's been avoiding me."

He does a quick U-turn and pulls to the curb... the snitch sees him and begins to quick-pace away.

"Hey, asshole, stay right there!"

Hank's out of the car, catches up with the man and slaps him up side of his head. I can't hear what he's saying, nor do I really care...... We're in the office by ten-thirty. Jade's alone, no sign of Gustav, Victor, or Wilson. She greets me with a big, warm smile.

"Good morning, agent Russell, how's the new day treating you?"

"Better, thanks."

"Better than what?"

"Better than yesterday and the day before."

"I'm so very pleased to hear that."

"Where's Frick and Frack this morning?"

"Off on an assignment for Randolph."

"Wilson?"

"At a meeting somewhere."

"I could use a cup of coffee. How about you?"

"Yeah, sure. Hank, cover the phones."

"Consider them covered."

Hank gives me the evil eye, raises his hand and wags a finger. I stick my tongue out. In the break room, we sit quietly stealing nervous glances like two teenage high-schoolers with the hots for one another.

"One of us has to say something."

"Okay, something."

"Ah, the lady has a sense of humor."

"We have to be careful in the office, Wilson won't stand for an office romance."

"So that's what this is?"

"What?"

"An office romance?"

I can always tell by someone's eyes when their wheels are turning, and Jade's are.

"You're thinking."

"Trying to figure out how this is going to work. In case you haven't noticed, no one gets a free pass out of here."

"We can't let that stop us."

"You don't get a vote, Billy, neither do I."

Reaching for her hand, I wrap it in mine. She smiles that warm smile of hers that melts my heart every time.

"Come by tonight?"

"Yes. I'll bring food."

I dig in my pocket and pull out the keys.

"These are for you."

She gives me the biggest, warmest smile yet.

"That makes it official."

She slips the keys in a pocket of her black jeans. I take her hand and squeeze it.

"You're a romantic at heart, Billy Russell."

"Go on, get back to work, lady."

At nine-forty-five, Wilson shows up. Chris arrives at nine-fifty. Neither Hank nor I pay him any attention. After a brief conversation with Jade, she sends him to Wilson. A half-hour later he and Wilson come out and he introduces Chris to Hank and me.

"You'll meet Gustav Heinz and Victor Augier when they return. Go sit with Jade, she'll get you up to speed."

When Jades finishes with Chris, she sends him off to meet Randolph. A half-hour later, he's back and takes up residence on my old desk between the interrogation room and the men's room. Come lunch time, I offer to take Chris to the clothing store.

"How did it go with Wilson and Randolph?"

"Like you said, neither came right out and explained what we do when we catch the bad guys. Randolph welcomed me to the hunting party. I thought that was kind of weird."

"He's missing a few screws, he's dangerous, don't cross him."

"I don't intend to."

On the chance he might see Jade's comings and goings at the apartment, I level with him about our evolving relationship.

"Lucky you. She's one hell of a catch."

While he's scrounging around for some new clothes at the store, I buy another jacket... this one's not UPS brown, it's black.

• • • •

AT SEVEN-THIRTY THAT evening, Jade arrives with a pizza and a six-pack of beer.

"Wow, I haven't had a pizza in—actually, I had one with Jules."

"There's other things you need to catch up on."

"Do I hear a complaint?"

"On the contrary, you did quite well."

Did I just blush? Yes... and yes, again.

"Let's eat and move on to more primal nourishment."

And that's exactly what we do after devouring the pizza and beer. The dessert course that follows lasts far longer than the pizza... for which I'm grateful...... It's nine-thirty before we roll out of bed. I ask her to stay the night, but for the second time I'm unsuccessful.

"Soon, Billy, soon, be patient. It's complicated."

And with that, the lady I now hold close to my heart, is gone...... Turning on the TV, I arbitrarily punch in channel twenty-three... it's a nature program about a pride of lions on the Serengeti. I'm not particularly interested, but leave it on while I gather up the empty pizza box and the beer cans. I hear four loud beeps... they came from the TV... I swing back just as the Lions are replaced with a one-word graphic—BULLETIN.

"We interrupt this program to bring you this special report. World Council member Henry Dion has died of gunshot wounds in New York's Central Park."

"What?"

The screen is filled with a headshot photo of Dion.

"Commissioner Dion was struck twice in the chest at a gathering at Central Park's Bethesda Fountain. Paramedics pronounced him dead at the scene. New York police officials are investigating a rogue white supremacist group as the possible perpetrators. We have obtained cell phone footage of the shooting. Viewers should be warned the video you are about to see is graphic."

The scene changes to video footage of Dion addressing the gathering. He's holding a bullhorn to his mouth, he speaking, but there's no audio. Thirty-second into the video, the bullhorn slips from his hand and he clutches his chest and staggers back, then recoils a second time, wobbles back two more steps and collapses to the platform he was standing on. The images blur as whoever's taking the video swings the phone wildly swishing one way, then the other until it comes to a stop on Dion's still body.

Several people rush to his aid... the pictures blur again as the cell phone swings around to the panicking crowd... people scatter and run for safety. Wait—there! What was that? If I had blinked, I would have missed it.

"Jesus Christ!"

The pizza box and the beer cans slip from my hands to the floor. The reporter's speaking again.

"The World Government headquarters in Marseilles has condemned the shooting vowing to use all available resources to bring Commissioner Dion's killers to justice. We will bring you more information as it becomes available."

The lion documentary returns. I'm sure of what I saw in that crowd, damn it, I'm sure... I don't know what to do next. Gideon's phone number, what did I do with it? Think, damn it, think. The desk, I tossed it in the drawer with no intention of ever using it... I find it and stare at the number trying to decide what if anything I'm going to do.

"Screw it, do it now."

I dial Gideon's number, but almost immediately, I get cold feet... but do I really want to get involved in this? No, no! I Disconnect before the first ring. I'm not getting involved, no way, I have enough troubles... let the madness not be mine... let the human race destroy itself if that's its destiny. God knows we've been working on getting it right for centuries only to have failed time and time again. Go to bed, Billy, pull the covers over your head and shut it all out, this is not your problem... don't play hero...... Minutes later I'm under the covers... damn it, sleep won't come... I can't get the image of Dion lying dead out of my head. Okay, stop fighting it, stop finding excuses... you know what you should do, what you have to do, so get your ass up and do it. I'm out of bed trotting into the living room and dialing the number again, hoping against hope I'm not making a mistake. Four rings, five rings... someone answers.

"Leave a message."

"Jesus, an answer machine. Okay, this is 556. Call me as soon as you can."

I pace, hoping Gideon will call right back before I change my mind, but he doesn't. An hour passes and then another. Now I'm questioning my decision again. I'm under covers just about to enter the dream stage when the phone rings... it jolts me and I bolt to a sitting position... I'm out of bed following the sound of the ring... it's coming from the living room, but I can't find the damn phone. There is it, there it is, peeking from between two sofa cushions. I snatch it up.

"Hello!"

"You called?"

"Gideon?"

"No names."

"I saw the news... terribly tragedy."

I'm expecting Gideon to express great sorrow over Dion's death, but there's no response.

"Are you there?"

"Yes."

"I saw something."

Silence again.

"Damn it, are you there?"

"Yes."

"We need to meet. I saw something."

Silence again... I can hear him breathing.

"Norman will pick you up in thirty minutes. Be out front."

"Make it the newsstand on the corner."

The line goes dead... as dead I could be if I'm wrong about this. I'm dressed and ready to go in minutes... how to sneak out without disturbing Jules? The last thing I need is to explain where I'm going at this hour. He's sleeping like the rest of the world, so stop fretting...... At one-thirty, I quietly make my way down the steps to the front door, turn the key and slip out, quietly locking the door behind me. I look up the street to the newsstand... Norman's Lexus is parked there... I don't walk, I trot my way to him... he's alone.

"Good morning, Mr. Russell."

"Nothing good about it?"

"Villains have silenced Mr. Dion. May their black souls rot in hell. Come, sit up front with me."

When I get in, he hands me the hood.

"Jesus, Norman, not again."

"I'm afraid so, sir."

I pull the hood over my head and he drives off. For the next twenty-minutes not a word passes between us. Either he runs every red light, or he's hit them green because we don't stop until we reach our destination. Once inside, Norman sits me down in my favorite chair and removes the hood... Gideon is there along with Jason.

"Coffee, Mr. Russell?"

"Lots."

"Jason, would you mind? How do you take it?"

"Black, and call me Billy."

Gideon looks washed out like he hasn't slept. He's dressed casually in gray slacks, a dark blue blazer, and a light blue shirt open at the collar. He sinks into a chair across from me.

"I'm sorry about Commissioner Dion."

"Truly, truly tragic. Henry was our knight in shining armor."

There is anguish in his voice... he leaves the sentence hanging.

"He leaves behind his wife, a grown son, daughter, and two grand-children."

"Why was he holding another rally? Wasn't the Paris attack warning enough?"

"Henry always said that to only look ahead without looking sideways and over your shoulder was to miss important signals. He quoted Winston Churchill—you do remember England's Prime Minister Churchill?"

"I paid attention in history class."

"Churchill said, 'The farther backward you can look, the farther forward you are likely to see.' That was true then, it remains so now. To your question. Unable to get a direct flight to Boston, Henry flew from Marseilles to New York planning to catch a connection to Logan Airport. At the last moment, he made a fateful decision to layover in New York for one night, insisting we arrange a rally of supporters in Central Park. We had to scramble to make that happen."

Jason's back with my black coffee.

"Thanks, Jason. Gideon, to the point, I think I know who's behind Henry's murder."

"Gustav Heinz and Victor Augier."

"Whoa, how could you possibly know that?"

"Have you not questioned why it takes four men to assassinate one?"

"You've lost me."

"Drug Enforcement, Unit 13, acts as Heinz and Augier's cover. In reality, they are the regime's assassins, taking their orders directly from Randolph... orders he receives from Marseille. Their real job it is to remove anyone who might be foolish enough to challenge the government.

"Now it's all coming together. Hank Drummond suspected as much. I'm certain it was them on the video."

"Ah yes, the video footage. Cellphones are banned from public gatherings. Those foolish enough to be caught using one pay a steep price. That footage was taken by a government agent following the agents who started the fracas. They wanted those images out there never believing for a moment someone would identify Heinz and Augier fleeing with the crowd."

"It was the briefest of glimpses. If I had blinked, I would have missed them. What happens now?"

"Nothing changes, we proceed as if Henry was still with us."

"Whatever he had, it better be bullet proof."

"I assure you, it is, Mr. Russell."

"Will you please call me Billy."

"Very well, Billy... have you made your decision?"

My life's in dire need of a refresher course, let's hope this is it.

"I wouldn't be here if I wasn't."

"You will not regret your decision. If all goes as planned, you will soon be free to seek employment in a less demanding enterprise."

He takes out a cigar, lights it and paces a few steps before speaking.

"Many years ago, in the early 90's, the United States Senate Chaplain spoke these insightful words: 'We now demand freedom without restraint, rights without responsibility, choice without consequences, leisure without pain. In our narcissistic, hedonistic, masochistic, valueless preoccupation, we've allowed ourselves to become dominated by lust, avarice, greed, and violence.'

Gideon pauses and stares blankly across the room for a few seconds before proceeding. I think he does just to hold my attention.

"Unfortunately, Billy, society failed to heed the chaplain's words."

He strolls to the chair and sits.

"By their greed—dare I say stupidity—the Marseilles mob has done the world a great favor, as they will soon discover. Never in the history of human civilization have the masses been so united against evil."

"And Dion's message will call them to action?"

"When they hear what Henry reveals, they will act as one and rise up for the good of all."

"Dead men don't speak."

"After the Paris incident, Henry knew his life was in danger, so he taped his message before departing Paris. We will see to it that it is broadcast as planned."

"How you gonna" pull that off?"

"You will know soon enough."

"You still don't trust me."

"It is not a matter of trust, Billy."

"Then what?"

"Go about your business, discuss with no one what I have shared with you. I will be in touch."

"Alright. If it all happens the way you say it will, I have nothing to lose and everything to gain. I might want to bring someone with me."

"Might that be Christopher Henley?"

"How do you people know this stuff?"

"Approach Mr. Henley with caution. He could choose to turn against you and, in turn, us."

"He won't."

"Then I will trust in your judgement. Goodnight, Billy."

"Wait a minute. There's one itch you need to scratch. If this Volte-face organization is as big as you say it is—"

"It is."

"How has it been kept under wraps? It only takes one tongue to slip."

"Volte-face is the people's opportunity to take back what was stolen from them. They will not allow it to slip away because of a slip of a tongue."

"Just one more issue. You know all about me, yet I know nothing about you."

He hesitates... he looks like he's not going to answer me. I'll toss him a reminder.

"Trust, remember. It starts here."

"You're right. We must share complete trust. I'll make this brief. After graduating Oxford University, I become a solicitor in various government positions eventually becoming chief legal advisor to the British Ambassador to the United Nations. While Henry was a U.S. Senator we met on a number of social occasions. When the new government was formed and Henry became a member of the World Council, he engaged me as his chief of staff. That's the long and short of it."

"Family?"

"Widower I'm afraid—two grown daughters, three grandchildren back in England."

"Your name, I need to know your name."

"Why?"

"Trust."

"Very well... Oliver Neville. It's getting late, I've kept you far too long. Goodnight, Billy."

And off he goes. This guy sure knows how to make quick exits.

"I'll take you home now, Mr. Russell."

Norman hands me the hood.

"Not again."

"Perhaps for the last time, sir."

During the drive back, I fail miserably to engage Norman in conversation... all I get is an occasional yes or no. At the newsstand, he bids me goodbye and drives off. It's now six-fifty-five in the morning. If I return to the apartment, Jules might be up and grill me why I've been roaming the streets at this hour. The newsstand is open... I grab a newspaper and a cup of black coffee from Sully and slowly make my way to the office. I'm there by seven-twenty-five and surprised to find Jade already there.

"Sleep here last night?"

"Couldn't sleep."

"Me neither."

I take a seat next to her desk and stare.

"Did I forget to put my makeup on?"

"I'm dazzled by your beauty."

"Wow, it's way too early for compliments. You, on the other hand, look a bit distressed. What is it?"

"You saw the news?"

"If you mean Commissioner Dion, yes. Tragic. He's been a thorn in the government's side to the extent he was labeled a traitor by some Council members. I doubt any of them are upset by his death."

I want to share with her what I know, to take her into my confidence, but I'm not going to involve her or place her in jeopardy if this all goes badly.

"The world is spinning at a faster rate than I can catch up."

"You've only been back for a short time, Billy, give it a chance."

"Give what a chance? If we haven't got our act together by now, what makes you think we ever will?"

"Because I have faith that what we're experiencing is not our permanent reality. It will change."

"Let's hope so."

She has this wonderful habit of taking my hand and cradling it in hers like it's my security blanket... she does it now.

"If it's of any comfort, I'm here for you today, tomorrow... for as long as you want me to be a part of your future."

That nearly brings me to tears. She squeezes my hand tightly.

"You're a good man, William Evan Russell."

Leaning to her, I kiss her gently.

"Look, ah, tell Wilson I ate something, I got a touch of food poisoning and I'll be spending the day in the John. I need time to think, to sort things out. The new guy can ride with Hank today."

"The good guys are going to win, you'll see."

"You have a crystal ball?"

"Trust in what I say, you'll see. I'm free tomorrow night. How about I come by around seven? I'll bring Chinese this time."

"Haven't had any in—"

"Fifteen years, got it."

• • • •

THE SUN IS UP AND IT'S warmed a bit. *I walk along Broadway at a snail's pace in no hurry to return to the hovel I call home. At least Henley is there now, I have someone to talk to who shared the cold cell-like sleeping quarters, dust swirling, lung-destroying mine shafts, bad food, and all the* *rest of the crap that went with life on Europa...... When I reach the apartment, decide not to go in and keep walking. A block down I spot Harold and Catherine. We exchange glances, I want to stop and ask how and why they ended up here on the streets. I move toward them, but there are other street dwellers around, so they slink away... they don't want to be seen talking with a cop....... Later, I hit the sack for a nap following a quick lunch of Chef Boyardee's SpaghettiOs © with little meatballs that was part of my welcome package. I remember it fondly from my childhood and was happy to see they still made it after all these years. As a kid, I ate it cold right out of the can, which drove my mother nuts. When I awake from my nap, it's five-forty-five and I feel like shit... so much for a nap. In the kitchen, I rinse out the empty SpaghettiOs can as I was taught to do as a kid, toss it in the trash that's in need of emptying in the trash bin out back, wash the fork and put it in the drawer. I hear a door close in the hall, Chris must be home. Do I dare do this, do I risk his telling me to go to hell, to leave him out of whatever I've got myself involved in? Maybe he'll fail to understand what's at stake... maybe he's happy to be free of what he left behind on Europa and willing to do what he's told to do at unit 513... I mean, it's not like he hasn't killed men before. Sooner than later he'll have to reach the same conclusion I have... what we're asked to do is inhumane, immoral, and every other word in the English lexicon that describe an assassin. Screw it, I'm gonna" do it, I have to trust that he trusts me. Crossing the hall, I knock on his door. He answers in his underwear.*

"Hey Billy, Jade said you weren't feeling well."

"Can you come over?"

"Not if you have a bug pal."

"I need to chat. Put your pants on first."

He laughs, I don't.

"I'll leave my door ajar."

Ten minutes go by before he shows up wearing a blue T-shirt and a pair of jeans, he bought at the clothing store.

"What's up?"

"Want a beer?"

"Where'd you get beer?"

"Want one or not?"

"Yeah, love one."

Grabbing two cold beers left from Jade's visit, I join him on the sofa.

"Why the long face?"

"I always feel like crap when I get up from a nap."

"A nap is the thing to do when you're sick."

"I'm not sick."

"But Jade said you were."

"I lied."

"Why?"

Before I go further, I have to be certain where his head is at. If he chooses to stay clear of this, he could go to Wilson and Randolph and expose the whole thing. I don't believe that, but it's possible... screw it, I have to chance it.

"During the year we spent coming home, we became good friends, didn't we?"

"Yeah, why?"

"I mean, good friends, friends who trust one another."

"Yes, Billy. Why all the questions?"

Here goes nothing... hope the hell I'm not shooting myself in the foot.

"You're aware a man by the name of Henry Dion was shot and killed in Central Park?"

"Yeah, it was on the news... tragic, just tragic."

"Maybe I know who shot him?"

Chris' face screws up like maybe I've lost it.

"How could you know that?"

"First, you need to know there's a movement to overthrow the government, and Dion was behind it."

"Same question, how could you know that?"

"The movement has a name—Volte-face."

"Sounds like a French movie."

"It is French... it means change."

"You were on Europa way too long, pal, your brain's fried."

"This is real, Chris. It's going to happen."

"When?"

"I don't know, soon maybe."

"And you're involved?"

"Yeah."

"Jesus, Billy!"

"If it works, you and me could be free of this mess we're in."

"Or we could find ourselves dead. How the hell is this Volte-face thing going to overthrow a government that controls the military? Huh? Tell me that."

"It's not, the people will."

"Oh yeah, right, the very people who put these guys in power in the first place. Don't make me laugh, ain't gonna" happen."

"Don't be so sure."

Okay, I'll play. Let's get to the part where you think you know who shot Dion."

"Gustav Heinz and Victor Augier."

That stops Chris cold... his face goes slack.

"Did you hear what I said?"

"You're telling me that two guys we work with assassinated a member of the World Council?"

"Yes, and other people too."

Chris is on his feet headed for the door.

"Where are you going?"

"Away from this wacky conspiracy theory."

"Chris, listen to me, I've had a couple of meetings with Gideon and—"

"Who?

"His real name is Oliver Neville. He runs the Volte-face organization. Henry Dion was to deliver a message that was so explosive, it would bring down the Laurent regime."

"Henry Dion is dead."

"Right. But he had the presence of mind to record the message before he left Paris. Oliver Neville said it would be the Black Swan Event that would crumble the regime."

"A Black Swan Event... mumbo—jumbo. What's on the tape?"

"I don't know."

"And you believe him? Jesus, Billy, what's wrong with you?"

"Okay, answer me this. Why did you execute those two Afghani slugs?"

"For the same reason you executed your wife's killer."

"Because we both served up justice when we believed the system might not."

Now he's at the door, his hand on the knob turning it, he stops, turns back, but doesn't speak.

"You and me Chris, we're bought and paid for assassins—at least we will be when we actually do it—and I for one want the hell out before that day comes. This is our chance, maybe our only chance, to break free of the stranglehold they have on us."

"And what happens if this uprising fails? We'll be tried, convicted, and sent back to prison or worse a firing squad."

My phone rings once, twice, three times.

"Are you gonna' answer that?"

"Are you gonna' answer me?"

He doesn't. I sweep up the phone and listen.

"Yes... yes. Midnight at the newsstand. I'll be there along with the other gentleman we spoke of... yes, I'm sure. Okay, see you then."

I hang up and toss the phone on the sofa.

"That was the call, it's going down day after tomorrow."

Chris is looking pretty angry with me.

"You were that sure of me?"

"If you're looking for an apology, forget it. You're either in or out."

"Goddamn you, Billy Russell."

"Yes, goddamn me, Chris Henley."

"Okay, okay."

"Okay, what?"

"I'm gonna" trust you haven't lost your marbles and you know what you're getting us involved with."

"I'm proud of you, brother Henley."

"But know this... if I get killed, I'll never speak to you again. "

"Deal."

"So, what did the Sheppard say when the storm was rolling in?"

"Get out of here, get some sleep."

Chapter 23
There but for the grace of God

*T*uesday *morning, Chris and I walk to the office after a quick stop by Sully's for coffee. I introduce Sully to Chris, make up a story about Chris being transferred to Precinct 513 from his former post in Dallas and taking up residence in my building. As we turn the corner of Broadway, Chris laughs.*

"You were born a professional bullshitter."

Gustav and Victor are still not back. Wilson wants Chris to get a taste of the streets, so he sends him out with Hank and me to cruise around. It doesn't take Chris long before he realizes how bad the situation is.

"Hank, how do these people survive out here?"

"Huh, many of them don't. Most of them are hooked on cheap drugs and turn to petty crime or worse to get them. If you lived out here, you'd do the same."

At 11:45 we go to Maggie's for lunch. The insult routine between her and Hank amuses Chris.

"She seems to enjoy the jabbing."

"She does, she dishes it out pretty good, too."

I can see it on Chris' face, he's totally bummed out by what he witnessed out on the street.

"How do they expect to get the drug epidemic under control unless they solve the homeless problem first. Those people need jobs, homes, and medical care."

Hank shrugs, leans closer like he doesn't want anyone to hear him.

"We can double, triple our staff, run twenty-four-hour shifts, and it won't dent either the manufacturing or the distribution. There's no solution as long as this government is driving this train wreck with their failed policies. They complain the drug problem hamstrings their ability to govern, when in fact they're the goddamn problem. It'll take an enormous uprising to bring those bastards to their knees."

Chris shoots me a knowing look...... It's four-forty-five by the time we return to the office. Jade is there alone. I smile my usual smile.

"Alone again?"

"Wilson left for the day. Gustav and Victor are back... down the hall meeting with Randolph. Why don't you guys split for the day, there's nothing going on."

Hank's on his feet heading for the door.

"You don't have to ask me twice. Billy, Chris, you guys want a lift?"

"I'll walk."

"Yeah, me too, I'll walk back with Billy."

As we reach the door, Jade stops me.

"Hey, almost forgot, the Lieutenant left something for you on your desk."

"I'll meet you outside, Chris... five minutes."

On my desk is an envelope with my name scribbled on it. Inside, I find a short-handwritten note from Wilson... Randolph wants to meet with me first thing in the morning.

"Jade, do you know what this is about?"

"What?"

"A meeting between Randolph and me in the morning."

"Hmm, that can't be good."

"Well, hell, I'm not going to fret over it."

I crumple the note and toss it in the basket when I spot a small slip of paper on the floor next to Gustav's desk. I scoop it up... I'm about to toss it in the basket when I glance at it. What I see causes me to do double-take... my eyes go to Jade, she's typing. I stuff the slip of paper in my pants pocket... got to get out of here quick. Don't alarm Jade, act casual, make a joke.

"Hey, need a bucket of water?"

"What?"

"You're going to burn up that keyboard."

I don't think she caught it. She stops typing and swivels toward me.

"Leaving?"

"Yeah."

"Hey, Billy, what's with the long face?"

"Just tired, I guess."

"I'll see you later for Chinese."

"I'm really whack out, how about a rain check?"

"Oh, okay, not a problem, we'll do it tomorrow night."

"Great."

"Go home, get some rest. See you in the morning."

I'm out the door, down the stairs... Chris is waiting on the sidewalk.

"Come on, we need to get to the house."

"What's the hurry?"

"Someone's going to die."

"Who? What the hell are you talking about?"

"Come on, I'll explain when we get back.

• • • •

AS SOON AS WE'RE BACK at my apartment, I dial Gideon's number.

"Who are you calling?"

"Shh, Chris, wait!"

Four rings later someone answers... It's Norman's.

"Norman, it's Billy."

"Yes, Billy."

"Where's the man?"

"He's not available at the moment."

"Where is he?"

"Home resting, I'm taking his calls."

"Call him now, tell him to turn off all lights and lock his doors."

There's no response.

"Norman?"

"Why?"

"He's in danger."

"What sort of danger, Billy?"

"Norman, stop talking, get in your car, and pick me up at the newsstand as quickly as you can."

I wait, but the damn fool doesn't answer.

"Norman, did you hear what I said?"

"What sort of danger is he in?"

"Damn it, you can keep asking questions, or we can get to his house ASAP, what's it going to be?"

Again, there's silence.

"Norman, we need to act now!"

"Um, okay, but it'll take me twenty minutes to get to you."

"Call the man first."

"Yes, yes, okay, I will."

I hang up and bark to Chris.

"Chris, get your gun."

"Not until you tell me why?"

I dig in my pocket, find the slip of paper, and hand it to him.

"That was on the floor next to Gustav's desk."

Chris's forehead crinkles.

"Neville."

"Oliver Neville, code name Gideon. What do you see below his name?"

"Two letters—PM."

"Go get your damn gun, I'll explain on the way."

Exactly twenty minutes later, we're standing in the dark in the cold next to the closed newsstand.

"My guess is Marseille knows something's about to happen and Oliver Neville is Gustav and Victor's next victim. PM—that can only mean tonight, Chris."

"And what if you're wrong?"

"Only one way to find out, we need to get to Oliver."

Norman arrives and we get in, me in the front seat, Chris in the back.

"Norman, Chris Henley, Chris, Norman... I don't know Norman's last name."

"It's Rodgers."

"Did you call Oliver?"

"Yes, he's doing as you asked, but wondering why. So am I."

"I'll explain on the way. Let's go."

"Oliver lives on Beacon Street in Beacon Hill. It's a thirty-minute drive."

"Don't give me direction, get us there. Drive, man, drive."

As Norman navigates traffic, I fill him in.

"Marseille must believe eliminating Oliver is the way to stop whatever they suspect is happening. Why else would they target Oliver?"

"And if we're too late?"

"Don't even go there, Norman."

Fortunately, Norman proves to be adept at navigating traffic and makes the drive in twenty-five minutes flat by running a couple red lights. On Beacon Street, he pulls up short of a high-rise condominium.

"Mr. Neville resides on the seventh floor. There's a doorman in the lobby."

"He knows you?"

"Quite well."

"Let's go, man, let's go."

When we enter the lobby, the doorman greets Norman with a hesitant smile.

"Hi Walter."

"Good evening, Mr. Rodgers. Is everything okay?"

"Why do you ask?"

"Two policemen arrived a while ago. They're up with Mr. Neville."

Damn it, damn it, Gustav and Victor are already here!

"The officers insisted I let them go up unannounced."

"Nothing to be concerned with. There's been a terrible misunderstanding. These officers are here to clear it up. I'll escort them up."

Good for you Norman, you're thinking on your feet. Chris and I open our coats revealing our badges. Walter glances at them and nods.

"Thank you... goodnight, Walter."

"Goodnight, Mr. Rodgers."

Good for Norman, he's thinking on your feet. He leads us down the hallway, then turn left to two elevators—one to our right, one to our left... Norman hesitates.

"What's wrong?"

"This elevator stops at each apartment on the East side, that one on the West. If we require an element of surprise, I suggest we use the service elevator in the garage."

"We could have driven in?"

"Sorry, I wasn't thinking."

"Alright, we're wasting time, let's go."

Norman leads the way down the hall through a door at the far end that opens to the parking garage. Around the corner to our right are oversized elevator doors. Norm punches in a four-digit code... the doors open and we enter. He taps in the number seven and we're moving. Less than a minute later we arrive on the seventh floor... the doors open to a small lobby.

"Through that door is Mr. Neville's apartment."

Norman approaches the door... I grab his arm.

"Wait."

Placing my ear to the door, I listen.

"There's voices... can't make out what they're saying."

On a wall-mounted keypad, Norman punches in a code. The door lock slides open.

"Let's hope they didn't hear that."

Taking out my weapon, I motion to Chris to do the same.

"Norman, your gun?"

From under his coat, he takes out a stainless-steel Walther PPK.380 that he had tucked in his belt. I point to the doorknob, Norman turns it slowly and quietly opens the door... we're in. We can hear a voice clearly now... it's Gustav.

"I'm losing patience, Mr. Neville."

"I've already told you, I have no idea what you're talking about."

Then comes the sound of Oliver being slapped. Norman bolts forward, I grab his arm and hold him back. Another voice, this time it's Victor.

"Let's try this again."

"Please, please, I don't know what it is you want."

Oliver is slapped again... I motion to Norman that we're going in and to lead the way. He points and whispers.

"They're in the living room."

As we begin to move, we hear Victor speaking again.

"It would be a shame to spill your brains all over this beautiful Persian rug."

Now Gustav's speaking.

"Victor, we have our orders. Let's just end this."

With weapons raised, we move cautiously down the darkened hall past a bedroom, through the kitchen to the dining room. Norman stops us and points to the living room beyond. With our weapons raised, we move forward until the three of them come into view. Gustav and Victor's backs are to us, but we can they both have their weapons out. Oliver's in a chair facing them... his hands are tied behind his back... he sees us, his eyes widen... damn it, he'll give us away... do it, do it now. I take two quick steps forward.

"Either of you bats an eye you'll become corpses."

Gustav and Victor spin around to find three guns pointed at them.

"Russell, what the fuck are you doing here?"

"Making sure you don't screw up the world more than you already have, Gustav. Oliver, you okay?"

"Yes, yes, I'm fine."

"Now, let's take this by the numbers. Place your weapons on the floor and kick them over here. Do it slowly, do it now."

To my relief, they do as I ask... I don't know what Chris might have been thinking, but I was prepared for a shootout right here in the living room.

"Chris, handcuff them. Norman, untie Mr. Neville."

Norman rushes to Oliver's side and frees him.

"Are you alright, Mr. Neville?"

"Yes, Norman, thank God, they were about to shoot me."

With his hands freed, Oliver pops to his feet and moves quickly to my side.

"How did you know?"

"Thanks to the German here."

I move to Gustav, take out the note he dropped on the floor, and hold it up to his face. His eyes widen in disbelief.

"How could you be so sloppy, Mr. Heinz?"

"Where did you get that?"

"Where you left it, asshole."

I show it to Victor. The blood drains from his face and he whips his head to Gustav.

"De quoi parle-t-il?"

"Norman, what's he babbling about?"

"It appears he's quite pissed at Heinz."

"And well he should be. Keep an eye on them."

Oliver is pale and he's shaking... I take him aside and show him the slip of paper.

"But for this note, we would have never known."

"And I would be dead."

"Does this change your plans?"

"On the contrary, it solidifies them."

"Alright, your shaking, try to calm yourself."

"Easier said than done. What do you propose to do with them?"

"Don't you worry about them, leave that to us."

I turn back to Frick and Frack just as Gustav is about to say something... I wave him off.

"Don't say a word. You two no longer have standing in the human race."

"You're a fool, Russell, this won't change's anything."

"Unfortunately for you, you'll never know. Oliver, call your door man, tell him all's well and you sent us on our way on the service elevator."

"Will do."

· · · ·

THE ELEVATOR TAKING us down *to the garage and I'm having an internal argument with myself trying to decide what to do with Heinz and Augier. Listen to your gut, Billy Boy, you know what you want to do, what you have to do, so get on with and stop wasting precious time.*

"Norman, where's the nearest body of water?"

"The Charles River."

"How far?"

"A couple of blocks from here on the edge of Lederman Park."

'Get the car, meet us here in the garage."

"We'll have to leave the car in the Vesta garage and cross the street... Lederman is for pedestrians only."

"Better yet."

"What are you thinking, Billy?"

"Nothing good, Chris."

It takes Norman ten minutes to get to back to us. Chris sits in the back seat with his gun trained on Gustav, Victor. Norman drives us to the mostly empty Vesta garage, then we're off on foot to Lederman Park across the road. It's dark and it's getting colder... not a soul in sight... that's a break. So far, not a peep out of Gustav or Victor.

"Norman, is there a boat ramp?"

"Next to Fielder Field, yes."

"Take us there."

Down the Esplanade we march.

"Billy, what we're doing?"

"Reinstating the rule of law, Chris... kind of."

"Huh?"

"Trust me, Chris, trust me."

It takes us seven-minutes walking along the esplanade before we reach the boat ramp... we cross over the short walkway to the edge of the water.

"Set them down on their knees on the edge."

"Billy, I see where you're going with this... we better think this through."

"I have."

I gotta believe by now Frick and Frack know what's coming.

Gustav is glaring at me.

"In the end you will all fail."

"Maybe, maybe not. Either way, you won't be around to find out. Norman, set them down."

"With pleasure, Billy, with pleasure."

Chris grabs my arm and spins me toward him.

"Think twice, Billy, don't do this."

"In Afghanistan and Providence... did we deliver justice?"

"That was different."

"No, Chris, it wasn't. These two assassinated people who had the courage to speak out against the evil empire. They left behind wives and children, and parents. We owe this to their memory. Enough talk."

I place my gun within inches of Gustav's head and pull the trigger... his skull explodes... the force topples him into the cold waters of the St. Charles River. I never gave a thought to the moral implications, not for a second... I did what had to be done... it feels right and righteous. I move to Victor, but before I can do him in, Norman grabs my arm and nods... I see in his eyes what he's about to do. Placing his weapon to Victor's head, he pulls the trigger... Victor slumps into the water next to Gustav.

"That was for Mr. Neville."

Chapter 24

Failure Is Not an Option

*T**he original plan was for Norman** to meet Chris and me at the newsstand at midnight and drive us to wherever this Black Swan Event was to take place. But I feel unclean, I need a hot shower and a little time to reflect, so I have Norman drop us off at the house.*

"I'll return at midnight as planned."

"See you then, Norman."

Chris and I linger on the sidewalk before going in.

"If you have something to say, Chris, say it now."

"You did what you felt was right. It's done, we move on."

"You're okay with that?"

"Yes."

"Let's have a couple of stiff drinks before I wash off the stench."

There's no further mention of what took place in Lederman Park... that's fine with me... what's done is done... what matters now is what is ahead of us later. When Chris leaves, I strip down and stand in the small shower stall, my hands flat against the wall as the steaming water cascades over me, washing away the past... bringing in the future.

· · · ·

AT FIVE TO MIDNIGHT, Chris and I are pacing by the closed newsstand when Norman arrives. Someone is with him... I assume it's Oliver. Chris goes around to the street side and opens the rear door, the overhead light comes on, we slide into the back seat and close the doors. The light goes off before I see who's sitting up front next to Norman. As we pull away, whoever it is in the front seat speaks.

"Norman filled me in on your earlier exploits. Nice work."

Are my ears playing tricks?

"Holy shit, Hank?"

"In the flesh my friend."

"What are you doing here?"

"Gideon—Oliver—recruited me six-weeks ago."

"Why didn't you tell me?"

"I wanted to, but it was taking you a year and a day to commit, so he told me to keep my mouth shut."

"So, it's you who's been feeding him office info."

"Nope."

"Who then?"

"Enjoy the ride. Glad you could join us, Chris."

Chris cackles like only he can.

"And the plot thickens."

Norman catches I-93 North, crosses Boston Harbor, Southwest on Edwin H. Land Blvd., West on Main Street, Southwest on Vassar, past the Massachusetts Institute of Technology, right on Massachusetts Avenue to a driveway at the corner of Massachusetts and Albany Street. We pull up to a big double metal gate attached to a cement block wall that surrounds a large compound. Hank leans forward and looks curiously at the gate.

"Well, now, welcome to Fort Trouble. What is this place, Norman?"

"It was a local television station before the government took over."

"And now?"

"Oliver will explain, sir."

Norman flashes his headlights three times, waits two beats before flashing them twice more. The right gate swings inward... he drives through to a dimly lighted parking lot... a dozen or more vehicles are already there. One is a white maintenance van with black lettering on the side panel... 'Menwith Relay Station'. In front of us is a two-story building... the windows on the first and second floors are boarded over and painted the same off-white as the building. On the right side of the building are four large satellite dishes. Norman parks next to the maintenance van.

"Okay, gentleman, if you'll follow me."

The entrance to the building is two oversized metal doors. Hank was right, this place looks like a fort. Norman presses a buzzer mounted on the wall to the right of the doors. A slot in the middle of the right door opens and two eyes peer out. The slot closes, the door swings open and we're greeted by a heavyset, balding man in his forties.

"Norman, gentlemen, come in."

He closes and bolts the door behind us.

"How are you, Zach?"

"Apprehensive, Norman... today's the big day."

"Zach, this is Hank, Billy, and Chris."

"Welcome, gentlemen, if you'll follow me, please."

Zach takes us through a maze of hallways and empty offices to a large open area that must have functioned as a TV studio at one time. There's a couple dozen people already there. Folding chairs have been set up in front of a large video screen. A long table has been set up with an impressive spread of food and drinks.

"Zach, I'll let Mr. Neville know they have arrived."

"Thank you, Norman."

I spot Oliver on the far side of the room speaking with two men.

"Zach, who are all these people?"

"Mr. Neville will explain."

Norman crosses the room to Oliver and points to us... Oliver smiles, waves and heads in our direction.

"Good evening, gentlemen."

Except for a small bruise on his face, Oliver looks no worse for wear.

"How are you doing?"

"Fine, Billy, fine. I have not shared with anyone our earlier misadventure. It would serve no purpose, so mums the word."

"Our lips are sealed."

"Suffice to say, I will be forever in your debt. Dare I inquire about the fate of Heinz and Augier?"

"Our lips are sealed on that too."

"We'll leave it at that."

"Meet Chris Henley."

"Thank you for joining with us, Mr. Henley."

"Make that Chris."

"Come with me."

I'm curious as hell to know who all these people are and what role they might be playing. Hell, I'm not exactly sure what our role is, let alone theirs, which leaves me feeling uneasy. Oliver introduces us to the two men he had been speaking with when we entered.

"Gentleman, this Billy Russell, Hank Drummond, and Chris Henley. This young man is Brian Adams, the facility engineer, and this is Joseph Natali."

Natali, Natali, where do I know that name? We shake hands all around.

"Your name is familiar, Mr. Natali."

"Until last night it was General Joseph Natali, military Commander of the North American-Caribbean Region."

That all but knocks me off my feet... what's he doing here? I look to Oliver... he smiles at my obvious surprise and turns to the gathering.

"The pedigree of those gathered here would surprise you as well, Billy. They are all world patriots. Gathered here are four of Henry's World Council colleagues, a Constitutional scholar, and a United States Supreme Court Justice. The others are Volte-face leaders from around the world. Along with millions of others across the globe, they are here to bring to an end the totalitarianism that has sucked the air out of humanity, and to return all of the world to a free and vibrant society."

"A very tall order."

"Indeed, Hank, indeed. Now, Brian will take you to the engineering room and explain what is to take place exactly at nine this morning. We will speak further when you return."

Brian leads us down a dimly lit hallway to an elevator that takes us to the second floor. Across from the elevator is a steel door. He unlocks it and we enter a room that is cold and brightly lit. The left wall is lined with racks of blinking electronic equipment. A man is at the end of the racks with his back to us... he turns... it's Officer John Goulding.

"John! Jeez, is everybody in on this?"

Goulding tosses up his hands and laughs.

"Just about, Billy. Hank, how are you doing?"

"Nervous like everyone else."

"John, this is Chris Henley."

"Hey Chris, glad you could join us."

"Just call me the nervous new guy."

Brian waves us over to the fourth electronic rack.

"Okay gentlemen... a quick tutorial. All relay stations are completely automated and only require a single engineer to keep them humming along. At this facility, it's yours truly. All broadcasts, whether they be from a government or commercial channel, are beamed first to Menwith Station in England before being relayed via satellite to relay stations. It's done this way so that Marseille can control content. Theoretically, relay stations cannot record or send signals beyond those received from Menwith."

"Theoretically?"

"Hank, I didn't get a degree in broadcast engineering just to play mechanic to a bunch of electronic equipment."

With a couple of twists of a Philips screwdriver, he removes a small faceplate on the third rack. There in all its glory is a DVD player/recorder.

"Suffice to say, that's not supposed to be there."

From behind the DVD player/recorder, he retrieves a large manila envelope and removes a plastic DVD box.

"At Oliver's direction, I installed this DVD player as a fallback in the event Mr. Dion decided to record his message instead of delivering it live. As it turns out, Mr. Dion, God love him, had the presence of mind to record his speech before leaving France. At precisely five-seconds before nine AM Eastern Standard Time, two engineers at Menwith Station—both Volte-face members—will cut Menwith's satellite feed and replace it with the one coming from this facility sending it to every relay station across the globe. I've returned one of the satellite dishes to send capabilities."

"How long do you get to stay on the air?

"Ah, good question, Chris—until they pinpoint the signal's source."

I can't help but visualize the possible firefight that would take place here if this place was pinpointed before the broadcast has completed. How would our small group stop a full-on attack? Brian voice snaps me back.

"I assure you none of this is being done helter-skelter, gentleman. Every possibility has been carefully scrutinized and evaluated. Four of Menwith Station's security teams —also members of Volte-face—will see to it that no one enters the room while Henry's message is being broadcast. Your job, gentlemen, is to insure no one breaches that door over there if it comes to that. John, if you would please."

John disappears around the back of the racks and returns with four AR-15's.

"There's five additional magazines for each."

Brian checks his watch.

"It's two-thirty, lots of time to kill. I suggest we return to the studio and get food and strong coffee."

"Brian, do you know what's on that DVD?"

"Mr. Neville and I checked it."

"So, you know what's on it."

"I do. It was very difficult to watch, first because of the death of Mr. Dion. Beyond that, the material is disturbing, and that's putting it mildly. Let's go get that coffee."

When we return to the studio, I look to the gathering... they're braver than we are. If someone was to breech this place, their first in the line of fire. I pose the question to Oliver.

"I'll let Mr. Natali explain."

"Well, Billy, if this building is breached during the broadcast, the engineering room will be their target, not these people. Having said that, I have every confidence that the military will stand down on orders from General Couture."

"Couture?"

"Yes, Hank, the very same General Couture who heads the world's military. He's one of us."

"General, I have a question."

"Not general anymore, Hank... just plain civilian Joe. What's your question?"

"Do you all know what's on Dion's tape?"

"Oliver, you want to answer that?"

"No, Hank, they will all hear it together."

"And they're confident it'll bring about the revolution Dion promised?"

"They had complete trust in Henry when he was alive, that has not waned now that he is gone."

As we make my way to the refreshment table, several guests express their appreciation for what we've agreed to do. I find it embarrassing, I don't take compliments well, never have. Even back in Providence when my career was moving on the fast track, for me it was always about the work. Kudos from the brass meant little, welcomed for sure, but it was never what motivated me... the work did. I fix a cup of the black brew and grab a whole grain bagel. I'm about to take a bite when someone taps me on the shoulder. When I turn, I almost choke... the bagel slips from my hand to the floor... I'm face-to-face with the one and only Jade Miro.

"Hello, Billy Russell."

For one of the few times in my life, I'm at a loss for words.

"Jade?"

She looks to her left, then to her right.

"Let's find a quiet spot."

Floored at the idea that she's involved, I follow her to a quiet corner of the studio.

"Go ahead, ask."

"You're the last person I expected to find here?"

"There you see, Billy, my cover worked."

"You're the office mole?"

"Guilty as charged."

"And you kept it from me."

"I wanted to tell you, but as long as Oliver remained unsure of you, he held me to secrecy."

"When did you come aboard?"

"I was already involved when I was with the Boston police. It was Oliver who encouraged me to apply for this job."

"So, you became their spy."

"Jesus, Billy, you make it sound like I'm a criminal."

"Sorry, that came out wrong."

"I certainly hope so."

She places a gently hand on my arm... her expression softens.

"What matters now is that you and I have something good going, I don't want that jeopardized."

"Neither do I."

"Second, and equally important, what is about to go down here to-day will determine the future. If those self-serving megalomaniacs in Marseilles have taught us anything, it's that we can't live with our eyes closed. When we do, we leave the door open to the Laurent's of this world."

"You are amazing."

"I am?"

"What if Randolph had uncovered the real reason behind your be-ing there?"

"Gustav and Victor would have paid me a late-night visit and you and I would have never met."

"Perish the thought."

"I'd like to see the look on Gustav and Victor faces when this all goes down."

Should I tell her how they met their end in the Charles River? No, absolutely not, that remains my secret never to be brought up again.

. . . .

BY THE TIME THE SUN comes up, everyone is pretty much a basket case. Jason's making fresh coffee and replenishing the supply of food. Tension is high... still an hour and a half to go before the shit hits the fan. Jade is across the room, mingling with others... from time to time, we steal glances. I spend time conversing with several others whose impressive credentials not only impress, but inspire... like the Supreme Court Justice, and the philosophy professor, he's is still teaching the subject at a major Pennsylvania university. Joseph Natali summed it up this way.

"I too believed that a world government had an excellent chance of working. But the bastards pulled the wool over everyone's eyes, and we fell for it. It was time to shut them down, so here I am along with other active duty generals who will make their voices heard in a couple of hours."

. . . .

AT EIGHT AM, OLIVER is calling for everyone to take their seats.

"Let me begin by thanking each of you. Without your support, without the support of millions from around the world, and without Henry Dion, today would not be happening. His message to us was clear... we must never be afraid of speaking to power. Justice requires action and voice. Today, your voice becomes Henry Dion's. Millions around the world are poised to tune at nine o'clock Eastern Standard Time. If all goes well, they will flood the streets in the largest protest—dare I call it a revolution—the world has ever experienced. In support of the public response, there are men and women prepared to move quickly to seize control of the Marseille government. To insure their success, General Couture, Commander of world forces, will issue orders for the military to stand down."

Murmurs of excitement ripple through the gathering.

"That same order will also be conveyed to every local police force around the world."

Spontaneous applause breaks out.

"Each of you has an assigned contact. Two minutes to nine make your connection and begin relaying information as you receive it. Does anyone have a question?"

A distinguished older woman in the fourth row raises her hand.

"Yes, Gloria."

"I just want to say, God bless everyone here, God bless each and every member of Volte-face, and above all, God bless Henry Dion."

Again, there is applause.

At eight-thirty, Hank, Chris, and I return to the engineering room with Brian. I look to Jade as we leave, she purses her lips and blows me a kiss, I blow one back. Back in the engineering room, Brian holds up a satellite phone.

"At five minutes to nine, Menwith Station will ping this phone once. They'll be a five-second pause followed by five additional pings, the signal that it's a go. If only three come, it's a no go. If all is well, precisely at nine, I'll hit play and Henry's speech will begin. If's only three pings are received, it's a no go."

The clock's ticking, Chris, Hank and I pace the engineering room like caged bears. The large oval clock on the wall now shows ten to nine. Brian takes the DVD from its case and inserts into the player. At one-minute to nine, the satellite phone pings once... it gives us all a start. Five seconds later a second ping sounds, then a third, fourth, and fifth. Brian takes a breath and places a finger on the 'play' button keeping his eyes on the wall clock. As the sweeping hand reaches nine o'clock, he takes a breath, and presses the play button. A second later the screen comes alive. Henry Dion is standing in a non-descript location. He looks tired.

"Citizens of the world, my name is Henry Dion. Most of you watching know me as one of the Commissioners on the World Council. I was born sixty-eight years ago in the State of Massachusetts in the United States of America at a time when basic decency and the rule of law was respected. In the years that followed, like everyone, I watched as progress and technology became the focal point of our lives. Unfortunately, while many prospered, many more were left behind. Many world leaders, drunk on power, placed their ambitions above those of their charges, betraying the people's trust time and again. We have paid a dear price for those past blunders, for today every segment of society finds itself in crisis. In seeking a solution, we fell victim to the false promises of a few privileged men whose only goal was greater power and wealth for themselves. Their greed, their ineptness, has led to a struggle just to maintain the very basics of daily life... while they continue to reap the spoils. Today, that ends."

My eyes shoot to the clock, we're four minutes in and I'm getting more anxious by the second. Come on Henry, come on, get on with it.

"Today, we of the Volte-face movement will take back our lives. To that end, I present here evidence of what will truly shock you, as it did me when I learned of it. It wasn't enough for these men to take over the world in order to enrich themselves. No, they deemed it their right to take it an abominable step further. And although their sins are many, this one will end their reign of terror... this one is the smoking gun. What you are about to see is difficult to watch, difficult to even imagine. But, as history has recorded, it has occurred before. Hidden deep within the wildlife refuge, PARC Naturel Regional de Millevaches en Limousin, Southwest of the town of Claremont-Terrand, France, is a human breeding farm—yes, a human breeding farm. One thousand white women from all over the world were abducted for the sole purpose of delivering offspring sired by the men presently in power. Each offspring would carry their genes to insure the future of the white race. No doubt some would rise to become future world leaders. By our actions this day, we will end what is taking place there, as well closing down the citizen retraining camps, which are nothing more than death camps. Watch now and rise up, let our voices be heard."

Jerky, grainy, video comes on. The opening shot is of a row of buildings that resemble military barracks... as many as twenty all lined up in a single row. Other than several armed guards, there is no one in sight. Now the video has switched to the inside of one of the buildings. It is dark and the pictures are grainier. As many as fifty beds line each side of a center aisle, down which the camera is moving. Each bed is occupied by young white women all dressed in identical white nightgowns. Many of appear to be teenagers... many are clearly pregnant. As the shot continues down the aisle, a door opens at the far end. A young woman in her early twenties is led out by an older woman who is holding the young girl's arm. The girl's shoulders are bent forward, her eyes to the floor. A man comes through the door, he's smiling and buttoning his shirt. He says something to the girl, then leaves. The older woman takes the girl to a nearby bed, says something to her, and helps her lay down. In the background, another young woman is led through the door of the back room... a man follows and closes the door behind him. The video ends. I'm horrified by what I have just seen. Dion is back on screen.

"These images were obtained at great risk to the man who was brave enough to have secretly taken them with, would you believe, a button on his shirt that was in fact a camera. As I speak, armed men are moving into the camps to shut them down and return the women to their families. Now, you must do your part. Begin this second, take to the streets without fear, let your voices be heard. In the days ahead, new leaders will come forth... lend them your support. Together we will create a democratic society across the globe for all. Thank you."

And with that simple ending, Henry Dion delivered the coup de grace to the evil empire. History would surely record this moment as the time when one man's devotion to truth moved an entire civilization to act... I hope. I look at the others... they are stunned and speechless. John moves to the door and listens.

"I don't hear anything. Take your weapons, let's join the others."

When we arrive back in the studio, everyone is on their phones. Zach comes rushing in with a surprised look on his face.

"The gate is still closed. There's no one out there."

Joseph Natali lets out a hoot.

"Damned if General Couture didn't come through."

A woman on the far side of the studio shoots up from her seat and excitedly calls out.

"London! London is reporting thousands in the streets."

A man in the middle whoops loudly.

"Moscow too."

And then a chorus of frenzied voices.

"New York's reporting traffic's at a standstill because of enormous crowds that have flooded streets!"

"Same in Miami!"

"Chicago the same!"

"The World Headquarters in Marseilles is surrounded by thousands!"

"Los Angeles is reporting thousands!"

"Pretoria, South Africa!"

"Berlin!"

"Ditto Toronto!"

"Sydney, Australia!"

"Beijing!"

As the chorus continues, Natali calls to us.

"Come on, guys, let's see what's going on. Zach, open the front door."

Hank, Chris, John and I follow Natali to the front entrance. Zach slides back the peep slot and glances out.

"As I said, not a soul out there."

"Open the door."

"You sure, Mr. Natali?"

"Open her up, Zach. You guys wait here."

Zach unlocks the door and swings it open.

"Wait here. Hank, give me your weapon."

Natali takes off at a quick-pace to the gate and listens. Now he's waving his arms and calling to us.

"Zach, open the gate."

Zach flips a switch just inside the door, the gate begins to slowly swing open, we can see people out on the street, damn there's lots of them. Natali's waving to us again... his face is one big smile.

"Come on, come see this for yourselves."

We step out, each of us with our rifles at the ready and to the gate.

"Leave your weapons here."

Setting the AR-15's down, we step through the gate. To our astonishment, Albany Street is clogged with thousands of people. Chris lets out a loud hoot.

"Holy Moly!"

Natali, smiling from ear-to-ear, says to no one in particular.

"If there's a heaven, I know where Henry Dion is."

This is cause for celebration, and I want to share it with Jade. I turn and begin to head back in... Hank calls to me.

"Hey, where're you going, stay and enjoy this."

"There's someone I need to see."

"Need I ask who?"

"I think you know."

As I enter the studio, Oliver is calling for everyone's attention.

"Ladies and gentlemen, your attention, please. I've just been informed the government headquarters in Marseilles is in friendly hands. As planned, former United Nations Secretary General Arturo Cordozar has taken charge. The search is on for President Laurent and the members of the World Council. We can safely assume they're running for their lives."

Oliver comes to me and shakes my hand.

"Everyone here played a special role... but none greater than yours... you saved my life, Billy. Now, how about a hug?"

"Ur, let's not and say we did."

He laughs, grabs my hand again and shakes it vigorously.

"I recall telling you that if this went down as planned, you'd be looking for new employment. When the dust clears, I may be of assistance in that area."

"Thank you. Would you excuse me, there's someone I need to speak with?"

I cross the studio to where Jade it speaking with two women.

"Excuse me, ladies, may I steal Ms. Miro for a moment?"

"Yes, of course, young man."

"Thank you."

"What's on your mind, William Evan Russell?"

"You, me, the future, Jade Miro."

"Where do we begin?"

"How about we get out of here."

"I think the streets of Boston will prove impossible to pass at the moment."

"Yes, and don't ever call me William again."

This is a moment of celebration not to be wasted. I sweep her up in my arms and kiss her.

Chapter 25
Closure and Renewal

The first thing I did was to have my GPS Tracker removed from my arm. True to his word, Oliver Neville arranged positions for Jade, Hank, Chris, and myself with the Boston Police Department. It took a little legal wrangling to keep Hank out of jail because of his participation in executions. However, once it was proven that he had done so under the threat of severe repercussions, he was set free. As for the uprising... in the immediate aftermath, there was, as expected, uncertainly and confusion of what was to come next. Never before had a world-change of this magnitude taken place this quickly. The Marseilles regime had crumbled in less than an hour—that had to be some sort of a record in itself. Because everything was happening fast, it was paramount that the masses be reassured the world had not gone from the fire into the frying pan. Arturo Cordozar, chosen as temporary world administrator, appeared on worldwide television to reassure people that reform would come quickly, beginning with the reinstatement of the World Council, the quickest mechanism that would get the ball rolling in the right direction. Four scholarly representatives from each of the six continents were selected in temporary appointments... Oliver Neville was one of them. Cordozar promised that a worldwide referendum, voted on by all people, would determine if a world government system was to be retained, or whether countries would go back to self-governing. It appeared, at least on the surface, that some semblance of sanity had returned. The challenges, however, had just begun, not the least of which was, how to handle widespread poverty and drug addiction. There was talk of creating a Nuremberg-type Tribunal. Jean Lumiere and thirty-two of the thirty-six members of the defunct World Council were quickly rounded up and jailed, as were those who commanded the drug enforcement units—so much for the Randolph's and Wilson's of the world. As for Jules, well, Jules is Jules, he'll always be his old lovable self. Daily he razzes *me about Jade's comings and goings. He even had the audacity to ask what my intentions were. I assured him Jade and I had become partners for life. As the world moved on with the business of restoring what had been lost, the question remained... would all of humanity come together for the benefit of all mankind, or would they revert to their old ways? If we were not morally offended by the Laurent regime's atrocities, then what might that say about us? The lesson I hope that we have learned is, if a person gains great wealth and position in life, that does not make them a moral person, nor does it insure they will express empathy for those citizens less fortunate... or will they simply pursue their greed for greater wealth and power. We must now and forever take that into consideration when selecting our elected officials. Ours must be a quest for the good we seek in life, and for the value and importance of truth, fairness, and equality. We must decide once and for all what the definition of citizen is, that in fact, every human being on the planet deserves and is entitled to be called citizen, and to be treated and respected as a citizen of the world. Otherwise, we'll be back to playing the race card, the religious card, and the political card... in which case we'll be repeating the mistakes of the past yet again. Although he was before my time, one of my heroes in life was scientific visionary, Steven Hawking. I studied him in school and over the years have read everything about his life that I could get my hands on. He once said... 'We have this one life to appreciate the grand design of the universe, and for that I am extremely grateful.' With Hawking's words of wisdom in mind, I wonder... if everyone were to see and experience what I saw peering out that portal on Europa-2... what would they see?*

The end... or is it the beginning?

Preamble to the Declaration of Independence

We hold these truths to be self-evident, that all men are created equal, that they are endowed by their Creator with certain unalienable Rights, that among these are Life, Liberty and the pursuit of Happiness.

<u>Other Novels by R.J. Eastwood</u>
"The Autopsy of planet"
Winner of the 2018 Readers' Favorite in Fiction
The 2018 Book Talk Radio Book of the Year
The 2017 Author's Circle Novel of Excellence Award for Fiction

"The idea for **The Autopsy of Planet Earth** by R. J. Eastwood is pure brilliance. That an alien would show up on our planet one day, claiming not only to have created Man but to have deliberately abandoned us, is quite a lot for a novel to take on. To go a step further and have the alien claim to want to correct their mistake and put Mankind on the road to evolutionary success is a massive assignment for any writer, but R.J. Eastwood manages to pull it off with style and flair. The fact that this is a massive undertaking doesn't seem to give R.J. Eastwood any reason to hesitate. I like the fact that this is a globe-spanning novel with experts and scientists from around the world, representing international scientific and cultural achievements."

Reviewed by Ray Simmons

• • • •

"SCIENCE FICTION FANS are delivered a surprisingly wonderful treat with The Autopsy of Planet Earth by R.J. Eastwood. The author does an excellent job of taking what is familiar and crafting a new world that is relatable and allows readers to logically suspend disbelief. The majority of the chapters end on hooks, so there are no stopping places. Great job with this! The dialogue throughout the book is strong and true to each character. Everyone in the story is well motivated, and that helps drive the plot."

Reviewed by,
Nicole, Judge, 25th Annual Writer's Digest Self-Published Book Awards."

• • • •

"A SPELLBINDING SCIENCE fiction novel with a very original concept and great potential for entertainment. The reader meets Legna, an alien on a mission to restore humankind to its original place of peace, harmony, and balance with the earth...but at a price that mankind may not be prepared to accept. The conflict developed in this book is monumental. The writing is excellent, with vivid descriptions that allow the reader to have clear images of elements of the setting. Here is a story that will entertain readers and force them to look at the earth with new eyes. Brilliantly plotted and accomplished with a master's touch. A great read, indeed."

Reviewed by Divine Zape

Author Robert J. Emery
(Pen name R. J. Eastwood)

Robert J. Emery writes under the pen name R.J. Eastwood. Over his long career as a member of the Directors Guild of America, he has written, produced, and directed both feature films and television programming and everything in between. His production work has garnered him over 75 industry awards along the way. To date, Mr. Emery has published seven books, four of which were nonfiction based on his Starz/Encore television series "The Directors." His first novel (as Robert J. Emery) was chosen as one of the top five finalists in the Next Generation Indie Books Awards.

In the Fall of 2017 he published the science fiction adventure "The Autopsy of Planet Earth." It won the 2018 Readers' Favorite Gold Award for Science Fiction, the 2018 Book Talk Radio Book of the Year, and the 2017 Authors Circle First Place Award for Fiction

With the release of his newest novel, "Midnight Black", he is busy working on his next entitled "The White Prize." When not writing, Mr. Emery can be found in the kitchen creating and preparing sumptuous Italian meals. He credits his culinary expertise to his Sicilian mother, who took the time to teach him to cook.

Visit Mr. Emery's author web site to learn more about his background as a writer/director in the entertainment industry as well as his book writing. He enjoys hearing from readers and encourages them to connect with him through his website (where there is an email address) as well as his social media sites.

http://robertjemeryauthor.com

http://www.facebook.com/robertjemeryauthor.

http://twitter.com/bobemery

http://www.goodreads.com/author/show/ 1169565.Robert_J_Emery[1]

---

1.   https://www.goodreads.com/author/show/1169565.Robert_J_Emery

Don't miss out!

Visit the website below and you can sign up to receive emails whenever R. J. Eastwood publishes a new book. There's no charge and no obligation.

https://books2read.com/r/B-A-XDBH-JDNW

BOOKS 2 READ

Connecting independent readers to independent writers.